# Family

## is life

# HIDDEN ELEMENTS

## THE DÚBAILTE CHRONICLES
### BOOK ONE

M.A. KILPATRICK

ISBN: 979-8-9888864-1-9 (Paperback)



Third printing edition 2025


Cover Design by Magaidh Dunbroch
Developmental Editing by Heather Creeden
Irish Culture and Language Guidance by Louise O'Hanlon and Erin Hartnett


makilpatrick.com

# DEDICATION

*For my family and friends who always support me, including my kids, Kiah McDaniel, Zane Scheffler, and Tayler Kilpatrick, and my sister, Sabrina Butler. For my mom, Kathy Butler, who is my biggest cheerleader and fabulous for my self-esteem. And for all the people who helped me figure out how to make this book a reality, especially my daughter, Kiah. I truly couldn't have done it without you.*

*And for Brad. I know you're proud of me.*

# TRIGGER WARNINGS

Attempted rape, stalking, spiders, verbal abuse, emotional abuse, bigotry, fat shaming, cursing, illness, near drowning

Please accept my apologies in advance if there are any I have missed. I assure you, it was unintentional.

# GLOSSARY

Author's Note: You will notice some of these terms are spelled in a slightly different manner throughout the story. In the Irish language, depending on how the term is being used (how many people are being addressed, vocative versus nominative cases, etc.), different letters and modifiers are added.

All terms are Irish, unless otherwise noted.

> *A rúnsearc (uh-ROON-shar(ch)) — Secret love, a term of endearment*
>
> *A stór (uh-STOR) — Dear, a term of endearment*
>
> *Aengus Óg (AIN-gus-OHG) — God of youth, beauty, and love*
>
> *Aibhleog (AV-lohg) — Ember, also Calder's nickname for Keegan*
>
> *Áine (AWN-yuh)*
>
> *Aintín (an-T(ch)EEN) — Aunt*
>
> *Aisling (ASH-ling)*
>
> *Anamchara (AH-num-KARR-uh) — Soul friend, another term for soulmates*

*Anord (uh-NORD)* — Chaos

*Anseo (an-SHOW)* — Here, often used as a greeting, paired with a person's name, when answering the phone (ex., Niamh anseo.)

*Aoife (EE-fa)*

*Aos Sí (ES-shee)* — Irish Fae

*Athair (AH-her)* — Father

*Athrú (ah-ROO)* — Change

*Badb (BAV)* — War goddess, one of the three goddesses making up The Morrígan

*Balor (BAH-lor)* — An ancient Fomorian enemy who looked like a hideous, one-eyed monster

*Banduri (BAHN-duh-ree)* — Female Druid, sometimes used as an honorific

*Banríon (BAHN-ri-uhn)* — Queen

*Bean (BANN)* — Woman or Mrs.

*Blathnaid (BLAW-nid)*

*Bríd (BREED)* — Goddess of fire, but also spring, fertility, and life

*Cáer Ibormeith (KARE-IH-bor-muh)* — Goddess of dreams and prophecy

*Cailín (kah-LEEN)* — Girl

*Cailíní (KAH-LEEN-EE)* — Girls, plural

*Cara (KARR-uh)*

*Céad míle fáilte (KADE-MEE-lah-FALL-cha)* — A hundred thousand welcomes, a formal Irish welcome

*Céilí (KAY-lee)* — Party

*Chica (CHEE-kah)* — Girl; Spanish

*Chico (CHEE-koh)* — Boy; Spanish

*Cliodhna (KLEE-OH-na)* — Irish goddess of the sea and the name of the Ó Faoláin woodworking business

*Codalaígí (KOH-da-LEE-gee)* — Sleep

*Cois an chlaí amuigh (KUSH-ahn-K(h)LEE-ahm-WEE)* — By the wall outside

*Corley (KOR-lee)*

*Craic (KRACK)* — Fun

*Croía (KREE-ya)*

*Cú Chulainn (KOO-(c)HUL-in)* — Ancient Irish hero and demi-god

*Cuppa (KUH-puh)* — Cup of tea

*Cute Hoor (HOO-ER)* — Unashamedly sly person

*Da (DAH)* — Dad

*The Dagda (DAG-duh)* — Father-figure god, associated with fertility, agriculture, manliness, and strength

*Daideo (dah-D(j)O)* — Grandad, sometimes used as an honorific

*Damhsaigh na Tine Mór — (DOW-sa-na-TIN-eh-MOOR)*

*Danu (DAH-noo)* — Mother of the gods

*Daugherty (DOW-er-tee)*

*Deartháir beag (DREH-hur-B(y)UG)* — Little brother

*Deartháir mór (DREH-hur-MOOR)* — Big brother

*Deirdre (DEER-druh)*

*Deirfiúr (DEH-fur)* — Sister

*Delaney (duh-LANE-ee)*

*Devlin (DEV-lin)*

*Dia duit (DEE-uh (hw)IT)* — God to you, a formal Irish greeting

*Dia is Muire duit (DEE-uh-ISS-MWEAR-uh-(hw)IT)* — God and Mary to you, or Hello, in response to Dia Duit

*Do athair fíor (DOH-AH-her-F(y)OR) — Your real
    father*
*Do na Páistí (DOH-nah-PAWSH-tee) — For the chil-
    dren, also the name of the charity Liam heads*
*Domhan Nua (DOW-uhn-NOO-ah) — New World*
*Donn (DOWN) — God of the dead*
*Doran (duh-RAN)*
*Dossers (DOSS-ers) — Slackers*
*Dúbailte (DOO-ball-cha) — Double, also a term used
    to describe Fae with dual powers*
*Éabha (AY-va)*
*Eejit (EE-jit) — Idiot*
*Éiníní (AY-nee-nee) — Little birds*
*Étaín (eh-TAYN)*
*Fáilte (FALL-cha) — Welcome*
*Feis (FESH) — Clan gathering*
*Feiseanna (FESH-uh-NUH) — Feis, plural*
*Fiadh (FEE-uh)*
*Fianna (FEE-uh-NUH) — Ancient band of roving
    warriors/hunters*
*Fiona (fee-OH-nuh)*
*Fionn mac Cumhaill (FI(yun)-mah-KOOL) —
    Ancient Irish hero and leader of the Fianna*
*Goibniu (GUB-nuh) — Smithing god, the metalsmith
    of the Tuatha Dé Danann*
*Himbo (HIM-bow) — Him plus bimbo, a promiscuous
    male*
*Hola (OH-la) — Hello; Spanish*
*Keegan (KEE-gin)*
*Laoise (LEE-shuh)*
*Lí Ban (LEE-bahn) — An ancient Irish mermaid with
    an otter companion*
*Lugh (LOO) — All-wise and all-seeing god repre-*

*senting the sun and light; also the name of
Keegan's horse*

*Macha Mong Ruad (MA-k(h)ah-MONG-ROO-uhd)
— Macha Red-Haired, the only queen included in
the list of the High Kings of Ireland*

*Máire (MOI-ra)*

*Máthair (MO-her) – Mother*

*Máthair Chríona (MO-her-K(h)REE-uh-nah) —
Wise Mother, sometimes used as an honorific*

*Mija (MEE-hah) — My daughter, also a term of
endearment; Spanish*

*Mijo (MEE-hoh) — My son, also a term of endear-
ment; Spanish*

*Mo bhuachaill (muh-VOO-k(h)ahl) — My boy*

*Mo chroí (muh-K(h)REE) —My heart*

*Mo chuisle (muh-K(h)USH-LAH) — My pulse; the
pulse of my heart*

*Mo fhíorghrá (muh-eer-GRAW) — My true love*

*Mo ghrá (muh-GRAW) — My love*

*(The) Morrígan (MOR-i-gin) — Shapeshifting,
triune war goddess, associated with death and
crows, also the name of Siobhán's horse*

*Muireann (MOY-rin)*

*Niamh (NEEV)*

*Niamh Cinn-Óir (NEEV-KEEN-oir(d)) — A beau-
tiful Fae who fell in love with the mortal Oisín*

*Nuada (NOO-uh-duh) — God with a silver hand and
the first king of the Tuatha Dé Danann*

*Ó Faoláin (OH-FAY-lin)*

*Ó Loingsigh (OH-LEE(in)-shee)*

*Ogma (OHG-muh) — God of speech and language*

*Oíche Shamhna Shona Daoibh (EE-ha-HOW-NA-
HO-na-DEEV) — Happy Halloween*

*Oisín (UH-sheen) — Son of Fionn mac Cumhaill, he spent three hundred years in Tír na nÓg with Niamh Cinn-Óir*

*Papi (POP-ee) — Dad, also a term of endearment; Spanish)*

*Póigín (POH-gheen) — Little kiss*

*Púca (POO-ka) — A shapeshifting, mischievous spirit, also Lir's type of familiar*

*Regan (REE-gun)*

*Rhiannon (REE-uh-nun)*

*Sadbh (SIVE) — Goddess of deer and transformation*

*Saoirse (SEER-shuh)*

*Shifting (SHIF-ting) — Kissing*

*Siobhán (shi-VAHN)*

*Sláinte (SLAWN-cha) — Health, an Irish toast, the equivalent of cheers*

*Slán (SLAWN) — Goodbye*

*Slán agat (SLAWN-AH-git) — Goodbye, when leaving*

*Spéir (SPARE)*

*Tá áthas orm bualadh leat (taw-AW-hiss-OR-um-BOO-lah-LAT) — Pleased to meet you*

*Tá brón orainn — (taw-BROH(n)-or-um/or-in) — We're sorry or there is sadness on us*

*Tabhair aire (TOOR-AIR-uh) — Take care*

*Taoiseach (TEE-shock) — High Clan Chief*

*Teas (TESS) — Heat, as well as the term for a Fae artifact used for gathering heat.*

*Tionól (TIN-all) — Assembly, and also the name of the village surrounding the World Tree in Tír na nÓg*

*Tír na nÓg (TEER-nah-NOHG) — Land of Youth, the Fae realm*

*Tuatha Dé Danann (too-AH-day-DANN-uhn) —*
*Tribe of Danu*
*Ula (ULL-uh)*
*Wander (WAHN-der) — Walk*
*Wanker (WAYN-ker) —Jerk*
*Wean(s) (WEEN(S)) — Child(ren)*

Family
is life

# PROLOGUE

The blackbird trilled with pleasure as it swiped a piece of scone from Aisling's plate. "Rhiannon, ye tiny thief!" she exclaimed, swinging her napkin at the retreating bird, narrowly missing her. The bird perched on top of a shelf, greedily devouring her stolen morsel. Aisling chuckled under her breath and shuffled over to sit at the table in the corner. She picked up one of the scrolls lying there, squinted at the cramped text, then leaned over to grab the lamp from the small table beside her favorite chair.

After re-reading that particular scroll for the hundredth time, Aisling sighed, pinching the bridge of her nose. "Something is missing!" she cried, slapping the table, the noise making Rhiannon startle and flutter briefly around the small room. She picked up the stack of papers and began sorting through them, separating them into various piles before changing her mind and reorganizing them into a different set of piles. After several minutes of this, Aisling rested her head in her hands and let out another major sigh. "I wish I knew what I don't know," she said quietly. Then, with a flick of her wrist, a gust of air lifted the scrolls and floated them up to the shelf where Rhiannon had just finished her snack.

There came a brisk knock at the door, then an Ovate-in-training poked her head in, bowed, and said, "Banduri." Aisling straightened in her chair and replied, "Deirdre, thank you for stopping by. Please sit." Deirdre raised her head, stepped into the room, and walked to the empty seat across from Aisling. She sat and placed her hands in her lap, looking expectantly at her mentor. "I have decided we must move beyond half-measures. There is something we are missing! There is evil coming, and all Aos Sí must prepare. You are one of the strongest Ovates I have ever trained. I need your help to trigger a vision."

Deirdre's eyes widened, and she gasped, "Banduri, you know how dangerous that can be! Isn't there another way?" Aisling tucked a few stray silver curls that had escaped her thick braid behind her ears, then shook her head. "I'm more afraid of what we're missing. I must take the risk. Make your preparations. I must meditate and center myself." Aisling looked up at Rhiannon and nodded. The blackbird let out a squawk and flew out the open window.

The Head Ovate dimmed the lamp and made herself comfortable in her favorite chair. She went through her meditation rituals, finding her center and clearing her mind. Deirdre quietly gathered the items she would need to initiate the process. This was done so rarely that she had to keep checking an obscure text, hoping she didn't forget something vital. Once all the materials were in place and Aisling's slow, even breathing signaled her readiness, Deirdre began the ritual.

She started by placing a blanket across Aisling's lap and laying a stone bowl on top. She added various herbs to the bowl, then lit them on fire, letting them burn for just a few moments. She blew out the flame and let them smolder, filling the room with a sweet, slightly spicy smoke. Then Deirdre moved behind Aisling's chair and placed her hands on the ancient Druid's shoulders. Rhiannon flew back in through the window, followed by her two sisters, and all three birds landed in Aisling's lap, standing around the perimeter of the stone bowl.

Aisling began breathing deeply, inhaling the smoke, willing it to trigger a vision. *What am I missing?* Deirdre started chanting, calling forth her gift and channeling it into her mentor. The Head Ovate could feel Deirdre's energy flowing down into her center, then moving outward, tingling as it went. Just when Aisling thought she couldn't contain another drop, Rhiannon and her sister ravens began to sing.

Suddenly, Aisling's eyes opened and rolled back in her head, showing only the whites. She opened her mouth, and, with an ethereal voice, she began prophesying.

> *Radiance blinds the masked peacock.*
> *The hawk protects the luster, feeding the fire.*
> *Dúbailte.*
> *The charming wolf keens her loss, drowns her sorrows, and life*
> *springs forth.*
> *Dúbailte.*
> *The hidden seeks out likewise, unknowing.*
> *When anamchara relent, the Aos Sí undergo athrú.*
> *Dúbailte, Dúbailte bring forth athrú and anord.*
> *Embrace them, and na páistí will bring forth an*
> *Domhan Nua.*

Once the last word left Aisling's mouth, she crumpled like a marionette with the strings cut. The birds were startled and flew out the window. Deirdre rushed to her mentor's side and checked that she was still breathing, letting out a great sigh once she confirmed the Druid was just unconscious. The Ovate-in-training re-read the prophecy her mentor had risked her life to deliver. "What does it mean?" she wondered aloud.

Tremendous pain suddenly erupted behind her eyes, and she pressed the palms of her hands to her temples, attempting to slow her breathing and think through the agony. *Deirdre,* a sibilant voice whispered her name inside her mind. *I felt something just now. What has that old crone been up to?* Deirdre immediately tightened the barriers in her mind, taking care to let nothing slip through. *A minor prophecy was revealed, nothing of note,* she thought, careful to keep her reply nonchalant. *Make a copy and bring it to me as soon as she dismisses you,* the voice said. *I'll be the judge of what's important.* Deirdre replied, *Of course.*

The presence quickly left her mind, and she let out a sigh of relief at the abrupt cessation of pain. She took a few deep breaths, trying to calm herself and decide what to do. Aisling slept peacefully in her favorite chair, the rigors of a forced vision taking their toll on the elderly Druid. "Oh, Banduri," she whispered. "I'm so sorry for what I must do." She then sat at the table and began making a copy of Aisling's prophecy. As she approached the end, an idea occurred to her. *I cannot disobey a direct order, but perhaps partial compliance may avert disaster.* She continued copying but omitted the last line. Then she made a third copy, also without the last line. Finally, she rolled up the original, complete prophecy and tucked it into the bodice of her dress. *I will keep this safe until I can figure a way out of this mess.*

Aisling's eyelids fluttered open, and she pushed herself higher in her chair. "What did I miss?" she joked weakly. Deirdre smiled at her mentor and handed her one of the edited copies. "Here it is, Banduri," she said. Aisling read through the prophecy, then looked up at Deirdre and said, "Well, that's clear as mud." Deirdre put her hand on the Head Ovate's shoulder and replied, "I'm sorry it didn't answer your questions." Aisling patted Deirdre's hand and said, "It's not your fault, my dear. Sometimes the answers only lead to more questions. But that's no reason to give up. I'm going to rest my eyes for a moment, then I'll take another crack at it." Then she closed her eyes, laid her head back against the back of her chair, and within a few moments, was lightly snoring.

Deirdre straightened up the room, spread the blanket over Aisling's lap, and paused momentarily, looking at her sleeping mentor. "I'm trying to save us all, Banduri," she whispered. "I hope someday you can forgive me." She wiped a lone tear from her cheek, checked to ensure the original prophecy was still safely tucked away, and quietly left the room, heading for the shore and an unwanted meeting.

# Family

## is life

# ONE

Keegan was sitting at her favorite thrift store find, a vanity with various flowers and vines painted on it, twisting her long, auburn curls into a messy bun. She momentarily looked at her pointed ears, the most apparent sign marking her as a Fae. She loved that feature, even if she couldn't go out with them like that. With a sigh, she made a twirling motion with her fingers, turning her pointed ears into ordinary, rounded human ears, at least to human eyes. Other Fae could see through the glamour, but that was hardly a problem, stuck as she was on Earth.

She took a look around her room. It was mainly decorated with items she had found at yard sales and thrift stores, like her vanity. Her tastes tended toward edgy flower child. But even though they had never had a great deal of money, her mom had always managed to come up with furnishings that were tasteful, if somewhat worn. Until recently, she hadn't minded being poor. She had her mom, her friend and cousin, Cara, and her familiar, who was currently busy abusing her dinner.

"Áine, for the last time, quit tormenting that cricket! Either eat it or let it go, but for heaven's sake, stop torturing it!" Keegan said with exasperation. Áine, a scarlet macaw parrot, let out what could only be described as a grumble, then snatched the poor cricket up and swallowed it whole. Keegan grimaced but said, "Thank you. I don't know why you insist on playing with your food."

Áine looked back over her shoulder at Keegan and said, "I play with my food because I'm bored. Someone with my level of intelligence should be continuously challenged. The most challenging thing around here is when Niamh turns on Jeopardy. And even that's not the same without Alex." She let out a mournful sigh at the thought of her favorite game show going on without its iconic host.

Keegan rolled her eyes and said, "Yes, yes, the world lost a light when Alex Trebek died. We know how you feel about him." She gave her hair one last look and said, "How do I look?" Áine shook off her melancholy and cast a critical eye over Keegan. "Not bad. Not as gorgeous as me, but that's an incredibly high bar." Keegan just shook her head and said, "Come on, your gloriousness, I'm going to be late for work if we don't leave soon."

She grabbed her purse and phone, blew out the candles she always had burning in her room, and bounded down the stairs to the living room. Her mom was lying on the threadbare couch, wrapped in her favorite fleece blanket, staring off into space, humming one of the myriad songs Keegan remembered from her childhood. They were all familiar to Keegan, but since they were from another world, she had never heard any of them anywhere else. She stopped and looked critically at her mom. Niamh was pale and drawn-looking, but she smiled at her daughter and said, "Off to work, a stór?"

"Yep, I'm closing tonight. Cara is too. She had to go in early, so she took the bus, but I'll give her a ride home." Keegan cleared her throat, fidgeting with the clasp on her purse. "So, how are you feeling today?"

"I'm fine, Sweetheart, just fine," she replied. "Please stop worrying about me." Keegan narrowed her eyes and said, "I'll stop worrying when you start getting better. You are not just fine, Mom. We need to find you a new doctor. Nobody we've seen up to this point seems to know their head from their a--"

"I take your point, Keegan," Niamh replied, "But that is a problem for another day. Right now, you need to go to work. Off with you now."

Keegan said, "Fine, I'll drop it for now. But we will finish this conversation. Soon." Niamh looked at her stubborn but compassionate daughter and couldn't help but let out a little giggle. "Think so?" Keegan raised an eyebrow and said, "Damn straight." Áine flew over the couch and dropped a stuffed animal in Niamh's lap, which she promptly threw at Keegan's head, saying, "Such a saucy little pup!"

Keegan ducked and replied, "You wouldn't have me any other way." Then she gave her mom a cheeky smile, narrowed her eyes at Áine, and said, "Come on, you traitorous bag of feathers, we're going to be late!"

She pulled her bright blue Volkswagen Bug into the newly vacated parking space about half a block from the upscale Kansas City restaurant where Keegan worked. "Score," she said, excited by the closeness of the spot. Nearby street parking on the Plaza was hard to find, so it seemed appropriate to celebrate her good fortune. *Let's hope my luck continues,* she thought. *I've got to figure out how to pay for the specialists so we can figure out what's wrong with Mom.*

She speed-walked the half block to her work while Áine was weaving back and forth overhead, doing barrel rolls and fancy flips, displaying her aerial prowess for the bystanders. Most of them were charmed by Áine's antics, a few even giving her a quick round of applause. "Thank you!" she squawked loudly, then for Keegan's ears alone, said, "I'll be here all week." Keegan laughed and said, "Show off," then she pushed open the door at the staff entrance, grabbed her timecard, and clocked in mere seconds before she would be considered late. "Whew, just in the nick of time," a familiar voice said behind her. Keegan turned around, crossed her arms emphatically, and said to her best friend, Cara, "I made it, and that's all that counts." Cara raised an eyebrow and said, "Just keep telling yourself that. Áine, you'd better take a form that's easier to hide. Carlos is on a rampage tonight, and making him worry about the health inspector will not improve the situation." Áine gave a harrumph and transformed into a tiny, bright red mouse. Then she scampered down Keegan's arm and jumped into her apron pocket. "Happy now?" she squeaked sarcastically.

Cara leaned over so her big, cinnamon-colored eyes were level with Keegan's apron pocket. "I suppose that will do." She straightened up, elbowed Keegan, and said, "Come on, we're already getting slammed."

Cara and Keegan were kept busy serving the various customers who came through the restaurant for the next couple of hours. More than once, though, Keegan had to clear her throat loudly or fake a cough because Áine couldn't help but make a sarcastic comment about a customer. Right before Keegan's scheduled dinner break, three fashionably dressed women were seated in her section. As she took their order and began serving them, she couldn't help but overhear bits of their conversation.

"I still can't believe they refused to vacate the premises just a couple of hours early. All they're doing is a poker tournament for some charity. We weren't asking for that much. Now who knows if we'll get it all done," a woman with heavily highlighted blonde hair commented to her friends, shaking her head and taking a huge swig of her chardonnay.

"Oh, get over yourself, Heather. We'll have plenty of time to decorate for the event. It wouldn't be an issue if you didn't insist on the theme and decorations being so over the top. An "Under the Sea" theme would be fine if you didn't feel the need to include real aquariums. Who has actual fish at prom? If we need to scale things back, that's what we'll do," commented another blonde with similar features. *Likely Heather's sister,* Keegan thought. "Oh, and that poker tournament raises thousands of dollars every year for Children's Mercy Hospital. We're planning a party for a bunch of high schoolers. Let's get our priorities straight here."

"Nobody asked for your commentary, Hillary," Heather snapped. "Just because I stay on top of trends and you don't, doesn't mean you can belittle me for my ideas."

A brunette, with a look on her face that said this wasn't the first time she'd been caught in the middle of these two, said very diplomatically, "Ladies, we all want the same outcome here…a quality event that will give our kids a night to remember. Can't we try a little harder to get along and work together?"

"Stacey, it will all be fine. It always is. Heather makes grandiose, over-the-top plans, and I scale things down and bring us back to reality," Hillary replied.

Keegan was freshening up their water at the time when she heard the tiniest little mouse voice start singing a relevant section of "Lose Yourself" by Eminem, and she frantically clamped her hand over the pocket, trying to cover the sound of her little superstar's impromptu performance.

All three women looked at her strangely, but she kept her composure, cleared her throat, and said, "Does anyone need anything else?"

"No, we're good," replied Hillary. So, Keegan turned and quickly made her way to the break room. She caught Cara's eye on her way and signaled for her to join her. Keegan grabbed a Coke on her way and sat down in the thankfully empty break room. A few seconds later, Cara joined her.

"What's the emergency? I already had my break, so Carlos will completely lose his shit if I'm in here for more than a minute or two."

"Well, little Miss Thang here decided to do her best Eminem impersonation in front of a table of soccer moms. I think I covered okay, and it was actually pretty funny. But that's not why I wanted to talk to you. The moms were talking about a prom they were planning, and one of them was upset because of the poker tournament taking place before their event. When I heard that, I remembered that you signed up to work that tournament, didn't you?"

"Yeah, the caterer is a friend of a friend, so I'm helping her out. Why?" Cara replied. "Because I need you to get me a job working the tournament, too." Keegan paused and thought, *I wish I knew another way, but I'm afraid we're running out of time!* She finally said, "It's the answer to all our problems."

"Huh?" Cara said. "I am so lost right now." Keegan took a long drink of her Coke, sighed, and said, "We're going to rob the poker tournament."

"What the actual fuck, Keegan? You've completely lost it!" Cara exclaimed. "You want to steal money meant for a children's hospital? Are you some kind of monster?"

Keegan had the grace to look ashamed but said, "I know, I'm a horrible person. But I won't steal it all, and I swear on my moth-er's life, I will pay every cent back. I just need a quick influx of cash so I can find out what is wrong with my mom. I don't know what else to do, Cara. I'm afraid if I don't get her help soon, she's going to..." She couldn't finish that thought. She tried to blink back tears, but one escaped and trickled down her cheek. "Please help me."

Cara stared at Keegan for a moment, then sighed and said, "Fine, but you'd better come up with a foolproof plan. Because I love you like a sister, but I am not going to jail for your ass. I'm too pretty, what with this glorious caramel skin and these gorgeous black curls. I'd be somebody's bitch before dinner." She smirked, came over and stood behind Keegan, planted a kiss on the top of her head, and hurried back to work before Carlos could pitch a fit.

Áine poked her head out of Keegan's apron pocket, then crawled up her arm and nuzzled beside her cheek. "It will all work out, a stór. I feel it in my bones." Keegan sighed and said, "I hope so, Áine, I really do. Because I can't lose her. I won't." Then she tossed the empty soda cup in the trash and got back to work.

# Family

## is life

# TWO

Calder took a deep breath and began moving through his favorite yoga moves. A warm breeze ruffled his dark, slightly wavy hair, and he smiled, enjoying the view of Kansas City from the rooftop of his downtown business. He looked over at Lir, his goat companion, who was munching on some clover Calder had planted up here just for him. He was also doing a little dance and humming under his breath as he snacked. It was almost impossible to be upset or sad around Lir. Calder chuckled and returned his concentration to his yoga. As he moved through the progression of moves, he felt himself releasing the stress he'd been carrying around because of his brother, Liam, and his stupid poker tournament. *No, that's not fair,* he thought. *The poker tournament is a fantastic event that raises money for an incredibly worthy cause. I just wish Liam would back off a bit! He's so bossy, and he always has to get his way.*

Calder shook his head and tried to bring his focus back to his breathing. He took a deep breath...and his phone rang. It was Liam. Of course, it was. With a sigh, he admitted defeat and walked over to the bar he'd had installed. While he worked on making himself a cup of tea, he answered his brother's call.

"Dia duit," he said, annoyance apparent in his voice. "Whoa, little brother, why so cranky?" Liam replied. "Don't give me that, Liam," Calder said. "I know you're calling to pester me until I agree to host your poker tournament. And you know I'll wind up doing it because it's a good cause, and I want to help the sick children. But I don't have to pretend to like it, especially not with you."

Lir sensed the anger and frustration in Calder's voice and stopped eating, beginning to move over by him.

"Now listen, a Dheartháir Beag," Liam scolded, "I know you don't like being in the spotlight, but we all have to pitch in to make this event work. We don't want to disappoint the children."

"Liam, I may be your little brother, but you don't need to speak to me like I'm a child. And this isn't about everyone pitching in; this is about you pushing me to find a date. I don't know what your fascination is with my love life, but I can handle things just fine all by myself. I'm twenty-five fecking years old, I'm not exactly pining my life away alone. Just do us both a favor and fuck off!" Calder exclaimed, getting more worked up the longer they spoke. *My brother could always get a reaction from me. Damn it.* Lir rubbed himself against Calder's leg, offering comfort, and Calder reached down to run his hand across the silky black hair.

"Fine, Calder, I'll leave it alone. Just remember, I've got your best interests at heart. Yes, I can be pushy. It's just my nature. I see something I think needs fixing, and I fix it," Liam tried to explain.

Calder knew he should take the olive branch Liam was trying to offer with this explanation. His brother wasn't conciliatory very often. But...nope, not today. "Yes, Liam, but I don't need to be fixed. Trust me to live my life in whatever way works best for me!" Calder retorted.

"Okay, a Dheartháir Beag, have it your way. I'll let you learn things the hard way since you seem bound and determined to make your own mistakes," Liam snapped. "Don't forget, there's a meeting with the event planner on Thursday at six o'clock. Your attendance is required." Then he hung up without waiting for a reply.

That was just too much. Calder barely restrained himself from slamming his phone down, but he couldn't contain a short shout of frustration, "Fuck!" Unfortunately, that startled Lir, who locked up and fainted, falling over onto his side for a few seconds.

Calder was immediately remorseful and bent down to comfort Lir while he recovered from his shock. "Sorry, Lad, I let Liam get under me skin," he apologized, the Irish lilt coming through a bit stronger with his heightened emotions. "Let's go work in the studio and get our minds off all this nonsense. Let it sort itself."

By that time, Lir was wholly recovered, so they headed downstairs to get to work. He gently head-butted Calder and said, "Fine, but I get to pick the music."

Down in the studio, Calder uncovered the project he was currently working on. It was an intricately carved resin river table. He had several traditional woodworking tools lying around, and he even used them occasionally. But the real secret to Cliodhna Wood Artistry was Calder.

He might use a tool once in a while, and he certainly utilized his earth power when working with the wood. But the primary thing he used when carving these gorgeous, functional pieces of art—coffee tables, rocking chairs, any home furnishings really— was water. He combined a thin stream of water with sand and wielded it like a scalpel, making intricate, detailed masterpieces. He wasn't supposed to have a second elemental power. Then again, he wasn't your average Fae. The only problem was he had to keep it hidden. But since he and his family, members of the Earth Clan, had been keeping this secret since he was a child, it was second nature by now.

Today, he was still roughing out the riverbed, which would eventually be carved in such intricate detail that you could see individual rocks, plants, and even fish. Calder lived in the details and loved every minute of it. Since this was rougher work, he chose to do this part with the traditional tools, with occasional help from his earth power. He picked up a chisel and mallet, turned to Lir, and said, "What music do you want today, Lir?"

Lir looked up at him with those strange but somehow adorable golden goat eyes. "Actually, Calder, I was hoping we could talk first," he said. Calder stopped, put the tools down, and said, "Of course, Lir. What's on your mind?"

Lir gave him a long look and said, "I'm just wondering why you let Liam push your buttons the way you do. Do you know why you allow him to do that?"

Calder sighed and sat back on the worktable behind him. "Liam and I have a complicated relationship, you know that," he said.

Lir responded, "I know that you think it's complicated, but I'm not so sure. You have both assigned yourselves *unnecessary* blame; I know that, too. But I think if you could let go of that blame, then maybe you could just be brothers."

"I don't know, Lir. I feel like I have tried to be his brother, but he always insists on acting like he knows so much more than I do. It's infuriating."

"Instead of Liam trying to step in and be a father figure to you, and you rebelling almost as much as you would have for do athair fíor, maybe try to approach your relationship more like a friendship, at least in the short term. Now, if you really want to get to the core of the problem, you need to learn how to communicate with each other in a healthy way. I know you two don't really talk about your feelings, but..."

Calder interrupted, "I think that might be a step too far, at least for now. But I will try to at least be open to Liam's suggestions and not shoot them down simply because they're coming from him." He paused momentarily, then continued, "Sometimes I forget how wise you are, Lad. Thank you for reminding me."

"My pleasure," Lir responded, then he looked up at Calder, gave his best version of a goat grin, and said, "How about we listen to some Metallica today?" Calder chuckled, picked up his tools, and said, "Excellent choice. I'm feeling like some 'Enter Sandman.'"

# Family

# is life

CHAPTER

# THREE

Máire looked at herself in the full-length mirror critically, turning every which way. Then she scowled, ripped the dress roughly over her head, and threw it on the floor. "Nothing fits right! It's almost time for dinner, and I have nothing to wear. M'athair will pitch a bloody fit if I don't look impeccable!" she bemoaned to her best friend— a white, long-haired chihuahua named Laoise. She threw herself back on her bed in a fit of dramatics. She usually didn't allow herself this kind of tantrum, but it had been a hell of a day, and she decided a tiny bit of indulgence was acceptable.

Her room, while currently a hot mess, was decorated in various shades of rose, pink, and silver. There were luxurious pink silk sheets, soft silver blankets, and a furry rug, all in shades of pink, shaped like a rose. Her four-poster bed had dark rose-colored gauzy material draped around the posts, entwined with faery lights and tiny white silk roses.

Laoise hopped up from her soft, fluffy, pink dog bed at the foot of Máire's bed and knelt beside her head. "I know your da has ridiculously high standards, but you're an adult, Love. You can set your own standards now," she said, giving Máire's cheek a lick.

"It's not that simple, Laoise," she whispered, tears pooling in her pale green eyes. "I wish it were, but it isn't." The dog nuzzled Máire, gave her one more lick, and replied, "Yes, a stór, I do know." She paused momentarily, looking over the vast majority of Máire's wardrobe, which was currently strewn about the room, and said, "How about that high-waisted, mossy green linen dress? It should be a little more flattering and forgiving than most of your other clothes. And it really makes your eyes pop. Surely that would be acceptable. Oh, and those new strappy sandals you just got would look adorable with it!"

Máire sat up, tapping a finger against her lips as she considered the suggestion. "Yes to the dress, no to the sandals. I love them, but Athair would consider them too casual for dinner. I'll wear the nude pumps." Re-energized by the suggestion, she jumped up, found the dress and shoes, and began dressing. She paused momentarily to give Laoise a quick kiss, "Thank you, a chara. You're a lifesaver, as usual."

She sat down at her vanity and began pulling her shoulder-length strawberry-blonde hair into an updo. Then she put a quick glamour over her features, giving the illusion of some light makeup. Typically, she would have done her makeup the old-fashioned way, but she was in danger of being late, which was utterly unacceptable.

As she was rushing out the door, she looked back at Laoise, then at the absolute disaster she had made of her room. Her forehead furrowed, and it became apparent that she was so afraid of being late, but the uncharacteristic mess was causing her serious turmoil. Laoise transformed herself into a diminutive Fae, about the size of a six-year-old child.

"Go, Love. I've got this," she said. Máire flashed her a brilliant smile, threw a "Thank you!" over her shoulder, and rushed from the room.

Máire rushed down the stairs and around the corner, careful to run on her tiptoes so her heels wouldn't make any sound. When she was just a few feet from the formal dining room, she stopped, took a deep breath, and walked gracefully into the room, the picture of poise.

Her father, Cass, was seated at the head of the table, dressed in an impeccable silver suit. His slightly wavy, ginger hair was meticulously groomed, and his dark grey eyes were piercing. Máire's mother, Étaín, was seated at the other end of the table, looking just as polished. Her blonde hair was perfectly coiffed, and her makeup, jewelry, and dress were all the latest style and incredibly flattering. Her greyish green eyes flicked to Máire's as she entered, the only warning she would get that her father was in one of his moods. Steeling herself, Máire took her seat, flicking her napkin open and placing it gracefully over her lap, the perfect smile never leaving her face.

Just then, the antique grandfather clock struck the hour. Cass's eyes narrowed slightly, and he said, "Cutting it pretty close, aren't we? Were we interrupting something more important than dinner with your loving family?"

Máire froze the smile on her face, turned to her father, and said, "Certainly not. Time just got away from me; I do apologize." Then she lowered her eyes to her plate, hoping that was conciliatory enough to placate him.

Unfortunately for her, Cass was not in the mood to let imagined slights slide. "And when you do show up, you have the nerve to wear a barely serviceable frock and a glamour instead of taking the time and effort to apply your makeup yourself. Sure, the tide wouldn't take you out," he said, disdain dripping from every word. With each word, Máire sank a little lower in her chair.

"Now, Cass, I think she looks pretty in that color. Can't we just eat dinner in peace?" Étaín pleaded quietly, not even daring to raise her eyes.

Cass turned his attention to his wife, placing his forearms on the table and leaning forward aggressively; he bit each word off sharply, "And why would I want the opinion of someone such as yourself? You barely look any better. I really don't understand why I put up with this shite from the two of you." Then he clapped sharply twice and snapped, "Dinner will be served now!"

Servants quickly entered with the first course, several of them nearly tripping over themselves to serve the food quickly and get the hell out of that room.

Unseen by anyone, a tiny white spider crept along the base-board, darted over to Máire's chair, and climbed up into her hair, right next to her ear. She settled in to wait and see how she could help her beloved friend. Cass's narcissism had been growing lately, and his emotional abuse was at an all-time high. Laoise had done what she could to try and help mitigate the damage, but she was afraid it was taking a toll. Máire was becoming increasingly callous and bitter. Laoise was worried that if her friend didn't get away from Cass soon, she might be beyond saving. *Not if I have anything to say about it,* she thought.

The family ate in blessed silence for a few minutes. Máire was taking slightly larger bites than usual because, with the mood Cass was in, she was afraid he might just tell the servants to clear the table, and she would be unable to eat the rest of the evening. He had done it before and no doubt would do so again. While she was preoccupied with getting as much of her dinner eaten as quickly as possible, she missed the telltale signs that her father was becoming increasingly worked up again. Her mother flashed her several looks, hoping to clue her in, but that was as much help as she was willing to risk. Étaín was terrified her husband would leave her. So terrified, in fact, that as much as she did love her daughter, she was unwilling to risk Cass's disapproval to help Máire. The occasional look or nudge to try and warn her she was heading into dangerous territory was the best she felt she could do.

Laoise, on the other hand, was willing to do anything she could to help Máire. She let out a quiet "psst" beside her ear. Máire startled slightly, but luckily, Cass was looking at his food at that moment. "Slow down and take smaller bites," Laoise said. "D'athair is looking at you sideways."

Máire immediately slowed down and chewed her food more slowly. She took a drink of water, then paused for a couple of deep breaths. She began eating again, more slowly, taking smaller bites. She risked a glance at her father, but unfortunately, he was staring at her and took that as another opportunity to criticize.

"Have you been getting fatter?" he asked bluntly. Étaín gasped, then quickly covered with a cough and whispered, "Pardon me." Máire set her fork down, wiped the corners of her mouth with her napkin, and looked up at her father. She said, "I have gained a couple of pounds. But I've started working..."

"Nobody wants to hear your fucking excuses!"

Máire blushed and stammered, "I was just trying to..." Cass slapped his hand down sharply on the table, wincing slightly and pinching the bridge of his nose. "Don't bother. You are excused."

She knew it wouldn't matter, but she couldn't help looking briefly at her mother. Étaín dropped her eyes and continued taking tiny bites of her dinner. Máire took a deep, hitching breath, wiped the corners of her mouth with her napkin, and laid it across her plate. Then she stood up ramrod straight and walked from the room with as much dignity as she could manage, a tiny white spider whispering soothing words in her ear as tears silently streamed down her cheeks.

After Máire left, Cass looked at his wife and said, "You are excused, too. Get out of my sight." Étaín didn't bother arguing; it would do no good anyway. She simply stood, dropped her napkin on her plate, and walked from the room.

Cass dropped his head in his hands, trying to relieve the building pain behind his eyes by rubbing his temples and taking deep breaths. After several moments of ever-increasing agony, he stood up, swiped his dishes from the table, and screamed, "Leave me the fuck alone!"

The pain receded somewhat, begrudgingly, it seemed. He sat back down, breathing heavily. Then he smoothed back his hair, straightened his tie, and shouted, "Someone come clean up this mess and clear the table. Dinner is over." Then he stood and calmly walked toward his library, deciding there was still time to work on his latest project.

Family
is life

# FOUR

Keegan took off from the corner of the gymnastics mat, exploding into her favorite acrobatic sequence, and grinned at Cara as she stuck the final landing. She lifted both arms, turning and facing all four directions as if she were in a competition and posing for the crowd. Cara giggled and jumped up, clapping and screaming, "Woo hoo!" Áine took off from where she'd been perched on the upper uneven bar, zipping back and forth in the air, screeching, and hooting like a lunatic. Keegan responded with multiple dramatic curtsies and bows, occasionally throwing kisses to the crowd of two.

The two Fae collapsed into a giggling heap on the mat while Áine settled back on the bar and began preening herself. When they finally stopped cackling, Keegan said, "Man, I needed that. I haven't laughed like that in so long." Cara reached over and gave her hand a quick squeeze. Then she sat up and said, "What next? Balance beam? Uneven bars?"

Keegan cleared her throat, sat up, and said, "Nah, we do those all the time. I think it's time to christen Maria's new parkour course." Cara gasped, "I totally forgot! She finally got it; she's been talking about this forever!"

Maria was their former high school gymnastics coach, now retired and running a gym of her own. She mostly got gymnasts in here but recently had gotten a lot of requests for a parkour training facility, so she decided to add a course and see how things went. She had a soft spot for Keegan and Cara, so she gave them the code to the door and let them use the place after hours, provided they always cleaned up after themselves and locked up when they left.

Excited to try out the new course, they both hopped up and ran down the hall on the left to another room, this one set up with various obstacles for practicing parkour. Áine fluttered down from the uneven bar and began slowly walking after them, somewhat underwhelmed at the thought of the new course.

As they skidded to a halt in the new room, Keegan took in the latest addition to the gym, let out a shrill whistle, and said, "Kick. Ass." Then she began bouncing around the course, adding flips and spins randomly along the way. Cara joined in, and the two Fae spent the next half hour running, jumping, spinning, and flipping their way around the course at a speed the average human would be hard-pressed to emulate. Áine finally waddled into the room, looked the course over briefly, and said, "Awesome, something new to bounce around on. I can hardly wait." Then she hopped up on a bench along the wall, stuck her head under her wing, and promptly began snoring.

After a while, they finally started slowing down, and Cara flopped down on the floor, barely breathing hard. "That was bloody brilliant," she said with excitement. Keegan laughed, grabbed a towel from Áine's bench, and sat beside her on the floor. Then she wiped her face and the back of her neck with the towel, leaving it draped over her shoulders as she leaned back with her arms behind her. Looking over at Cara, she said, "So I think we need to talk about what's going to happen at the poker tournament."

Cara matched her position, sighed loudly, and said, "Not this again, cousin. I got you added to the servers for the tournament because I know you're trying to make as much money as possible to pay for your mom's doctors. I get that. But this talk of robbing them? It's nuts. What will your mom do if you end up in jail, huh?" Cara stood and began pacing, rapidly getting herself worked up.

Keegan jumped up and grabbed her arm, spinning her around to look her in the eyes. "I don't know, Cara. Just like I don't know what the fuck I'm supposed to do if she dies. Aside from the fact that she has been my whole world for my entire life, she has told me only the bare minimum about my fire power. I think she's trying to protect me, but all she's really accomplished is leaving me completely unprepared to deal with a major part of who I am. You've at least been able to help some with my air power and explain a bit about home, but I'm still so ignorant about the Fae homeworld and even how my powers work! I don't know what I'm doing," she ranted back at Cara.

"I know it's not right, Cara. And I know my mom would be ashamed of me for stealing. She taught me better than that. I've been wracking my brain for months, and I just can't think of anything else! We've never had a lot of money, but since Mom got sick and had to quit teaching a few months ago, what little savings we had is almost gone. If I knew we had enough time, I'd work my ass off and save up the old-fashioned way. The right way. But if she dies and I could've saved her? It will break me." The tears came then, spilling down her cheeks like water overflowing a dam.

Cara's large, cinnamon-colored eyes also welled up immediately, and she threw herself into Keegan's arms, saying, "I know, a stór, I know." Keegan was stoic for a moment, then she broke down and let herself have a moment of vulnerability with her best friend, finally allowing herself to release some of the stress and despair she'd been carrying for the past several months. As her mother's health declined, Keegan had built a wall around her emotions, but Cara's simple kindness allowed her to lower that wall and actually feel what she needed to feel.

The ruckus had finally awoken Áine, who fluttered over from the bench and wrapped her wings around both girls' heads, creating her version of a group hug. She was also quietly humming a lullaby, which took things to a whole new level. After a few moments, Keegan giggled and dried her eyes, saying to Áine, "Thanks, but I think we're good now." Áine lowered her wings and said, matter-of-factly, "Well, of course you are. My power to comfort is unsurpassed. You're welcome." The familiar did, however, decide to stay perched on Keegan's shoulder, nuzzling her hair slightly.

Turning to Cara, she said simply, "Thank you. I obviously really needed that." Cara smiled and said, "Anytime, you know that."

Keegan nodded, then sighed and said, "I know it makes you uncomfortable, but we really need to plan what we're going to do." Cara matched Keegan's sigh but said, "I know. Tell me what you had in mind."

Keegan's silver eyes lit up, and she said, "Okay, so I know you've done this tournament before because you kept talking about how well they paid the servers. But didn't you tell me you also helped collect the money from the various tables?"

Cara replied, "Yeah, two of us had these little carts, and we went around to the different tables, picking up their money in these little locked bags. Once we had all the tables done, we rolled the carts into this room, unlocked the bags, piled all the money into a safe, wrote down the total, and locked it up. Then we took the bags back to each table, and the process started all over again."

Keegan had been pacing back and forth during Cara's

description, but she stopped, crossed her arms, and began tapping her chin as she said, "Very good; I think that answers all my questions about logistics. Now, do you think you'll be able to get us both assigned to pick up the money?"

"Oh, sure. Derek always handles those assignments, and he's got a crush on me. He's a little socially awkward, but he's a sweet kid, and I've always been nice to him. He'll do me this favor, trust me." Cara replied with a grin. Derek was the sixteen-year-old son of the caterer, and Cara was one of his favorite people.

Keegan just nodded. Then, on a more serious note, she added, "Thank you, a stór. You have no idea how much this means to me." Cara took her hand and gave her a little squeeze. Keegan squeezed back, and her eyes lit up as she said, "Now it's time to go practice our getaway!" Glancing up at Áine, she exclaimed, "Come on, Lazy Bird, it's time to fly!" Then she pulled Cara toward the stairs leading to the roof.

A few minutes later, Keegan, Cara, and Áine finally made it to the roof after Cara reminded them that they needed to turn out the lights and lock everything up as promised. Áine complained loudly but picked up their sweaty towels and dropped them in the laundry hamper, doing her part to restore the gym to its former state.

Now that they were outside, looking out over the city lights, all three took a moment to enjoy the view. It was late at night, so it was calm and quiet. Cara began bouncing in place, saying, "I love it when we fly! This is the best use of our powers ever!" Keegan smiled at her friend and replied, "No argument from me." A thought occurred to her, and she said, "I know we've done this a few times with no problem, but remember to keep your focus. There will be no splatting on my watch!" Cara and Áine both nodded with serious expressions on their faces. Keegan glanced at Áine, grinned, and said, "I didn't mean you, dork. Flying is second nature for you." Áine lifted her beak in mock outrage and said, "Fine, see if I offer you my help as you go spiraling down to the cold, hard pavement. You're sure to be road pizza now." With that prophecy of doom, she took off, getting a head start on the flight home. Keegan yelled after her, "You are such a diva! But you know I love you!" A faint snort was the only reply.

Cara and Keegan quickly checked for any loose items on their persons, ensuring everything was tightened appropriately to avoid being lost on the trip. Then, Cara cast a quick invisibility glamour, and with one last look at each other, they took off running toward the gap. As they reached the edge, each pushed off and called on their air powers to support and boost them to the next roof. While more limited on Earth than on the Fae home-world, their powers were still sufficient to carry them easily from rooftop to rooftop.

At first, they would touch down for a few steps on each roof, but as they built momentum and gained confidence in their powers, they eventually became fully airborne, supported solely by their control over the air. At that point, Keegan and Cara glanced at each other and found they were both grinning like idiots, but neither could be bothered to care. When they finally landed in their backyard, Áine, who was perched on the back porch snacking on crickets, said, "Amateurs."

Family
is life

# FIVE

Lir looked over the tie choices with a critical eye. "I think you should go with the dark green one," he decided. Then with a grin, he added, "The color of money." Calder barked a laugh, picked up the lucky tie, and began tying it around his neck.

"I guess if I have to suffer through all the simpering entitlement, at least we can raise some money for the sick kids," he reasoned. "Goodness knows there are a few donors out there who have the best of motives. But for every one of them, ten others are only interested in giving if they get something out of it. It just gets old sometimes," he said with a sigh and shake of his head.

Finished with his tie, he ran his fingers quickly through his wavy, dark hair. Just when he thought he had it tamed, a rogue wave would pop up and look stupid. Finally, he snorted at his vanity and said, "Good enough." Looking himself over, he decided, *I guess I'm as presentable as I'm going to get.* He looked down at Lir and said, "Last chance, buddy. If you want to come tonight, you can. You can go as a goat or shift into something smaller and hang out in my pocket." Lir looked thoughtful, considering the matter. Seeing him on the fence, Calder added in a singsong voice, "There might be some delicious snacks!" Lir looked even more torn but then reached a decision and said, "Not tonight. I promised Reilly I'd take a look at the latest chapter in his novel. Besides, I've peopled really hard the past few days. I don't think I'm up for any more tonight. I'm going to shift into something with opposable thumbs and spend my evening read-ing." With that, he shifted into a chimpanzee, grabbed his copy of Reilly's in-progress book from the side table, and started for the door. As he crossed the doorway, he paused, looked over his shoulder, and said, "But if you see any snacks I might like, I wouldn't mind if you brought me a little treat." Calder gave a laugh and replied, "Will do."

Crisp, black, linen tablecloths provided the perfect background for the gorgeous floral centerpieces gracing each hi-top table. Tiny strands of faery lights were everywhere, sprinkling bits of light across the room. Dealers were taking their places at the various tables, ensuring everything was ready to go. The caterer had just called all the servers into the kitchen for a last-minute meeting, and the doorkeepers were getting ready to open the doors and allow entry to the guests. Calder stood on the mezza-nine balcony overlooking the bottled-up frenzy that was about to be unleashed. He took one last deep breath and prepared to descend into the fray.

Just then, the kitchen door swung open, and two young women, servers working for the caterer judging by their black pants and crisp white shirts, walked into the ballroom. The first was a pretty girl with caramel-colored skin and so many dark, black curls he wasn't sure how she contained them. She had kind eyes, the color of cinnamon, and Calder liked her immediately.

When Calder looked past her to the other woman, he forgot

to breathe. The setting sun streamed in through the big windows at the front of the ballroom, and as the fiery orange light hit her face, she seemed to be glowing, as if she were lit from within. She had sparkling silver eyes and riotous, red curls, almost as many as her friend, pulled back and held in place with a small section of braid.

A telltale sparkle around the tips of her ears hit him like a punch to the gut. *She's Fae,* he thought. *How is that possible? And how do I not know who she is?*

Calder had always believed that love at first sight was something found only in romance novels and faery tales. But since he was still having trouble catching his breath after only a brief glance at this unknown woman—scratch that, this unknown Fae—he was reevaluating that opinion. *At the very least,* he thought, *from now on, I will most definitely allow for the possibility of fascination at first sight. I'm not sure what I'm feeling exactly, but this girl is drawing me like a moth to a flame.*

Calder turned toward the staircase, ready to find the answers to his questions about this intriguing, captivating creature who'd just walked into his life and nearly ran into his older brother, Liam.

*Feck, feck, feckity, feck,* Calder thought. *I'm finally intrigued by a woman and want to pursue her, just as Liam had hoped, and now he's in my way. Sometimes I hate irony.*

"A Dheartháir Mór, everything looks lovely. I see the doors are about to open; I'd better get downstairs and get ready to mingle," he said, hoping to cut the conversation short and go find that redhead.

"That can wait. Before everything starts, I wanted to make sure you have everything you need," Liam said, looking up from his cell phone, which seemed to be an ever-present fixture with him lately. He hated that, but it seemed it was the cost of doing business. He focused his attention on his little brother, noticing that he seemed somewhat distracted. "Everything okay, Lad?" he asked.

Calder plastered a smile on his face and replied, "Never better. But I really need to get downstairs now. If I need anything, I'll come find you." Then he patted Liam on the shoulder and quickly headed for the stairs before his brother could do any more digging.

Liam watched him go with narrowed eyes. Something was up with his little brother, and he would figure out what it was. That was his job as firstborn, after all.

Keegan and Cara each picked up a tray of appetizers and got ready to mingle amongst the guests, who were just now entering the ballroom. Cara looked at her best friend's face, which looked more like she was about to face a firing squad than a bunch of hungry rich people. "Hey, dorkalicious," she whispered out the side of her mouth. Keegan was startled and looked over at Cara. "What?" she said. "You need to chill the hell out. You look constipated," Cara responded. "Help me out here, Áine."

Áine, currently in her tiny, red mouse form, poked her little head just barely above Keegan's apron pocket, looked up at her critically for a moment, then said, "That's not what she looks like when she's constipated, but I see your point. Keegan, you're gonna have to fake it 'til you make it, girlfriend. You're scowling so fiercely that your forehead wrinkles have wrinkles. Right now, if I had to pick someone guilty of something, you would be suspect number one."

Keegan looked back and forth between her two best friends in the world, shook her head, and took a deep breath, focusing on relaxing her face into something resembling calm. "Fine. But I'll have you two know I am not constipated."

A little mouse voice said, "Ew, TMI!" Keegan rolled her eyes and said, "You guys started it."

Cara said, "And it served its purpose by distracting you and getting you out of your head for a few minutes." Then she said, "Now, let's go feed some rich people."

The two Fae made their way through the growing crowd, offering appetizers to anyone interested. The turnout for this event was outstanding, but then again, it always was. You couldn't tug on the heartstrings any harder than an event to raise money for Children's Mercy Hospital. Everyone with a little bit of money wanted to be seen supporting this cause. And this charity, Do na Páistí, knew how to throw a party, that's for sure. But from what Cara could see, they also treated people well, which was far more rare.

Cara allowed herself a bit of people-watching. She was constantly amazed at what you would see if you just paid a little attention. As she and Keegan made their way through the crowd, Cara noticed that her best friend had drawn the attention of their host for the evening. He wasn't the charity's representative; she'd seen that one earlier, directing traffic when they arrived with all the food. However, he did look very similar. *Brothers maybe?* At any rate, neither one of them was very hard on the eyes, as Keegan's mom liked to say.

Keegan was doing a decent job of acting calm and relaxed, but Cara wasn't fooled. Her friend was still wound incredibly tight tonight. *Just let us both get through this without incident,* she thought. *A couple more hours, and we'll be home free.* They both ran out of food at about the same time, so they made their way back to the kitchen. As they were about to go through the door, Cara caught their host going all googly-eyed over Keegan. *Hmm, this could be an issue. I'll keep an eye on him and see how it goes.*

They made steady rounds through the crowd for the next hour. Keegan was hyper-focused and, therefore, oblivious to the gorgeous man practically panting over her. Cara just shook her head and smiled to herself. About this time, she felt her phone buzzing in her apron pocket. She checked it, and there was a text from Derek telling her it was time for their first money pickup. *Showtime,* she thought. She caught Keegan's eye and motioned with her head toward the kitchen. They both made their way over there and dropped their nearly depleted trays off.

In a pantry off the kitchen, there were two silver carts with several locking drawers, each with a big ring of keys attached to it by a retractable wire. They each grabbed a cart and started wheeling them out to the ballroom. Taped to the top of each cart was a list of which tables' money that cart should collect. So, they gathered the little zippered, locked money bags from each table, and once they had them all, they proceeded to the room with the safe and locked the door behind them.

They piled all the bags on the table, and while Keegan unlocked the bags, Cara began counting the money. It took a while; there was a lot to count. When she finally finished, she said, "Okay, that makes the total just short of thirty-nine thou-sand dollars."

Keegan stared at Cara for a minute and said, "Ho-ly-shit. And that's just from the first hour. Just wow." She shook her head and collected herself. "Ten percent, that's what we decided on. So, count out roughly four grand, and let's finish up before someone comes looking for us."

Cara said, "Way ahead of you, Sweetheart." She took the wad of cash she had set aside, wrapped a rubber band around it, and tossed it to Keegan. "Do your thing."

Keegan peered into her apron pocket and said, "You're up, hotshot. Make it quick; dawdling would be suspicious." She picked up Áine the mouse and said, "Ready?" Ever the performer, the little red mouse channeled her best Lady Gaga and sang, "Baby, I was born that way!" Unable to contain the eye roll,

Keegan said, "Oh, for crying out loud. You're going to need your wings, your excellence." She tossed Áine into the air, where she shifted back into a scarlet macaw and landed on Keegan's shoulder. She held out a claw, and Keegan handed her the money. Áine took it and flew up to the exposed ductwork near the ceiling. A backpack was waiting up there, placed in advance right after they arrived and were helping set up, to avoid suspicion. She managed to get the money inside the backpack and flew back to Keegan's shoulder.

Meanwhile, Cara had already recorded the corrected total, shut, and locked the safe. Áine shifted back to her mouse form and did a cannonball back into Keegan's apron pocket, making Cara giggle and helping to alleviate some tension.

Keegan took a deep breath and said, "One down, three more to go." Then they rolled the carts out of the room, across the ball-room, dropping off the money bags as they went, and parked them back in the pantry where they found them. Once that was done, they picked up freshly loaded trays and headed back to the ballroom to feed the hungry rich people.

Calder had spent the vast majority of the evening moving from one frustrating interaction to another, and he was quickly losing patience. First, he was required to hobnob and mingle with all the angel donors, so they would feel like they were getting their money's worth. He had no idea how a brief visit with him would accomplish that, but it seemed to be a necessity. Once he had finally made it through all the donors he needed to schmooze with, he had set out to find that intriguing Fae redhead. He was free for about two and a half minutes before being cornered by the very new, very nervous head of facilities, who was concerned about all the candles potentially setting off the fire suppression sprinklers. *Like I know anything about sprinklers?* he thought.

He might not know sprinklers, but he did know how to listen to concerns and find someone who might actually be able to resolve the issue, which in this case meant soothing the fears of an inexperienced but well-meaning facilities supervisor. It took him a while, but he eventually found the right person to talk the nervous Nelly down from the ledge.

After that, he was free for a whole five minutes before there was another emergency that only he could solve. This time, the caterer was convinced she hadn't prepared enough food. She was on the verge of running down to Costco to beef up the appetizers, but Calder convinced her that she had indeed prepared the appropriate amount of food. And even if they did run out, they had more than enough beer, wine, and liquor, which was what most people were interested in at this point in the evening anyway.

On the plus side, at least this crisis took place in the kitchen, so he was able to watch his new favorite redhead and her dark-haired friend as they dropped off empty trays and picked up two silver carts, pushing them out into the ballroom to collect the money from the tables. He tried to be low-key and not stare at her, drooling, but he was afraid he was only partially successful. At least he didn't think he had drooled on anything. Staring, however...he was pretty sure he qualified as a super stalker at this point. *There's just something about her.*

He had just left the kitchen, intending to finally start a conversation with his elusive redhead, when his brother, Conor, snuck up behind him, threw an arm over his shoulder, and said, "What's the craic, a Dheartháir Beag?" Calder sighed, pinched the bridge of his nose, and said, "Bloody hell."

"Oh, come now, I may not be a redhead, but surely you can manage a little love for your most handsome brother?" Calder just stared at him, stunned and speechless. Conor barked out a laugh and said, "You haven't exactly been subtle, Lad. I didn't notice your new obsession, but I have my adoring fans to keep me occupied. But big brother, Liam? He notices everything." Calder sighed and said, "I should have known." Conor replied, "Yes, you really should have. But at least in this case, you happen to be pursuing something our loving brother approves of. Which brings me to why I'm here. With you. Instead of the aforementioned adoring fans. Liam asked me to relieve you of your duties for the evening, so you may go pursue this intriguing redhead. Who happens to also be, stop me if you've heard this one, a Fae. And I am absolutely dying to know why I know nothing of this little hottie. Granted, I play for a different team, but I still like to know all the players. Anyway, I'm tagging in, so bring on the annoying fires; I'll put them all out. You can thank me later. And you should also thank Liam, you know. But I'll leave that between you and him. Happy hunting, bud! Slán!"

Conor slapped him on the back a little harder than was strictly necessary and started to walk away. Calder grabbed his arm, spun him around, and gave him a quick hug, whispering, "Thank you, brother." Conor smiled at him, showing off dimples that drove the other boys crazy, and replied, "My pleasure, Love. Go find her."

Calder quickly compartmentalized the gratitude he was feeling. Gratitude for Conor wasn't that unusual. Gratitude for Liam, however, was a different story. But he could deal with that later. Right now, he had a redhead to stalk.

He quickly scanned the ballroom and caught a glimpse of red curls disappearing around the corner. He quickly followed, hoping to catch her alone or at least with only her cinnamon-eyed friend. He wasn't quite quick enough, though, and the door to the safe room clicked shut as he turned the corner. *Crap,* he thought. *I left the venue keys in the kitchen.* He turned around and nearly ran back through the ballroom. Unfortunately, not everyone had gotten the memo that Conor was taking over for him. So, he had to gently but firmly extricate himself from a couple of different conversations.

He finally reached the kitchen, grabbed his keys, and headed back across the ballroom toward the safe room. The entire time, he was going over in his head what he would say. How he would introduce himself, ways he might compliment her...he really needed to make a good impression. He reached the safe room door, took a deep breath, unlocked it, and opened the door in one smooth motion. What he saw made him question his sanity.

Next to the safe, the dark-haired girl was putting the money, or most of it at least, into the safe and writing down the amount in the logbook. None of that was unusual, but the rest of the scene more than made up for it. The object of his infatuation was in the process of tossing what appeared to be a tiny, red mouse into the air. The mouse then shifted mid-air to a scarlet macaw, who turned back to face the redhead. As if that wasn't strange enough, the silver-eyed Fae took that opportunity to toss a big wad of cash into the air and gave a little twist with her hand, sending a gust of air to help guide the money into the parrot's waiting claws. The bird grabbed the cash, flew up to some duct-work near the ceiling, and dropped the money into what appeared to be a backpack partially filled with other wads of cash.

Calder kept looking back and forth between the two Fae, occasionally glancing up at the parrot, not wanting to believe his eyes. *I finally found someone I'm interested in. She's even a Fae, which causes some problems but eliminates others. And she's a bloody thief.* He shook his head, a look of disgust coming over his face. He stepped into the room, the sound causing all three females to whip their heads toward him and freeze. He closed the door behind him. *No need to involve anyone else in this circus,* he thought. As he took another step toward Keegan, her temporary paralysis dissolved, and she squared up to him and called fire into both her hands.

That stopped him dead in his tracks. *Another Dúbailte? (Damn, I hate that word.) How the fuck was that even possible?* His brain began spinning off in directions he couldn't keep up with. However, Keegan chose that moment to cause the flames in her palms to flare up, redirecting his attention nicely.

Áine leapt off the ductwork and shifted into an eagle, diving down to land on one of the tables beside Keegan, making her allegiance clear. Cara decided it was time for some damage control. She stepped up next to Keegan, put her hand on her shoulder, and calmly said, "Everybody take a deep breath."

Keegan said, her eyes never leaving Calder, "I'll breathe when I'm dead. Wait, that came out wrong." Cara patted her back and said, "Love, I think you can put the flames away. I don't believe we're in any imminent danger. But I do think we need to have a conversation, and time is limited."

Keegan glanced at her friend and then at Áine with a questioning look. "Don't ask me," Áine said with as much of a shrug as her eagle wings could manage. "I'm ride or die. I will light the place on fire and laugh as we watch it burn if that's what you need from me. But yeah, de-escalation is maybe not my strong suit." Keegan thought about it for another moment, then clenched her fists, causing the flames to die.

Cara said, "Alright then. Why don't we start with some introductions? I am Cara Delaney, a Fae from the Air Clan. At least my mom is of the Air Clan; my dad was human, so I'm a half-breed." The look of shame that quickly crossed her features at that term told Calder most of what he needed to know about her. He nodded politely at Cara, then looked at Keegan, waiting for her introduction.

Keegan stared back defiantly for a minute, then Cara cleared her throat and elbowed Keegan lightly in the ribs. "Ow! Fine. My name is Keegan Doran, and I belong to the Fire Clan. Obviously." Then she clamped her lips shut and refused to say any more.

Calder, slightly amused by Keegan's attitude, said, "But didn't I just see you use air power as well?" Keegan's eyes widened, and she stammered, "No, just fire. You must be mistaken." Calder crossed his arms over his chest and said, "Oh, really? I don't think I am. Right after you tossed the mouse/parrot in the air, you used air power to guide the money into its claws."

Keegan shook her head, "Nope, that was just a perfect toss." The look of stubbornness on her features convinced Calder to back off on that particular point for the moment.

Áine whistled and said, "You hoo, mouse/parrot over here. Since nobody else wants to introduce me, I guess I'll do it myself. The name is Áine. And I am most definitely not an 'it.'" She took that opportunity to shift back to her parrot form and continued her commentary, ostensibly talking to herself but at an increased volume. "How anyone could mistake me for anything other than a queen absolutely boggles the mind, but maybe he's a little slow."

Calder's lips twitched, but he mostly maintained a straight face. "Okay then, I guess it's my turn. My name is Calder Ó Faoláin, and my family belongs to the Earth Clan." Then he held his hand out toward a potted plant located near the curtained windows, whose buds were almost ready to flower. With a twist of his wrist, all the buds trembled, and gorgeous, deep red blossoms burst forth. It was so beautiful that Keegan couldn't contain a small gasp, and her defiant expression finally softened a bit.

Calder looked at Keegan, and she glanced away from the plant and back at him. *Do I trust her?* he thought. *I don't know anything about her. But she is Dúbailte, no matter what she says. I know what I saw. And there's that damn feeling again that I should keep her close. Protect her.*

Then he gave a slight nod as if coming to a decision. He reached his hand up, clenched his fist, and pulled downward. Suddenly, several tiny droplets of water appeared out of the air and followed the motion of his hand. He guided the water over to give the newly transformed plant a drink.

Áine let out a squawk and said, "Holy shitturds, Batman! I did not see that one coming!"

The three other Fae looked at each other, and all started cackling. After a minute, Keegan shook her head and mumbled, "Fuck my life."

Calder took a deep breath and said, "Alright, cailíní, let's begin again. Now that we both know about our special abilities, maybe you can explain why you're stealing money from sick children?"

Keegan pinched the bridge of her nose and shook her head. Cara said, "I told you. Monster."

Keegan said, "First of all, we aren't really stealing it. We're simply borrowing it because we will definitely pay it back." Now it was Cara's turn to pinch the bridge of her nose and shake her head.

Calder gave a short laugh and said, "Not sure where that present tense is coming from because you have been caught. Red-handed. You're not leaving here with that money. I can't be much clearer than that."

Keegan took a deep breath to retort, but Cara stepped between the two, lifted her hands, and said, "Time out."

Calder took a slow, deep breath and thought, *Not only is she a thief, but she's also a stubborn arse! She does have gorgeous eyes, though. Damn it!* He shook his head to clear his mind.

*I need that money!* thought Keegan, desperation increasing by the minute.

Cara lowered her hands and looked at Keegan, saying, "Of course, we're not keeping the money. Keegan, we'll be lucky if we don't go to jail." That gave Keegan pause, and she swallowed hard, thinking about the possible ramifications.

Calder stared at them for a full minute, then he started pacing back and forth in front of the door, obviously having an internal debate. *I don't have any reason to trust them. But I can't shake this feeling that I'm supposed to.* Finally, he decided to put them out of their misery. "I'm not going to send you to jail." They both let out audible sighs. "But I do think I deserve to know why you were trying to steal from us?"

Cara lowered her eyes and took a step back. This was Keegan's story to tell.

Keegan's eyes got a faraway look in them. She said, "When my mom found out she was pregnant with me, she was terrified. She'd grown up with that stupid prophecy; I'm sure you know the one I'm talking about."

Calder gave a curt nod and said, "The Aisling Prophecy. Also known as the Dúbailte Curse."

"The very one," she said with disdain. "So, she did the only thing she could think of; she ran. She came to Earth, had me, and that, she thought, was that. But a few months ago, right after my twenty-first birthday, actually, she started getting sick. She just keeps getting weaker and weaker, and nobody can tell me why. We don't have much money, and it costs a lot to hire specialists to figure it out." She paused and caught a hitching breath. "So that's why I need to borrow some money."

Calder said, "No, I won't lend you any money." She felt her eyes welling with tears, so she quickly looked at the floor. He stepped closer to her and lifted her chin with one finger until she looked him in the eye. *Her skin is so soft,* he thought. *Come on, man, focus!* "I didn't say I wouldn't help you. But I really don't think your human doctors will be able to help, no matter how much you pay them." Keegan blinked her tears back and said, "But then what can I do? I can't just let her die. I won't."

Looking thoughtful, he cocked his head to the side and said, "Let me go speak to my mother. If she doesn't know something that will help, she will insist on finding someone who does. Aos Sí have millennia of experience treating illness and injury. Someone will know what to do."

Keegan turned to Cara and collapsed against her friend, shuddering with relief at the thought of finally finding a cure for her mother. *Maybe I won't have to do something I'm ashamed of,* she thought. Cara stroked her hair and whispered soothing nonsense against her ear, swaying back and forth.

Calder turned partially away for a moment, giving Keegan and Cara a moment. Then he cleared his throat and said, "There's one other thing. If I'm going to be spending a great deal of time going back and forth to Tír na nÓg, and I truly don't mind doing so, but I'm going to need some help with my business. I have no doubt that you three can help keep me from falling behind. I will, of course, pay you for your labor. Extremely well, provided I get your best effort."

Áine waddled across the table toward Calder and said, "Can I get paid in crickets and jewelry?" With great difficulty, Calder managed to keep a straight face and replied, "Of course, a Bhanríon."

Áine stuck her wing out and said, "Deal." Calder gently shook her wing and repeated, "Deal."

Family
is life

CHAPTER

# SIX

The pilot announced they were descending at a private airstrip just outside Dublin. Calder stretched in his seat and then rubbed the sleep from his eyes. He looked over at Lir, curled up, sleeping, and snoring in his own oversized recliner, and grinned. He was glad for the excuse to visit Tír na nÓg and even more delighted to visit his mother. She was the matriarch of their family, and her boys loved her dearly. It had been a couple of months since he'd seen her, and that just felt like too long. Family is life.

He hopped up to make himself a cup of tea, trying to stay as quiet as possible so Lir could get a few more minutes of sleep. His friend was always good-natured, but he could get a little cranky if he didn't get his beauty sleep. But Lir was excited about the trip home, even on such short notice.

When Calder had finally gotten home from the poker tournament, he made the impromptu decision to call his family's pilot and fly to Dublin immediately. His mind was spinning from everything that had happened in the past few hours, and he felt a great responsibility to help Keegan figure out what was causing her mother's weakness. *Sooner begun, sooner done,* he thought. He

53

wished there was a quicker way to get to the Tír na nÓg portal, but faery trees weren't exactly easy to find. So, his only option was to make the long flight to Dublin and then a much quicker drive to the Faery Tree of Tara.

He took a sip of his hot tea, burning his tongue. *Damn,* he thought. *I am so off my game. That cailín has my head spinning!*

Lir decided it was finally time to wake up, stretching and yawning before popping his head up and saying, "Are we there yet?" Calder chuckled and said, "Yes, we're about to land. I brought you some clover and water. They're over at the end of the table."

Lir stood up, gave one more big stretch, then walked over for a little snack and a long drink. After a few moments, they felt the descent, and the plane touched down. Calder grabbed his overnight bag, then he and Lir departed the plane. A dark green BMW was waiting on the tarmac, and the two travelers wasted no time getting in. The driver from the Ó Faoláin estate, an older gentleman named Thomas, looked back at them and said, "It's lovely to see you, Lads. I'm so glad you're going to see your mam, Calder; it's been too long."

"I know, Thomas. I'll try to do better," he replied. Thomas nodded and began driving toward the road that led to the Hill of Tara.

Lir kept pestering Thomas until he finally opened the sunroof in the BMW and let the goat climb up on the center console so he could stick his head out the top of the vehicle. Once he got up there, he was so excited he was doing a little happy dance. Thomas kept shaking his head and whispering, "Silly bloody goat." But there was a smile on his face as he said it.

Lir and Calder, preoccupied though he was, enjoyed the

drive through County Meath. There was something so relaxing about coming back to Ireland. He loved aspects of Kansas City, but being amongst the green hills felt like home, with good reason. Tír na nÓg was a lush island paradise, not unlike the Emerald Isle, albeit the flora and fauna were a bit more eccentric. But even better than the gorgeous scenery was the power boost Fae received on the homeworld. A reasonably powerful Fae could do minor to mid-level magic on Earth without much trouble. But in Tír na nÓg? That same Fae would be able to handle upper-level magic pretty easily. This brought up another question: How in the world was Keegan so strong? When she had called fire into her hands, he had a moment of genuine surprise at the height of her flames and more than a bit of concern. Calder's best guess was that since she appeared to have grown up on Earth, she'd always had to work a little harder to make her magic work. So that meant when she finally made it to the homeworld, her powers would be off the charts. *Note to self: don't piss her off, especially not in Tír na nÓg,* he thought.

About this time, a bug flew straight into Lir's eye, which startled him, making his muscles lock up, and the poor goat toppled over into Calder's lap. He ran his hand over the silky goat hair on his side for the few seconds that Lir was paralyzed. When his muscles relaxed, the little goat ducked his head, embarrassed, and curled up into a tight knot in Calder's lap. Calder gave him a few pets and said quietly, "It's alright, pal. I wanted to do it, too." Lir relaxed a little more and gave a little sigh before nodding off for the last few minutes of the trip.

When they approached the Hill of Tara, Calder was pleased to see the light drizzle had kept the tourists to a minimum. Thomas parked the vehicle as far away from the other cars as possible. Calder had gently woken Lir and was gathering his bag when Thomas cleared his throat and began speaking. "Lad, I want you t' be careful. I don't know what's comin', but it's something big. I feel it in me bones."

Calder looked thoughtful for a moment, then replied, "I will be more careful, Thomas. Thank you for the warning." Whether or not Calder believed in the old man's vague premonition, taking extra care was never a bad idea, so it hurt nothing to agree. And he truly did appreciate the sentiment behind the warning.

He and Lir stepped out of the car, and as Calder straightened up, he threw a quick invisibility glamour over them. He shut the door, and Thomas slowly pulled away.

Thankfully, Lir and Calder could still see one another. Since they were on Earth, the glamour was only strong enough to work on humans. They made their way over to the Faery Tree, which was beginning to be covered with rags and other detritus left behind by some of the tourists that constantly visited. Periodically, Druids would come out and clear all the trash away; otherwise, the tree would sicken and eventually die.

Calder had called ahead when the plane landed to let the Druids know they were on the way. The four of them were making their way to the far side of the Faery Tree. They were also hidden from human sight; there was no reason to cause a scene with the tourists. It appeared the Druids were also strengthening the rain, hoping to keep looky-loos from stumbling onto the creation of a portal, potentially even falling through. *No, thanks,* he thought. *Not today.*

The Druids began quietly chanting, each one calling upon their elemental power. Fire was called, dancing up and down the hand and arm of a dark-haired Fae. Water joined next, weaving in and out of the fingers and around the wrist of the blonde-haired, green-eyed Fae whose hand hovered inches away from the first. Then it was Earth's turn—rock, dirt, and various plants and flow- ers, going through the growing cycle, blooming, dying, then growing and blooming again, swirling and spinning along the palm and forearm of a Fae with short brown hair. And finally, there was air. Wind swirled around a red-headed Fae who reminded Calder for a split second of Keegan. The breeze began swirling around all four Druids, drawing them closer until the moment their hands touched, and a buzzing began, followed by a bright light emanating from where their fingers touched. As they began stepping back, the light grew larger and larger, showing a rich green landscape on the other side with fuzzy edges, similar to the surrounding Irish countryside but different in many ways as well. The Druids then twisted their wrists, flipping the portal perpendicular to the ground instead of parallel.

Calder and Lir wasted no time, quickly walking up to and through the portal, disappearing from view.

There was an unsettling moment as the two traveled through the portal, but it passed as soon as they were both entirely in Tír na nÓg. Lir hadn't taken two steps before his whole body began to undulate, and he shifted into his púca form, a huge black horse with a wild mane and glowing golden eyes. He reared up on his hind legs, pawing the air, and bellowed out a neigh that definitely got your attention.

Calder shook his head and said, "Way to keep it low-key, Buddy. Care to give me a ride?"

Lir trotted over to him, and Calder grabbed a handful of mane and pulled himself up on the púca's back. "Let's see if you've still got it; what do you say?" he asked with a grin. Lir took that challenge seriously, pawed a couple of times at the ground, and almost growled, "Better hold on then, man."

Lir trotted to the edge of the gardens, then leapt forward as if he was spring-loaded, tearing across the grassy meadow. He could turn on a dime and took great pride in providing a thrilling ride. He was a self-respecting púca, after all.

The Ó Faoláin manor wasn't very far away, but it had been a long time since Lir and Calder had been able to enjoy a good ride, so Lir took the scenic route. He ran along the edge of the woods that backed up to the main house, ducking in among the trees. All of this was done at a speed that defied belief, but Calder hung on tight, cackling the entire way.

Calder's mother, Siobhán Bhean Ó Faoláin, a petite blonde woman with eyes the same shade of green as his, stepped out onto the back porch and took a look at what was taking her youngest so long. The Earth Druid at the World Tree had informed her as soon as they crossed over, but they should have made it home by now. She spotted Lir having a version of the púca zoomies along the tree line and thought, *Oh, for pity's sake.* Then she let fly a whistle that could stop a bird in mid-flight. And it did, indeed, stop Lir mid-antic. He calmed himself and trotted to the house as sedately as he could manage. Calder, however, could not wipe the ear-to-ear grin from his face if his life depended on it. Seeing that, Siobhán cracked a small smile herself.

Calder dismounted and headed toward his mother, but was shouldered aside by his supposed best friend, as Lir never turned down an opportunity for a good scratch behind the ears, and Siobhán gave the best scratches. Calder patiently waited while she indulged the needy púca, and once she gave him a final pat and pushed him to the side, he stepped forward and wrapped her in the biggest bear hug, even giving her a spin before setting her back down. "Oh, it's so good to see you, Mam," he said. "I've missed you."

"Well, of course you have, mo bhuachaill, I'm your mam, and you've been ignoring me for far too long," she gently chastised, softening the words with her palm on his cheek.

"I know, I know," he replied. "It's just hard for me to be here and have to hide half of who I am. Not to mention the awkwardness with Morgan." He paused momentarily, lost in thought, then shook himself and continued, "But that's no excuse for missing visits. I'll make a better effort, I promise."

"That's all I ask, Love," Siobhán said, with a peck on his cheek. "Now, come inside, and we can get to the bottom of whatever is bothering you. Don't ask how I know; it's a mother's job. Are you coming in, Lir? If so, pick a smaller form, please." Lir shifted back to his goat form, and she ushered them both inside.

The back door they entered through opened into a huge kitchen area, the heart of the Ó Faoláin home. A few cousins were working on the evening meal, and the room smelled amazing. Lir wandered over to a cousin who could always be counted on for a juicy tidbit. She quickly slipped him a morsel, and he hurriedly caught up with Calder and his mother, who were just taking a seat at the enormous, round kitchen table.

Calder had so many memories that had occurred at this table. He ran his hand along the intricately carved edge, proud of his family's skill with their earth power. Just then, his mother covered his hand with hers, giving it a quick squeeze. "What is it, Love?" she asked gently. "You know you can tell me anything."

"I know, Mam," he replied. "I've met someone who could use our help. I thought maybe you'd have some information I don't."

"Well, now I'm intrigued," she said. "Give me the details." She patted his hand, crossed her arms, and leaned forward on her elbows, obviously interested in hearing more.

Calder told her what he knew of Keegan's story: how her mother had become pregnant and run away to Earth and how she had never even been to Tír na nÓg. He told her Niamh's name and that she was part of the Fire Clan. Siobhán said, "Oh yes, the Doran family. Both parents were killed in an accident when Niamh and her sister were teenagers. I remember that one of them disappeared about twenty years ago, but I never knew what happened."

Then he took a deep breath and said, "There's something else." Siobhán raised an eyebrow at the seriousness of her son's tone but remained quiet, waiting for him to proceed. He opened his mouth to tell her Keegan's secret, but Lir cleared his throat and said, "Not to complain, but could we go somewhere I could lie down? It's been a long day. I'd go myself, but I'd like to be there for the discussion." Siobhán replied, "Of course. Let's go to my library."

She stood and led them from the kitchen, down the hall, and around the corner to the great room. The entire house was covered with ornately carved woodwork. Various family members would add or change scenes as they liked, so the styles from one panel to the next might vary greatly, but every inch was master-level work. The only part of the house that was never touched was the mantle in the great room. That scene had been carved by Siobhán's late husband, Fallon, and the craftsmanship was unmatched. It consisted of a large wolf pack sprawled across a grassy hill. The precision was uncanny, and the playful pups romping through a patch of wildflowers almost appeared ready to leap off the wall. There were adult wolves watching over the pups and sentries scanning their surroundings. Even the grass and flowers seemed to be waving in the breeze. It made Calder catch his breath every single time he saw it; it was so stunning, and today was no exception.

Siobhán gave it a sad smile as they passed through before taking another hallway to the right. At the end of that hall was her library, which she entered and proceeded to sit behind her desk. Calder sat on the other side, and Lir climbed up on the sofa. He was part of the family as well, after all.

So, what else did you want to tell me, Lad?" she asked. Calder leaned forward and said, "Keegan is Dúbailte. Fire, like her family, but also air." Siobhán's eyes widened, and she slammed her hand down on the table sharply. "I will comment on the content of that remark shortly, but firstly, don't you dare use that word in my presence! The superstition surrounding that gods-damned prophecy is the bane of my existence, and we will not further it in any way. Is that clear?" she snapped in a tone that tolerated no dissent.

"Yes, Mam," Calder replied, unable to keep a slight grin from his face. "Don't think I don't see that smile, Lad. Keep it up, and you'll be mucking out more than your fair share of stalls," she replied, pointing at him for good measure. "There's one more thing, and the most important reason I'm here. Aside from seeing your lovely face, of course," Calder continued, throwing in a little sugar for good measure. Siobhán's only response was an eye roll. "Niamh has recently begun weakening. They've tried human doctors, but they weren't able to help. Do you know what might be causing the weakness?"

She looked thoughtful, then said, "I have a few ideas, but I need to ask around and see what I can find out for sure." Calder nodded since that was precisely what he expected her to say. She was well-respected within the Earth Clan and Aos Sí in general. He had no doubt she could collect information to which he just didn't have access.

Suddenly, there was a knock at the door. "Yes?" she responded, and the door opened just enough for one of the cousins to poke his head inside and say, "Sorry to interrupt, a hAintín Siobhán, but Máire Daugherty is here, and she insists on seeing you."

*Of course she does,* Siobhán thought, her eyes narrowing slightly at the level of presumption she was showing. *That one bears watching.*

"Very well, Colin. Please show her into the Great Room. We

will be with her shortly." Her nephew nodded and left to deliver the message.

To Calder, she said, "Son, would you mind keeping her company for a few moments? I need to send some messages while this is all fresh in my mind. I won't be long." He replied, "Of course," and stood to leave the room.

Lir, who had been snoring off and on for the past few minutes, perked up and said, "I'll join you." Calder nodded and said, "Let's go," and they both left the library to attend to their visitor.

Máire was looking up at the extraordinary carving above the mantel with tears in her eyes, her feelings a mishmash of envy, awe, and intimidation. This home exuded a sense of comfort and love, which confused and disturbed Máire. She was so used to functioning in survival mode that any reminders that not all families had that level of dysfunction were most unwelcome.

She heard the sound of footsteps, oddly spaced footsteps at that, and quickly dried her eyes and schooled her expression to slightly bored superiority. The door opened, and in walked a silky, black goat, followed by Calder Ó Faoláin. She had always had a strange fascination with him, ever since he had been kind to her after a particularly embarrassing dressing down she'd received from her father. He had found fault with her performance at a school concert and had told her exactly what he thought of it in front of what seemed like everyone in the world. Calder had seen that debacle and had made a point of stopping to talk to her, complimenting everything her father had just picked apart. She was immediately entranced.

But shortly after that, Calder had suddenly left Tír na nÓg, apparently being sent to work for the Ó Faoláin family business on Earth. Máire had been devastated. Calder, however, had no idea of the part he played in her fantasies.

He entered the room behind Lir, smiling politely, and said, "Hello, Máire. My mam will be here shortly. Can I get you anything to drink while we wait?" He vaguely remembered cheering her up a few years ago after her father had been a complete arse to her. He hoped she had been able to get out of his shadow. Lir hopped up on a sofa, sensing there was some entertainment to be had with this one.

Máire's face lit up, and she rolled her shoulders back, putting her ample cleavage on display. "Calder? I had no idea you were here. When did you get back?" She batted her eyes, ratcheting up the flirtation to an almost comical scale.

Calder had a slightly confused look on his face as he attempted to discern precisely what was going on with the woman. "Well, I'm not really back, just here for a brief visit. But how have you been?" he said, turning the conversation back on her.

Máire took that opportunity to take the few steps separating them and latch herself onto his arm. She looked up at him and said, "Oh, I'm doing really well! I've been named to the Council, as you can see," pointing to the torque tattooed around her neck. It consisted of several strands of Celtic knotwork, braided together, ending in a triquetra on each side, just at the level of her collarbone. Little flames flickered throughout the knotwork, denoting her affiliation with the Fire Clan. He used that as an excuse to slip out of her grasp and point to the tattoo, taking great care not to actually touch her skin, and said, "That is beautiful ink, Máire. Just lovely." Then he quickly walked over to the bar and poured himself a glass of ice water. "Can I get you a drink?" he said, trying to appear busy enough to avoid any more physical contact, the message finally reaching him that she was giving off some serious stalker vibes.

She almost skipped over to the bar, leaning forward to, once again, put her cleavage to good use. "I'd love Sex on the Beach," she purred. Calder made a concerted effort not to roll his eyes, but was saved from having to respond by the entrance of Siobhán. One look from her and Máire promptly stood up straight, putting the girls back where they belonged.

"Cead mile fáilte, a Máire," Siobhán said as she crossed the room. "How can I help you?"

Máire looked slightly flustered, but she quickly pulled herself together, fixing her features into the slightly haughty expression that had become her resting face. "I was just stopping by to discuss that mare that Athair wants to buy."

"Then I'm sorry to say you wasted a trip. I've told your father more than once that Morrígan is not for sale. It would be tremendous if he would deign to listen this time," Siobhán replied shortly. "I look forward to seeing you at the Council meeting next week. Can you see yourself out, or should I call for Colin to escort you?"

Máire stuttered slightly when she replied, "N-n-no, I know the way." Then she turned around and left the room, risking a final glance over her shoulder at Calder, who made it a point to look elsewhere.

Once Máire was gone, Siobhán turned to Calder and said, "I've started the process of gathering what information I can about the family, as well as what might be causing her illness. But you know what you need to do if you really want an answer to this problem." She just looked at him for a moment, letting him take the time he needed to come to the conclusion he didn't want to reach. Finally, he sighed and said, "I need to speak to the healers, don't I?"

"Yes, Love, you do," she replied sympathetically. She knew how uncomfortable he was with that course of action.

He nodded and said, "Then that's what I'll do. But it'll have to wait until next time. I need to see Keegan again and get some more information. I'll be as quick as I can."

Siobhán gave him a small smile and said, "I know you'll do what's right, mo bhuachaill. You always do."

Family

is life

# SEVEN

Cara swung over the top uneven bar, winding up for her dismount. As her feet rose above the top bar, she let go and began her full-twisting double tuck dismount, sticking her landing, as usual. Keegan gave her the obligatory, "and the crowd goes wild, ahhh," and even Áine paused her preening long enough to add a meager "Woo..." before returning to her grooming.

"Thank you, thank you," Cara responded, throwing kisses to the crowd and gracing them with overly dramatic bows and curtsies. Keegan stood up from where she was stretching on the floor, chuckled, and said, "I think we missed our calling. We should be movie stars so we could have adoring fans clamoring for our autograph, wanting to take selfies with us." She did her best duck lips for emphasis.

Áine flew over to where Keegan's phone and Bluetooth speaker were sitting on the end of one of the benches. "Not movie stars," she said. "Rock stars." Then she turned on one of her favorite songs, picked up Cara's lip balm to use as a microphone, and began singing along.

Cara and Keegan began dancing and tumbling while Áine,

who actually had a gorgeous voice, even in her parrot form, was singing along with the first verse. Then the chorus hit, and they all joined in to sing Halestorm's "I Am the Fire" at the top of their lungs, "I am the fire..."

Áine joined in, adding her own aerial acrobatics, and for the rest of the song, the three Fae danced, flew, and sang their hearts out. It was just the stress release they all needed. When the song finished, they all collapsed in the middle of the floor exercise mat, giggling and breathing hard.

"Damn, that felt good," Keegan remarked with a contented sigh. "Yeah, we've needed that for a while," Cara agreed. "You're welcome," Áine commented, looking very pleased with herself. "Yes, yes, you have good ideas. Occasionally," Keegan teased. The parrot rolled her eyes and fluttered back over to the bench to finish her preening.

Keegan rolled onto her side, facing Cara, and propped her head up on her palm. "So, I've been thinking about our convo with rich boy last night." Cara giggled, then rolled over to face Keegan, mirroring her position. "I believe you're talking about Calder Ó Faoláin, whose family is very well-respected and power-ful, not just within the Earth Clan, but among the Council and the Fae people in general."

"So, he's a big deal on the homeworld, so what? I just can't figure out what his angle is. What does he get out of helping me and my mom? I hate to say it, but I wonder if we should just try again. Surely if we were able to get enough money, we could..."

"What the actual fuck are you talking about, Keegan?" Cara said in disbelief. "I know you're not used to trusting people, and I completely understand why. But you just had the best possible luck, while we were in the middle of committing a felony, I might add, and now you think we should just go try to rob somebody else?" She shook her head, looked at Áine, and said, "Care to tag in here? The cheese has slid completely off her cracker."

Both Fae sat up, and Áine flew over to join them, landing on Keegan's shoulder. She nuzzled her ear and said, "She's scared, Cara. You know that." Keegan started to take offense, then she stopped, thought about it, and said, "Fair enough. I am scared. And with good reason, I think."

Cara grabbed her hand and said, "You act so tough most of the time; I sometimes forget how vulnerable you really are. But trust me, a stór, he's one of the good ones. The Ó Faoláin family has been well-respected for generations. His mother is on the Council, and he and his brothers, while sometimes a little wild and rambunctious, have a reputation for being unfailingly fair and honorable. It's possible that he has some ulterior motive, although I can't think of what it might be, but I really, really doubt it, Love. He just felt really genuine to me. Didn't you feel that?"

Keegan thought about it and finally, reluctantly said, "Yeah. I felt it, too. There's just something about him that makes me want to trust him. It makes me suspicious."

"Everything makes you suspicious! Sometimes you just have to take a chance, Love. And frankly, what have we got to lose? If he can't help us, we'll fall back on your plans of theft and debauchery."

Keegan bumped her shoulder against Cara's, causing Áine to stumble a bit, putting one claw on each girl's shoulder. "I love you two dorks; you know that, right?" Cara nodded and said, "Uh-huh." Áine gave her a dose of side eye and said, "Of course you do."

Around eight o'clock the next morning, Cara yelled up the stairs, "We need to go, Keegan. Hurry it up!" Keegan's bedroom door opened, and Áine flew out and down the stairs, with Keegan following quickly behind. Cara looked her best friend over and shook her head. *She always has to do things the hard way,* she thought. Instead of picking out something flattering to wear and maybe fixing her hair and makeup, Keegan chose a different path. Never mind that a gorgeous, interested Fae had found her stealing and didn't call the cops. And not only that, but he had also volunteered to research her problem, was planning to make multiple trips to the homeworld at his own expense, and had given them well-paying jobs. She wore a clean but entirely shapeless t-shirt, faded shorts, and flip-flops. No makeup. Hair washed and brushed, but otherwise unstyled.

Cara couldn't help but let out a little sigh. Áine landed on the table beside her and said, "I know, I tried. She just kept saying, 'I'm not trying to impress anybody. If he has good intentions, how I look shouldn't matter.' After a while, I just gave up." Cara gave the bird a scritch on the head and said, "I know you tried. She's just as stubborn as a mule sometimes."

Keegan grabbed her keys and phone and headed out the door. Cara and Áine followed her to her VW Bug convertible, and they headed into downtown Kansas City to the Clíodhna Wood Artistry offices. The building had been around for over one hundred years, but it had obviously been cared for well. The walls were weathered brick with ivy growing in spots, and it had an abundance of windows, which made it appear to sparkle in the sunlight. Thankfully, it also had its own parking lot. Keegan pulled in, parked the bug, and they all piled out.

*It is nice to have a job Áine can openly come to,* she thought. Okay, *I will try to keep an open mind, but I make no promises.* By then, they had reached the front door, and Cara reached out and rang the buzzer. After just a minute or so, they heard Calder's voice say, "Good morning! Come on into the lobby. I'll be right down." Then a buzzing sound was heard, and they pushed the door open.

The lobby also doubled as a showroom, filled with master-works of art disguised as furniture. Chairs, tables, shelves, clocks, and just about any other home furnishing you could think of were there, of varying sizes and shapes, but everything was intricately detailed and exquisitely designed. They were a little starstruck as they looked around, whispering to each other over their favorite pieces.

Calder entered the lobby, cleared his throat, and said, "Hello, cailíní. You've seen our lobby; do you have any questions about any of the pieces?"

Áine piped up and said, "Uh, yeah, how do you make these? They're stunning." Calder couldn't help the blush that rose in his cheeks at her blunt praise. He gave a self-deprecating smile and replied, "Thank you, a Bhanríon." Áine positively glowed at that sobriquet. "I carve the wood using a combination of water and earth power. It allows for incredibly detailed work."

"It really is gorgeous," Cara said. "But I'm not sure how we can help. What did you have in mind?"

"Oh, well, I have a couple of ideas. There's always administrative work and shipping/receiving stuff. We can divvy that up amongst all of us. Even Áine, if she decides to shift into something with thumbs," Calder teased. "Not likely," she replied with a sniff.

"Very well," he said with a chuckle. "I'd also like to experiment with different ways we can manipulate the wood with our various powers. I think we could make some fascinating pieces."

Keegan looked thoughtful, then said, with a slight grin, "I could do some exciting things with fire." Calder couldn't resist and said, with a definite sexy undertone, "Oh, I bet you could." She blushed but smiled as well.

Áine, who had gotten bored and started flying around the lobby, happened to be swooping low over their heads at that exact moment, and she let out a squawk and said, "I can't even."

Cara barked out a laugh, which caused the other two to chuckle as well.

"Alright, how about I show you the rest of the place?" Calder asked after a moment. Keegan and Cara nodded. Áine ignored everyone and continued exploring the lobby.

Calder began leading them up the stairs, which were also a work of art, with intricately carved detailing on every step and a banister where each baluster was a separate flowering vine or branch. The vines and branches all flowed up to join the others to create a handrail. The effect was such that it felt like stepping inside a tree surrounded by vines and branches. It was a very comforting experience.

"Here on the second floor, we have several studios, most of which hold a project in some state of completion. There are also some storage areas, as well as a lunchroom. Feel free to wander around and look at whatever calls out to you. Let me know if I can answer any questions for you."

Keegan and Cara began strolling through the studios, looking at the various works-in-progress, feeling a little overwhelmed at the level of talent on display. Calder stood calmly against the wall on the stairwell landing, unobtrusive but available.

Keegan kept looking over at him, trying to guess what his ulterior motive might be. If there was one thing she had learned in her lifetime, it was that everyone had an ulterior motive. You just had to figure out what it was. *I'll figure it out. Then maybe I can decide whether to truly trust him,* she thought, her earlier intention to keep an open mind forgotten.

Cara traced her fingers ever so lightly along a particularly intricate portion of a rocking chair, amazed at the tiny details she found. Little bees and butterflies were scattered throughout the field of flowers depicted on the back of the chair. She whistled quietly and said, "Just wow. This detail is next level, Keeg." Her best friend nodded and said, "I know. It's almost surreal. Guess I can check 'use us for slave labor to churn out cheap home goods' off the list of possible reasons he's helping us."

Cara did a facepalm, sighed, and replied, "I just can't. Your stubborn refusal to see any potential for good in this man is driving me bloody batty."

Áine took that opportunity to make an entrance, flying up the staircase while singing the Halestorm song from the night before at a deafening volume. Calder couldn't hide a grin, crossing his arms and shaking his head slightly. Keegan and Cara walked back to the landing, allowing Áine to land on Keegan's shoulder as she belted out the chorus. The Fire Fae quickly reached up to clamp Áine's beak shut and scolded, "Crap on a cracker, Áine, are you trying to burst my eardrum? Take five already." Áine shook her head to remove the offending hand and said, "How rude!" Then she hopped over to Cara's shoulder in protest.

"Well, now," Calder said. "Why don't we go to the third floor and then the roof? I have a little surprise for you up there." Áine led the way, obviously still annoyed with Keegan, who threw her hands up at the attitude and followed her up the stairs. Cara and Calder brought up the rear.

On the third floor, there was a large conference room with all the latest electronic devices, allowing online meetings to be held with ease. This came in very handy since his brothers were often in Dublin, and he preferred spending most of his time in Kansas City. Calder was of the opinion that most meetings, or video calls, should really be handled via email, but he was routinely overruled.

The only other thing of note on the third floor was a small studio apartment where Calder often slept. He had a gorgeous house nearby in the Brookside area, but since his creativity often seemed to be at its peak late at night, that's usually when he found himself working. So, he often slept at his office. He even built a nice little bed for Lir. The setup was reasonably comfortable and saved him time, so he didn't really mind.

As he showed them the apartment, Áine said, "Wait a minute. Who sleeps there?" She pointed a wing at Lir's bed. "That, Love, is your surprise. Shall we head up to the roof and answer your question?" Calder replied, enjoying the suspense he was creating. He loved Lir so much and was so proud of him. He hoped they would also grow to feel some affection for the little goat. He headed toward the stairs to the roof and said, "Follow me."

They stepped out onto the roof, and Keegan was captivated. There was a covered area with a bar and some patio furniture that looked incredibly cozy. And the view was absolutely incredible, the Kansas City skyline on full display. She could even see a small stretch of the Missouri River in the distance, sparkling in the sunlight. But the most amazing thing about the space was the sheer abundance of flora. Small potted trees were dotted throughout the area, and she couldn't even count the number of plants and flowers she saw.

Near the bar was a small pool with a waterfall that fed a little babbling brook that wound its way around several trees and plants before heading back to the pool. Standing beside the pool was a small goat with silky black hair and huge, golden eyes. He was smiling at everyone and was so cute it was almost unbearable. Keegan was holding back a squeal, but just barely.

Calder approached his best friend and said, "This is Lir, and he's the best and brightest soul I've ever met. Lir, this is Keegan, Cara, and Áine." Lir said, "Pleasure to meet you all," and bent his front left foot, giving them all a bow.

Áine flew over to the pool and landed on the stone ledge, looking the goat over with a critical eye. "Hmm. We'll see. You might be an acceptable sidekick, with a lot of work on my part. It won't be easy, but I'm up for the challenge." Then she waddled even closer to Lir and began preening his coat like she would her feathers. He giggled and said, "That tickles!" Áine made a mildly disgusted sound in the back of her throat and said, "I've just met you, and you're already high maintenance. That's okay, though; I'll whip you into shape. Come on, you can help me look for crickets in the plants." Then she fluttered over to the nearest plant and began searching for her favorite snack. Lir followed, with a slightly confused but enthusiastic look on his face, and began helping her look for crickets. After a minute, he said, "Hey, let's look in my clover patch. I bet there are some in there." And he led the way to his favorite snack.

Calder motioned Keegan and Cara over to the bar area and asked them to sit. "Speaking of snacks, would either of you like something to eat or drink? I need to restock up here, but I have some trail mix and soda, water, or iced tea." Both women declined, so he sat across from them and paused momentarily, gathering his thoughts.

Keegan, who had been trying to figure out what ulterior motive he could have, finally said, "Just give us the bad news already! We've wasted enough time here if you're not going to help us." She started to stand, but Calder lifted a finger and gave her a stern look. "I'm not sure where you got the idea that I'm not going to help you, but that is most assuredly not the case. I've already made a trip to Tír na nÓg and put things in motion. Mo mháthair is currently researching the issue with her contacts, which are many and varied. I will be making another trip soon to meet with the best Aos Sí healers. I hope to have a definitive answer after that trip."

While Calder was speaking, Keegan had the grace to look

mildly abashed. Cara just shook her head, her expression displaying her frustration with her stubborn friend. "So why did you assume that I would not keep my word? Because, frankly, that has never happened to me before. My whole family is known for our fairness and honor. We say what we mean and mean what we say," Calder asked, truly confused by Keegan's distrust.

Keegan stood up, her frustration mounting until she had to move. She began pacing around the roof, getting a hold of her emotions the best she could. This strange feeling that she should really trust him had her off balance and irritated. It went against her nature, which had developed over two decades from all the secrecy and hiding. Calder stood and watched her, staying quiet, patient enough to wait for her to work through her thoughts. Finally, she stopped and turned to face him. "You say your family is 'known' for these things. And I'm sure that's true. In Tír na nÓg. But I've never been to the homeworld. I have grown up on Earth, and trust me, plenty of people are not known for fairness and honor. So, you'll pardon my caution, but I have no reason to trust you. Trust needs to be earned."

"Actually, I've found that trust should be granted freely. It can always be revoked. But showing trust often motivates people to reach their highest calling. That's how I see it, anyway," Calder replied sincerely.

Keegan looked thoughtful but unconvinced. Calder gave a small, slightly sad smile and said, "Just give it time. You'll see." *Such cynicism at such a tender age. She hides herself behind quite a thick wall. But there's a little ember there. And I think, with the proper handling, it could become a wildfire. That's a sight I'd love to see.*

Suddenly, Lir came skidding around the corner with Áine on his back, her claws gripping his hair to keep herself on his back. "Whoa, Goat Boy, slow your roll! You're about to fling me off the roof!" Lir giggled and said, "You know you can fly, right?" Áine scoffed and said, "That's not the point! Take me over to the big guy." Lir stopped in front of Calder as instructed. Áine looked at him and said, "There is a serious cricket shortage on this roof, buddy. And I haven't seen a single decent piece of jewelry anywhere. Better get to work on that because if we don't get at least some crickets up in this motherfu-" Cara quickly interrupted with, "And on that note, I believe we should go back downstairs. Come on, little Miss Potty Mouth." Then she opened the door to the stairs and ushered Lir and Áine downstairs.

Keegan approached Calder and said hesitantly, "I'm sure you can tell I don't trust easily. When you grow up hiding who you are, it becomes hard to let someone see the real you. And to trust that what someone shows you is the real them." Calder just raised an eyebrow, feeling that actually verbalizing the irony was unnecessary.

Keegan laughed and said, "Okay, maybe I'm preaching to the choir with that one. But hiding one of your elemental powers is different than hiding all your powers. You have no idea what that is really like. To have grown up that way. So, you'll have to be patient with me. But I wanted to tell you that I will try. To trust you. As much as I'm able to, at least. And hopefully, with time, you'll prove to me that my trust was not misplaced."

Calder looked deeply into her eyes, seeing just how much that cost her. He put his hand on her shoulder and gave a gentle squeeze. Then he gestured toward the stairs and followed her down them. Along the way, he thought, *I need to tread carefully. But I'm willing to put in the effort. Let's see if we can coax this little ember into a wildfire.*

Family
is life

# EIGHT

Keegan watched as the sun sank below the horizon, creating a deep orange, to white, to midnight blue ombré across the sky. Áine was dozing on the porch swing, snuggled in a blanket, her head tucked under her wing, a light snoring sound coming from her general vicinity. Keegan was sitting in one of the Adirondack chairs on her back porch, just going over everything she had learned from Calder. She had briefly discussed this new information with her mother earlier, but she wasn't sure she agreed with her mother's vague excuses when asked about living on the homeworld. She knew that Calder had to hide his secret—their secret—all the years he lived in Tír na nÓg. But if he and his family had been able to manage, why couldn't she and her mother have given it a try? At the thought of what might have been, tears welled up in her eyes, which she blinked back, refusing to give in to those kinds of self-defeating thoughts.

The sliding glass door behind her opened, and Keegan heard the sound of her mother's footsteps walking up behind her. Keegan felt her mother's arms wrapping around her from behind, then she leaned over and kissed her on the top of her head. She gave a small sigh and sat in another Adirondack chair across from her daughter. She looked into Keegan's silver eyes, sighed again, and said, "I get the feeling you'd like to talk to me, a stór. What would you like to ask?"

Keegan looked back into her mother's icy blue eyes and felt the rage begin to build. She tried to calm herself, take deep breaths, and think soothing thoughts. But the more she tried to stay calm, the madder she got.

Niamh watched as the various emotions passed across her daughter's face, a small, sad smile on her face. She knew what was coming, and she didn't blame Keegan one bit. She also didn't know what other choice she could have made. It was immaterial at any rate; the past was the past. But her daughter did have the right to get some answers to her questions.

"Why, Mom?" she asked. "Why didn't you stay on the home-world? It wouldn't have been that hard to hide my air power. We could've managed. And at least then, I could've openly used my fire power! I don't understand!"

As Keegan got increasingly upset, Niamh stood up and knelt beside her chair, folding her hands on her daughter's knee, and staring sympathetically into her eyes. Áine poked her head up but decided to give the mother and daughter some time on their own.

"I know, a stór, I know," she soothed. "I'm so sorry it turned out this way for you. But there are things you don't understand, Keegan. Things I've never really explained before, but maybe it's time for you to know." She paused and appeared to be gathering her thoughts. Then she continued, "You know that your father and I had a brief romance, that I became pregnant, which was strictly forbidden since he was from a different clan, and there-fore I chose to travel to Earth and raise you here."

Keegan nodded; none of this was new information. "But I never really explained how your father and I met. Or told you about my sister's family. Both of those are relevant to the story."

Keegan looked slightly puzzled, not quite following her mother's narrative.

"When my sister, your aunt, Étaín, turned sixteen, she met Cass Daugherty, another member of the Fire Clan. Cass was a handsome lad with wavy ginger hair and dark grey, smoky eyes, and he only had eyes for Étaín. At first. She had beautiful blonde hair and eyes the silvery green color of artemisia. And she was head over heels for him. She would have done anything he wanted. Then he met me. And like a typical child, he ignored what he already had and wanted only what he could not."

She paused and took a sip of the sweet tea Keegan had sitting by her chair. Then she continued, "I was two years older than Étaín, and I thought I needed to focus on what I wanted to do with my life. Our parents had died in an accident less than a year before, so I felt I needed to be the adult. A relationship was an unwelcome distraction. Also, Cass struck me as very conceited and often rude, which are not qualities I find attractive. So, I tried to ignore him, hoping he would eventually go away. But every time I rebuffed him, it just seemed to feed his obsession. And every time he came back at me, Étaín would watch, pretend it wasn't happening, and get sharper and sharper with me.

"Pretty soon, he was following me everywhere I went. Nowhere in Tionól was safe. I tried to stay around other people, but it's hard to do that all the time. Any time he would find me alone, he was very sexually aggressive. Luckily, I could always squirm my way out of his reach, or someone would walk by, and he would be forced to back off.

"I was beginning to panic, as I knew I couldn't keep this up much longer. One day, my worst fear came to pass. I was taking a shortcut behind the blacksmith's forge, and as I turned the corner, there he suddenly was, leaning against the back wall and grinning ear to ear.

"I quickly turned around, trying to retrace my steps, but he was too quick, and he grabbed my arms and spun me around, trapping me between him and the forge's wall.

"I released my fire power, letting it flare from my fingertips to my shoulders, causing Cass to yelp and pull his hands back. I tried to take advantage of my momentary freedom, but he flared his own fire power, forming a half-circle barricade of flames behind him. Since we are only immune to our own flames unless we consciously will immunity to another, it was an effective way of holding me in place. I called the fire back into my hands, determined to make him pay in pain for every unwanted touch."

A tear rolled down Niamh's cheek as recounting the memories brought back the pain and terror of that event. Keegan wiped it away, cupping her mother's cheek with her hand, her own eyes filling with tears. "I'm so sorry, Mom," she said. Niamh covered Keegan's hand and replied, "I know, Love. I don't like to think about that time, but it's over now. Let me finish the story while I still have the strength."

She paused a moment, then took a deep breath and continued, "After I burned him and he walled us in with fire, he got a look in his eyes that really terrified me. Before, he had always looked at me like I was something he wanted to worship. Now he looked at me like I was something he needed to dominate and control. I flared my flames and steeled myself for a fight.

"As he took a step forward, I heard someone walking toward us along the side of the building. As I turned toward the sound, I saw Shay Ó Brien turn the corner and immediately stop short as he caught sight of us.

"'Cass, I hope you have some reasonable answer as to what's going on here,' he said, his body entering that stillness you only really see when someone is readying themselves for a fight. I thought for sure that Cass would immediately back down. Shay's mother was the High Chief of the Council, the single most influential Aos Sí Fae. But Cass was out of his mind, too far gone in his obsession to make a rational decision. He turned to Shay and said with a sneer, 'Mind your business. There's nothing to see here.' Then he flared the flame barricade until I could barely see Shay on the other side of it. However, I could see the incredulous look on Shay's face. Then the Air Fae lifted his arm and made a flourish ending in a fist. Immediately, the flame barricade disappeared, which tends to happen when oxygen is removed from the area.

"Cass was stunned, mouth hanging open, eyes wide as he tried to process what just happened. He had always been one of the stronger Fire Fae, so he was not used to being bested, especially not that easily. I took the opportunity to step around Cass, hoping he would finally let me be, but I should have known better. I was almost out of his reach, but he grabbed my wrist at the last moment, turning me back to face him. My anger overcame my fear at that point, and I had had enough. I flared my flames where he gripped me, burning him badly. He shrieked and let go of my wrist, but he also fought back, launching his own fireball, and at such short range, it hit me square in the shoulder, also burning me. I fell backward into Shay, who caught me gently, his silver eyes full of kindness. Cass narrowed his eyes and began stepping toward me, so I quickly raised my own flame barricade, trapping him against the wall.

"He seemed stunned that I would dare to defend myself. He called his own flames forth again, trying to overpower my barricade with his own so he could walk through it. Shay saw what he was attempting to do and began feeding my fire with his air power. Soon, the flame barricade was taller than the Fire Fae it was blocking. Shay raised his voice to be heard over the fire and said, 'I can only guess at what was in that thick skull of yours when you came up with this plan, Daugherty, but hear me when I say that if you bother Niamh, in any way, ever again, you and I will come to blows that'll make this confrontation look like child's play. She and I are leaving now. I can keep this fire blazing from quite a distance, so I suggest you get comfortable until the fire dies and then go home and lick your wounds. While you're doing that, I'd also suggest you find a new hobby. One that does not involve Niamh.'

"Shay gently grabbed my arm, and we began walking backwards away from Cass and the wall of flame. We continued that way until our path took us around a corner and out of sight. 'So, can you still maintain the flame from this far away?' I asked. He nodded and said, 'I've been practicing my control for years. Control almost always beats raw strength.'

"Then he started leading me toward his family's estate. I tried to tell him I was fine; I just needed to go home. But he insisted on helping me clean my burns. So, he led me to the carriage house on his family's property, and we went inside to tend to my wound. We walked up the stairs to the stableman's apartment on the second floor. There was a fire in the hearth, and he put some water on to boil. Then he gathered some bandages and a cooling salve from the other room, laying everything out on a small table beside the bed.

"He was such a gentleman and so kind. After he had gathered all the supplies, he started to reach toward the buttons on my shirt, realized what he was doing, and turned bright red. 'Um, could you, uh, unbutton a couple buttons? I need to slide your shirt down to treat your burns.' He wouldn't look me in the eye while he was asking that, which I found slightly funny and a little charming, in a mildly awkward way. I was wearing a camisole under my shirt, so I unbuttoned it and carefully slid it over the wound, folded it, and laid it on the table.

"Once he finally looked at me again and realized I wasn't topless in front of him, he relaxed a bit and began cleaning and dressing my wound. I know that most healers are Water Fae, but Shay had the most amazing way about him. He was so kind and gentle as he worked, which was exactly what I needed. As he went about his task, he began humming...he has a beautiful voice. It was very soothing. And he also appeared to be pulling on his air power almost constantly. There was always just the tiniest breeze around him. Altogether, it finally allowed me to relax enough to break down. The trauma I'd just been through, combined with Shay's kindness, was more than I could handle, so I began sobbing. Ugly crying. It was definitely not pretty." Keegan let out a little giggle at that image. Áine snorted.

Niamh continued, "At first, I don't think Shay really knew what to do with me. But eventually, his compassion insisted he comfort me. By then, he had finished cleaning and bandaging my burns. They were painful but would heal quickly and cleanly. So, he scooped me up, sat on the bed, and carefully laid me in his lap, with my good shoulder against his chest and my head on his shoulder.

"My crying had quieted a bit, but it was far from done. So, he just held me like that, running his hand through my hair, singing me lullabies, and whispering soothing nonsense in my ear. We barely knew each other, but his kindness that night stole my heart."

Niamh's eyes were welling up again, so she paused, wiped her eyes, and took a deep breath. "Damn it all, I thought I could handle this," she said to herself. Keegan took her hand and laced their fingers together. "Take as long as you need, Mama," she said.

Niamh smiled at her daughter and said, "Thank you, Love. You have his compassion. And his eyes." Keegan smiled at that. She'd never met her father in person, but she loved it when her mother talked about him. She especially loved it when her mother pointed out something she had inherited from him. It made her feel closer to him in some small way.

"Once my tears had finally run their course, we stayed there for the longest time. I've never felt more at home than I did in his arms that night. I eventually lifted my head to ask him a question, and, at the same time, he lowered his head to say something. Whack! We head-butted each other. Talk about ruining a beautiful moment! But we both started laughing, which lightened the mood a bit. Especially since, as our laughter was dying down, our eyes met, and we leaned in for a kiss. I swear I felt tingles all the way to my toes. He had both hands buried in my hair and, well..." Keegan held up her hand and said, "Ew. I get the picture, Mom."

Áine added her two cents with a loud, "Boom chicka wah wah," causing both Niamh and Keegan to burst into laughter. When they finally were able to quiet themselves down, Niamh continued the story.

"So, afterwards, I had to sneak out of the carriage house, which turned out to be where Shay spent most of his nights. He said he found the sound of the horses calming. Anyway, I snuck home, exhausted and exhilarated in equal measure. I had no sooner shut my bedroom door than Étaín burst in, absolutely incensed.

"'How could you!' she practically screamed at me, fists clenched, and face flushed. 'I ran into Cass on my way home from a friend's house. He told me how you attacked him. He showed me the burns you gave him! How could you do that, Niamh!'

"She finally stopped to take a breath, and I tried to reason with her. 'It wasn't like that, a Dheirfiúr.' This was my little sister; we had always been so close. I couldn't process that she might take his side. 'I know you like him, but...'

"'Like him?' she practically screamed at me. Then she became eerily calm and looked at me with a desperate look. 'I love him, Niamh. He's all I've ever wanted.' She looked away and shook herself slightly. Then she looked at me again, a mask of disdain coming over her features, and said, 'You have to be lying. There's no other explanation.'"

I stared at her momentarily, unable to believe what I was hearing. Finally, I snapped back at her, 'Your beloved Cass is a stalker, you bloody fool! He cornered me and tried to assault me, Étaín! Yes, I burnt him, and he returned the favor in kind.' I pulled my shirt aside to show her my bandaged shoulder.

"Étaín narrowed her eyes at me and said, 'I don't believe you. He said you started things, that you wanted to kiss him, and when he refused, you burned him. Besides, he has me; why would he need to stalk you?'

"I rolled my eyes and replied, 'That's an excellent question. Maybe you should ask him. Now get the fuck out of my room.'

"Étaín gave me a dirty look, spun around, and stomped out of my room, taking care to slam the door on the way out.

Keegan watched as a pained expression passed over her mother's face. Niamh quickly schooled her face to calm, but Keegan could tell how much her sister's behavior had hurt her.

"So, for the next several weeks, Shay and I met secretly any chance we could. Aside from the rule against mating with other Clans, Shay's mother was also notorious for disapproving of her son's relationships. Any time Shay showed any interest in another Fae, his mother would make things difficult for his love interest, so much so that they would eventually leave to avoid the constant annoyance.

"I definitely wanted to avoid the ire of Mother Ó Brien, but since it was technically okay to have a sexual relationship with a member of another Clan, so long as no children resulted, I wasn't quite as careful as I should have been. I thought I was safe with the birth control I was using. Little did I know that no birth control is one hundred percent effective. Except for abstinence. Pay attention to this part, Keegan," Niamh said pointedly. Áine snorted again.

"Anyway, I was too excited to see Shay, and I got sloppy. Cass had never actually stopped stalking me; he just got a little more cautious. So, I was rushing to meet Shay at the carriage house, and Cass caught us just as Shay opened the door, wrapped me in his arms, and planted a big kiss on me.

"Cass began clapping, walking toward us, and loudly exclaiming, 'Well, isn't this a lovely surprise?' Shay shoved me behind him, or he tried to. I didn't exactly cooperate. He gave me a little side eye, then barked, 'Daugherty, get your arse in here!'

"A Cheshire cat grin slowly began spreading across Cass's face. Then he sauntered into the house. As he passed in front of Shay, a short but strong gust of wind pushed him from behind, making him stumble the first few steps into the carriage house.

"Shay slammed the door shut, then turned around, grabbed the front of Cass's shirt, and slammed him up against the wall. 'What the fuck are you playing at?' Shay hissed.

"Cass chuckled and said, 'I could ask you the same thing. Does your mother know about the fun you two are having?' He laid the threat right out on the table. At least he didn't beat around the bush.

"Shay pinched the bridge of his nose, leaned close to Cass's face, and replied, 'What I do is none of my mother's business. Nor is it any of yours. So, I would suggest you forget whatever you think you saw here and get the hell out of my house.' And he dragged Cass by his shirt over to the door, opened it, and threw him out.

"Cass sat there in the grass for a moment with that same stupid grin on his face. Finally, he stood up, dusted his pants off, and said, 'I will keep this to myself. For the moment. But unless you'd like our illustrious leader of the Council to hear about your little tryst, perhaps you can convince Niamh to be a little nicer to me. I'm not asking for much, just a little kindness and companionship now and then. That's not too much to ask, is it? Something to keep in mind.'

"In response, Shay slammed the door shut, then began pacing

back and forth. 'Bloody hell,' he finally said, leaning against the door. Cass's thinly veiled threat hung between us, and I didn't know how we were going to be able to continue seeing each other. It was breaking my heart.

"Shay looked at me and saw the tears streaming down my face. He quickly crossed the room, took me in his arms, and let me sob my frustrations out. After I had calmed down a bit, he said, 'I will figure something out, a rúnsearc.'"

Niamh paused again; all the emotions brought up by these memories were taking their toll on her. "So, we tried to continue as if nothing had happened. But every day, the tension we were feeling grew a little thicker. And every time I saw Cass, I was sure he would force himself on me again, and this time, I didn't know if I would be able to stop him.

"After a while, I thought the stress was getting to me, and I was throwing up daily. But, of course, it was more than just stress. When I finally figured out I was carrying you, I went to see Shay. You see, if I'd just been a little more careful, I could have perhaps stayed in Tír na nÓg and raised you there. Passed it off as a one-night stand with another member of the Fire Clan, and hid your air power, the way that Calder and his family managed to do. But because Cass knew we were seeing each other, there's no way we could have kept that a secret.

"Shay was heartbroken when I told him I was leaving. He wanted to be a part of your life, our life, so badly. But between the power it would give Cass and the havoc his mother would create if she knew, we both concluded that this was the safest choice.

"Please always remember that part, Keegan. Your mother and father both wanted you desperately. And we are so, so sorry we weren't able to give you the childhood you deserved."

Keegan knelt beside her mother and wrapped her in the biggest hug she could manage. She was quickly joined by Áine, who landed with one foot on each Fae's shoulder, enveloping their heads with her wings in an awkward but thoughtful group hug.

Cara chose that moment to step onto the back porch, took in the scene, and said, "I always miss the good stuff."

Keegan laughed, poked her head up over Áine's wing, and said, "I'll tell you about it later."

Cara said, "You'd better. And dinner's ready, by the way." So, they made their way inside to eat.

# Family

*is life*

# NINE

As Calder and Lir descended the steps from the plane, a dark green BMW pulled up, but instead of Thomas in the driver's seat, Calder saw his brother, Liam, driving with the twins, Conor and Reilly, riding along.

Lir noticed at the same time, and Calder saw his little hooves going tippy-tappy in his excitement. The brothers spoiled Lir horribly, but Calder couldn't begrudge him the attention. His best friend deserved it.

Conor hopped out of the passenger seat and opened the door to the back with a flourish. "Welcome to your ride, Your Highnesses. Ó Faoláin Taxi at your service." He finished with a grandiose bow.

Lir giggled and hopped into the back seat next to Reilly, who gave him a good ear scratch and then started feeding him strawberries, one of his favorite snacks. Calder just snorted at his brother's antics and slid into the seat beside Lir.

Liam began driving, but he didn't turn toward the Faery Tree when he was leaving the private airstrip. Instead, he began driving toward the family estate. Calder said, "Don't get me wrong, I appreciate the ride, but you're going the wrong way."

Liam glanced at him in the rear-view mirror and said, "Sorry, a Dheartháir Beag, but as your brothers, we have decided it's high time we got the details on the new hottie. We already sent a message to Mam, so she's not expecting you until tomorrow. So, for tonight, your arse is ours."

Calder couldn't help a slight eye roll, but then he sighed and said, "Fine. I knew this was coming, so I suppose it's best to get it over with. But over dinner. I will need some sustenance, and a pint or two, to put up with you lot."

Liam chuckled and said, "Fair enough, Lad. Fair enough."

It was only a short drive to the Ó Faoláin estate, but by the time they pulled through the gates and up to the front entry, Calder was already grateful that his brothers had chosen to kidnap the two of them temporarily. It had been too long since he had visited their place in Ireland. The fresh air, the gorgeous scenery, and a familiar place with his rowdy but loveable brothers...it was just what he needed. Although he was not looking forward to the grilling he was sure to get about Keegan.

Thomas was there to open the door for them with a huge grin. "Well, now, it's such a pleasure to be seeing all you lads together! How long are you staying this time?" Liam responded, "Calder and Lir will be leaving tomorrow morning, but the rest of us will be here through the weekend."

Thomas said, "Alright then, I'll take what I can get. Aoife, the boys are home! Best get something on the stove; you know how they like to eat!" His wife hollered back, "I've always got something on the stove, Tommy, you know that! Tell those boys to get in this kitchen and give me a póigín!"

He turned to the boys and said, "You heard her! Best get in there afore she comes and hunts you down. And you know she'll do it, too!" Lir, very familiar with the elevated level of Aoife's treat game, let out an excited bleat and trotted into the kitchen. The rest of the brothers chuckled and followed him.

Aoife, a boisterous, curvy woman with a long, silver braid, was busy "accidentally" dropping food on the floor, which Lir happily hoovered up. She looked up from her food prep and said, "Oooh, it's been so long since all of you have been home! Come give me a póigín right now!"

The four brothers happily stood in line to give her a kiss. When they were done, she bent down, presenting her cheek to Lir, and said, "You, too, little man." Lir giggled and gave her a big juicy lick on the cheek. She chuckled, stood up, and said, "It's good to have the house full again, even if it's only for a bit. We're having lamb stew, Loves. Conor and Reilly, I need potatoes and carrots peeled and diced. Calder, grab a fork and go harvest maybe ten good-sized leeks for me. You remember how I taught you?" Calder nodded. "Good Lad," she replied. "Liam, would you help Tommy set the table, Love?" Liam responded, "Of course, a Mháthair Chríona."

Calder grabbed a fork, and as he was heading past Liam to gather the leeks, he bumped into him and whispered, "Suck up!" Liam just smacked him in the back of the head and replied, "It's not my fault you aren't as polite as I am."

Aoife gave the roux she was working on one last stir, tapped her wooden spoon sharply on the side of the Dutch oven, and pointed it at Liam and Calder, saying, "Don't make me come over there!"

They both chuckled, mumbled, "Tá brón orainn," and went on about their chores.

A relatively short while later, the four brothers, Aoife, Thomas, and Lir, were all seated at the table, passing around a green salad, some savory lamb stew, and hot buttered rolls. Guinness was flowing as well. The conversation was understandably limited as everyone tucked into the fantastic meal. Calder sat back once his immediate hunger was satisfied and just basked in the comfort of home. It didn't matter that he hadn't actually grown up in this house. He'd grown up with these people, so home was wherever they were.

Liam sat back, pinned him with those green eyes, slightly lighter in color than his own but just as penetrating, and said, "Okay, little brother. What's the craic? We need details about that fiery little redhead you've been chasing. What's her story?"

Calder took a long draft of his Guinness, gathering his thoughts. His mother had taught them that family is life. They had learned the hard way that secrets are a terrible idea.

When Calder first began showing signs of having a water power in addition to the family's earth power, his mother had thought to keep it a secret from his brothers, hoping to avoid them having to lie to the rest of the world. So, for a few years, Calder and his mother kept his secret to themselves. It was incredibly difficult for them both.

Then one day, when Calder was about nine years old, the four brothers decided to go swimming in a pond near their home in Tír na nÓg. They were all good swimmers, so their mother didn't think twice about giving permission when they asked to go.

*We were so excited; it was the first time we'd been able to go swimming that summer. I remember spending several hours jumping, splashing, roughhousing...just having a good time.*

*We were all getting tired, but Liam, like a typical fourteen-year-old Fae, insisted on giving the backflip he'd been trying to perfect one more try before we left. The rest of us were gathering our clothes and putting on our shoes, but we paused momentarily to give him a proper audience.*

*Liam climbed back up into the branches of the colossal rowan tree that grew beside the pond, its branches providing the perfect place from which to launch his spectacular backflip. The tree was so laden with flowers that Liam was barely visible. All the previous attempts had been made from the lowest overhanging branches. So, this time Liam decided to give himself a little extra airtime and chose one of the higher branches for his launch pad. Standing with his back facing us and one hand lightly resting against the trunk to steady himself, Liam took a couple of deep breaths and prepared to jump.*

*He sprang upward, arms leading the way, arching his back, then tucking into a ball, bringing his knees up to his chest and wrapping his arms around them, spinning a full rotation before coming out of the tuck and slicing the water with a beautiful dive that barely made a splash. It was a thing of beauty! Right up to the point where his right arm crashed into a couple of sharp, heavy rocks on the bottom of the pond, getting wedged tight. Normally, he would have been able to move the stones with his earth power, but the pain of his broken arm made concentrating impossible.*

*On the bank, unaware of what was going on below the water, we started clapping and shouting, showing our approval of the outstanding acrobatic feat we had just witnessed. We kept clapping and shouting for what seemed like a really long time until, finally, we started to get worried.*

*"Liam! Liam, what's going on!" we shouted, unsure what to do. Conor and Reilly were quickly kicking off their shoes and pulling their shirts off, ready to jump in and try to help Liam.*

*But I was quicker. Afraid to wait any longer, I used my water power to part the pond directly over where Liam entered the water. At the bottom of the pond sat Liam, gasping for air now that it was available. His arm was still wedged in the rocks, but at least he could breathe.*

*Conor and Reilly kept looking back and forth between me, with my hands out in front of me, shaking with exertion, and Liam, sitting in the mud at the bottom of the pond with his arm under the rocks, panting and staring back at me.*

*"Uh, Lads, I can't hold this much longer!" I said, my breath labored as the stress of holding back that much water took its toll. The twins looked at each other, then immediately slid down the muddy bank of the pond, made their way to Liam, and freed his obviously broken arm from the rocks.*

*"Got him!" they shouted, walking back to the muddy bank to climb out of the pond.*

*"Hurry up!" I screamed, already feeling the water slipping from my grasp.*

*The three boys scrambled up the bank and out of the pond just as I collapsed, and the two separate sections of water crashed back together as one.*

*When I woke up a few minutes later, my brothers were gathered in a circle, staring down at me. I sat up, shaking my head to clear it. With his arm cradled against his chest, Liam spoke up first, saying, "Well, a Dhearthàir Beag, it looks like you've been keeping quite the secret." I looked down, unable to hold back my tears, afraid I had just lost my brothers forever.*

*But Liam reached out his good arm and put a finger under my chin, lifting my head until I could look him in the eye. "It makes no difference to us what your powers are, Lad. You're àr Dhearthàir Beag, and you always will be. No matter what." Then Liam looked to Conor and Reilly for affirmation, "Right?" But the twins were already nodding their heads in agreement. They each put a hand on my shoulder. "Of course," Reilly said, his pale greyish-green eyes looking at me intently. Conor grinned and said, "Who would we all pick on if you weren't around? Sure we need to keep you then."*

*"Now that that's all settled, can we please get me home so I can get*

this bloody arm fixed?" Liam asked, his pain apparent in his expression.

We all hopped up and began heading back to the main house. Thomas was outside working with the horses when he saw us coming and could tell something was wrong. "Aoife, Siobhán, come out here, please! It looks like the weans have gotten into mischief again!"

The two females came outside and watched as we made our way toward them, muddy, bedraggled, with Liam obviously injured. They both looked ready to tear into us, but then something happened with Liam. I swear I saw him turn into a man in front of my eyes. He straightened as much as he could, which made him roughly the same height as our mam. Then he said, "Could we please go inside? We have something to discuss as a family."

His words, and especially his tone, brought both females up short. Siobhán looked her oldest son over and seemed to make a decision. "Very well," she said, leading the way inside to our large kitchen table. Almost every major decision or discussion in our lives had taken place at that kitchen table.

Still cradling his broken arm, Liam stood up and said, "A Mháthair, you have always taught us that there should be no secrets among family. Yet today, it became apparent that Calder is a Dúbailte."

Siobhán slapped her hand on the table sharply, stood up, and said, "We do not use that term in this household! We will not spread that idiotic superstition!" Then she took a deep breath and resumed her seat.

Liam held up his good hand in a placating manner. "Apologies, I meant no offense. Whatever you want to call it, today we learned that Calder has not only earth power, but he can also control water. In fact, he saved my life with his water power." Liam gave Calder a grateful look, then looked around the table. "So, I won't speak for the rest of you, but as for me, I could not care less about some stupid curse. Calder is my a dheartháir beag. And that's all I need to know."

*Reilly and Conor both stood up and, in a moment of twin solidarity, said together, "Us, too!"*

*Siobhán looked over at Aoife and Thomas, distant cousins who lived with and contributed to the household. "Don't even insult us with the question," Aoife said. "Calder is family. Family is life. That is all we need to know."*

*Then Mam stood up at the head of the table, eyes brimming with tears. "You have no idea how much this means to me. To us," she said, glancing over at me. "Thank you for proving what I've always known. The Ó Faoláin family takes care of our own. And I have never been prouder to be a member."*

*Then she sat down and continued, "When Fallon died all those years ago, I didn't know how I would get through it. He was my world, and then suddenly, not only was he gone, but I also had a toddler and two newborns to care for. I was so overwhelmed and distraught; I didn't know what to do.*

*"Morgan Ó Loingsigh, of the Water Clan, had lost his wife earlier that year, and he was also grieving. We took comfort in each other. And Calder is the result. I despise that stupid Dúbailte Curse. I think Morgan and I could have been happy together, but it wasn't to be because of that superstition about dual powers supposedly bringing about the bloody apocalypse.*

*"So, now that it's all out in the open, I only have one regret." I looked up at Mam, suddenly fearful that I was her one regret. She saw my angst and smiled at me, saying gently, "Oh no, Love, not you. Never you."*

*She looked at the others around the table and said, "I regret ever trying to keep this secret from you all. No matter what happens, we are in this together. A family should not have secrets. I'm sorry I forgot that."*

*Then Thomas said, "Alright now, you're forgiven, of course. Never again, agreed?" Mam nodded and agreed, "Never again." Then*

*Thomas and Mam looked around the table until the rest of us also agreed, "Never again."*

With that memory fresh in his mind, Calder decided that his family deserved the truth about Keegan. Never again, after all.

"Well, that fiery little redhead happens to have dual powers as well," he began, eliciting more than one gasp around the table with that bombshell. "Although, in her case, they are fire and air powers. Her name is Keegan Doran, and she grew up on Earth. In fact, I'm almost positive she has never set foot in Tír na nÓg. When her mam found out she was pregnant, she just ran to Earth, and they've been here ever since. I'm still not entirely sure why, but I intend to get the full story soon." Calder paused to take a drink and collect his thoughts.

"As most of you know, I met Keegan at the poker tournament a couple of weeks ago. She and her friend, Cara-" Lir interrupted with, "Don't forget Áine!"

Calder barked out a laugh, "I wouldn't dream of leaving out her Highness! Áine is Keegan's familiar. Currently, she spends most of her time as a parrot, with occasional side trips as a little red mouse. Who likes to sing." He realized he was digressing as he watched his family's eyes glaze over.

"Anyway, you will meet Áine at some point, and you'll see what I mean. So, Keegan and her friend, Cara, who has air power, and Áine were all at the poker tournament. Keegan and Cara were working as servers, and they had also managed to get assigned to pick up the cash from the various tables and lock it away in the safe." He paused momentarily, thinking about how to phrase the next part of the story.

"This leads me to how we finally met face to face. I followed them after they had picked up the cash and walked into them skimming a percentage off the top and floating it up to Áine, who was depositing it into a backpack they had been filling all evening." He paused as the inevitable gasps sounded around the table.

"Give me a minute to finish, and you'll all understand. Keegan is desperate. Recently, her mam began experiencing a disturbing level of weakness. She's been to multiple human doctors, and they haven't been able to help her. Keegan is terrified she will lose the only parent she's ever known. So, with very limited funds and thinking human doctors were her only option, she began trying to find a way to raise a great deal of money, hoping that specialists might have an answer for her mam.

"Once I got the whole story from them, I realized I was in a position to help Keegan and her mam, Niamh. I visited the home-world and got Mam's help researching the illness. Aos Sí have been around far longer than humans, so it stands to reason we might have more luck diagnosing and treating something like this. Not to mention the fact that human healers are fairly hope-less when it comes to Fae. That's what this trip is; I'm going back to find out what Mam has discovered and to talk to the healers personally."

With that last statement, Liam and the twins looked at each other, understanding dawning as they realized who held the title of Chief Healer...Morgan Ó Loingsigh. Knowing Calder had an extremely complicated relationship with his biological father, the brothers looked at each other, and then Reilly said, "You know we've got your back, Calder. Just say the word, and we'll be there with you."

Calder smiled and replied, "Thanks, Lads, but I can handle it. Can't keep running away from the difficult tasks forever, can I?"

Conor shrugged and said, "I don't know; that actually sounds like a worthy goal to me." Reilly punched him in the arm and said, "Don't be a little shit."

Conor rubbed his arm and mumbled, "I still think it sounds like the way to go, but what do I know?"

Liam took that opportunity to say, "Well, I can't say I agree with theft as a way to pay for health care, but I also understand desperation. It makes us act in ways we'd never consider otherwise."

Then he stood and held up his glass for a toast. "Here's to successfully finding answers for your redhead. I will withhold the teasing I had planned for tonight. But once you've got your answers, the gloves are off, a Dheartháir Beag. Consider yourself warned. Sláinte!"

The table responded by standing, clinking pints together, and taking big slugs of their stout. "Sláinte!"

# Family

## is life

CHAPTER

# TEN

L ir was singing as he jumped up and down the wood pile, periodically stopping to munch on the Cheerios Thomas had gotten for him. Calder turned the corner, looking for him, just in time to see him wiggle his little goat butt in time to his rendition of "Bodies" by Drowning Pool. Calder watched him briefly, chuckled, and said, "Okay, rock star, time to go."

Lir looked over at him and said, "Woo hoo, it's almost púca time!" He hopped down from the wood pile and trotted over to his friend. "Let's go, Romeo," he said. "Oh, could you grab the rest of my Cheerios for the ride?" Then he held up a hoof and said, "No thumbs."

Calder chuckled again and said, "Áine has been a bad influence on you." Lir snorted and said, "I choose to be nice, but any púca worth their salt could mop the floor with Áine in the insult department. She does have potential, though. I can work with that." This time Calder snorted and said, "Come on, before your head gets so big it won't fit in the car."

105

Thomas pulled up near the Faery Tree, put the BMW in park, and turned to Calder, saying, "Lad, promise me you'll be careful. I know I've said it afore, but somethin' is coming, and it ain't good."

Calder looked back at Thomas and nodded. When Thomas got one of his feelings, it was wise to pay attention. More often than not, what he saw coming arrived. "I'll be careful, a Dhaideo. I know better than to ignore your warnings."

"Good Lad," Thomas replied. "You tell your mam to be careful, too. We worry about her when we're on this side of the portal."

Calder squeezed Thomas's shoulder and said, "Mam has plenty of cousins around, and she's a damn strong Fae in her own right. But I will tell her."

"That's all I ask," Thomas replied. Then he turned to Lir and said, "I expect you to keep an eye on the lot of them, understand?" Lir nodded solemnly, taking his protector's role very seriously.

"Alright, that's enough of this old man rambling. The Druids are almost here. Have a good trip, and I'll be here when you return. Safe travels, Lads," Thomas continued.

Calder got out of the vehicle and opened the door for Lir. They headed toward the far side of the Faery Tree, where the four Druids, shrouded in an invisibility glamour, awaited them. Once they crossed to the back side of the tree, they cast their own invisibility glamour, just in case any tourists wandered nearby.

The four Druids began chanting, each called their element, then joined hands in the center of their circle. A bright light appeared as soon as their hands touched, expanding as they pulled the circle back, a different landscape showing through. When it reached a certain size, the Druids twisted their wrists, flipping the portal sideways. Lir and Calder quickly stepped through, and the portal closed behind them.

As Lir's hooves touched down in Tionól, he transformed into his púca form. He tossed his mane and neighed loudly, overcome with joy as usual.

Calder couldn't help but grin at his best friend's excitement. "Come on, Lad, let's go!" he exclaimed, jumping on the púca's back, wrapping his hands in the wild mane, as Lir exploded forward, heading for the Ó Faoláin manor via the scenic route. After all, they needed a little time to get in a good run.

They made it to their home after a nice gallop through the woods. Siobhán had come out to the back porch, having gotten the Druid's message that they were on the way.

Lir skidded to a stop, showing off a bit and earning a laugh and a short round of applause from Siobhán. Calder slid off his back, slapped his haunch lightly, and said, "Do you want to come with Mam and me for our discussion, or would you like to go explore and see your old friends?"

Lir cocked his head and said, "Do you need me with you?" Calder smiled and said, "Thank you, but I'll give you all the details later. Find your friends and go for a wander. Could you stop by the healers in about an hour? I will meet you over there." Lir nodded quickly, whipped around, and took off at top speed.

Siobhán quickly wrapped her youngest in a tight hug. "It's good to see you again, a stór. I've found a few bits of information for you. Let's go to my library and have a cuppa."

Calder nodded and followed his mother into the main house, through the kitchen, down the hall, and through the great room, then turned right and took the hallway to Siobhán's library. Calder's cousin, Croía, a sixteen-year-old with dark auburn wavy hair and dark teal eyes, looked up from where she was straightening some books on one of the many bookshelves. She gave them both a big smile and said, "I'll finish up later, a hAintín Siobhán. You still owe me a horseback ride, Calder. Will ya have time this trip, maybe?" Calder smiled back at her and said, "I'll make time, Croía. Do ya feel up to taking Lir for a ride today?" She laughed and said, "Of course, I'd love it!" Calder looked at his mother and said, "How about you, Mam?" Siobhán raised an eyebrow and said, "We'll see if you two can keep up."

Croía giggled and left the room, closing the door behind her. Siobhán busied herself making tea for them both. Calder sat in an oversized armchair and picked up a copy of Shakespeare's collected works on the end table beside the chair. He flipped through to *A Midsummer Night's Dream* and perused the play while waiting for his tea. It was his favorite, of course, because of the homage paid to the púca through the character Puck. His own púca might not be as mischievous with his friends, but piss off Lir at your peril. He was like a harbinger of karma, and he was patient. He would get you when you least expected it.

Siobhán brought his tea over and set it on the end table. Calder replaced the book of Shakespeare on the table and began carefully sipping the hot tea. After a few moments, he said, "So what have you found, Mam?"

Siobhán put her tea on the table and sat back in the armchair that matched the one Calder sat in. "Well, I've found that Niamh Doran has a sad, sad family. As I mentioned on your last visit, her parents were killed when she and her sister, Étaín, were teenagers. Shortly after, Niamh quietly left for Earth. It wasn't widely known then, but there were whispers that Étaín's now husband, then betrothed, had become obsessed with Niamh, and that's why she left. Apparently, that was only part of the tale, however. I will put out some feelers and see what else I can unearth."

Calder nodded and replied, "That tracks with what I know of the story." Siobhán continued, "There's something else we need to discuss—Máire Daugherty."

A look of slight confusion crossed Calder's face. "What about her?" he asked. Siobhán said, "As I was piecing together Niamh's background, I also came across some rather unflattering opinions about Niamh's niece, Máire. Apparently, Máire's father, Cass, in addition to being obsessed with his wife's sister, is also just a general asshat." Calder's eyes bugged out at her choice of an Earth curse word; it was so unlike his mother.

Siobhán couldn't help but grin. "What?" she said. "I read Earth literature. I know how they speak. Asshat seemed an appropriate term in this case. I feel like it should be arsehat, but that just doesn't roll off the tongue quite as nicely, does it?" Once Calder got over his momentary shock, he started to chuckle. "Yes, the people of Earth certainly have a way with words, eh?"

"Quite," she replied. "Now, back to Máire. As I was saying, her asshat of a father has turned her into a scheming, obsessive mess. And unfortunately, it appears her current obsession is, well, you."

Calder's eyes bugged out for a second time. He hardly knew Máire existed. "That seems unlikely. I've barely met her." Siobhán shook her head. "I'm sorry, but you have a thriving relationship in her mind. And I'm afraid that if you reject her, she might snap. I don't think any of us wants to see that."

Calder shook his head, unsure exactly how things had reached the current state. "Okay, I will try to avoid her. If I can't, I will be extremely non-committal but definitely avoid outright rejection." He paused, refocusing his attention on solving Keegan's problem. "What about Niamh's illness? Does anyone know how to cure it?"

Siobhán paused to take a long sip of tea. "I'm afraid, Love, that the information I could find in that regard was pretty sparse. A few of the elders I spoke to thought they had heard of something similar, but none of them knew the cure for such an ailment." She took another sip of tea. "I take it you know what that means, a stór?"

Calder let out a sigh and said, "Yes. It means I need to go speak with the healers. With m'athair." Siobhán gave him a sympathetic look and replied, "I'll be here when you get back, Love."

Lir and Calder walked along the bubbling brook, making their way to the Healers' Grove, an area of forest with various structures, mounds, and white tents scattered throughout. The healers used these areas for whatever purpose might be needed: meditation, creating and dispensing medication, as well as various other therapies and treatments, magical and mundane. Just entering the Grove caused a sense of calm to come over them. All the colors were soothing pastels and earth tones, and the scents of the forest mingled with various aromatherapies, combining to create a unique and calming environment.

Lir kept grazing along the creek, keeping an eye on Calder but giving him space to do what he needed without an unnecessary audience. He knew this was difficult for his best friend.

Calder flagged down a passing healer, explained his situation briefly, then waited while she went to find someone to help him. In just a few minutes, he saw someone he recognized walking toward him. She had long, dark, wavy hair, currently pulled back in a messy bun, and dark, bluish-green eyes.

"Dia duit, a Chalder," she said in greeting with a slight smile.

"Dia is Muire duit, a Mhuireann," Calder replied nervously. "I've come to get help with an illness," he continued.

Muireann's brow furrowed as she looked him over for any visible symptoms. "Oh no, not me," he said. "I'm researching, uh, an illness for my friend," he stuttered.

She looked relieved and said, "Oh, alright then. Tell me the symptoms, and I'll see if I can help."

Calder explained the length and severity of Niamh's illness.

Muireann listened carefully, then replied, "I've never heard of a relatively young Fae experiencing anything like that. But Athair has far more experience. I can ask him for help if you'd like me to?" She looked Calder in the eyes while speaking, then dropped her gaze at the end, knowing that this would be difficult for him. Calder smiled at her sensitivity, touched her arm briefly above the elbow, and said, "If you could ask him if he could spare me a few moments, I'd appreciate it." She smiled back at him, nodded, and left to find their father.

While she was gone, Calder took a deep breath and thought about his relationship with his biological father. The few times he'd interacted with him had been awkward and stilted. It felt like they both wanted to reach out and have some type of relationship, but with the Dúbailte Curse and the superstition it created, there was no way to do that openly. So, they were left with this half-assed middle ground that was neither satisfying nor meaningful. And Calder didn't see that changing anytime soon, so it was best just to keep his distance. It was less painful that way. Or at least that's what he kept telling himself.

Lost in thought as he was, the sound of someone approaching startled him slightly. He looked up and saw Morgan Ó Loingsigh, his father, turn the corner and walk toward him. The resemblance, while not overwhelming, was definitely there. Father and son, and daughter for that matter, shared rich, dark brown, wavy hair. Morgan and Muireann also shared dark, bluish-green eyes. Calder's were similar, but more of a true, deep green, like his mother's.

Morgan looked over at the son he could not acknowledge. He could admit there were a few things he regretted over the course of his life. He wished he could recognize Calder as his own. He truly wished he could pursue a relationship with his mother, Siobhán. But he would never regret what he felt for Calder's mother or the son she gave him. And he was enough of an optimist to believe that there was always the chance things could change. Maybe one day.

"Dia duit, a Chalder," Morgan said as he approached, holding his hand out to shake.

"Dia is Muire duit, a Mhorgan," Calder replied, gripping his hand firmly and shaking it, the awkwardness already surfacing.

"Muireann mentioned you needed my help diagnosing an illness?" Morgan asked, hoping that things might go more smoothly if they stuck to the business at hand.

"Yes, my uh, friend's mother has been experiencing extreme fatigue and weakness for several months. My friend is very worried about her," Calder explained.

"How old is this Fae? We sometimes see these symptoms with Fae who are over five hundred years old. There are remedies, but I'll need some more information," Morgan replied.

Calder looked confused and said, "She's not quite forty. She's not an elder."

Now, Morgan looked confused and said, "I don't understand. It is highly unusual for a Fae that young to have those kinds of symptoms. Is there anything else out of the ordinary I should know about?"

Calder facepalmed and said, "I'm such an eejit. I completely forgot to mention that she has been living on Earth for the past twenty years or so."

Morgan smiled and said, "Well, that makes a lot more sense. Earth has a fraction of the ambient magic of Tír na nÓg. Since we draw magic from our environment, she didn't have as much to draw from, and she just used up her reserves and needs to recharge. It will take a while to fully charge her battery, so to speak, but once she's back in Tír na nÓg, her symptoms will resolve fairly quickly."

Calder looked thoughtful and said, "How long is a while? My

friend and her mother have made a home on Earth. I'm not sure they want to be away for an extended time."

His father frowned and said, "I'm afraid they don't have much choice. At least not if your friend wants her mam around for a while. Our magic is an integral part of us. The scarcity of ambient magic on Earth has caused a leaching of your friend's mother's magic to a dangerous level. If she stays on Earth, she will get weaker and weaker until, eventually, she dies. However, all she has to do to fix the issue is return home. That will sort things immediately. She will need to stay here for at least a decade, but with our lifespan, that's really not long at all.

"Has your friend lived on Earth her whole life, then?" Morgan asked. Calder nodded. "Well, chances are she hasn't used her magic as much as her mother would have. She probably isn't noticing any effects yet. But her battery will eventually drain as well, just as her mam's has."

Calder furrowed his brow, his mind processing this interesting development. *I need to speak to Mam. We need to figure out a way to get Niamh and Keegan to Tír na nÓg and come up with a back story for them.*

Morgan watched his son's emotions cross his face as he considered what he'd learned. He put a hand on his shoulder and said, "Calder, I don't know how close this friend of yours is to you, but I promise you, her mother will die if she does not return home. If you want to save her that pain, convince her and her mam to return."

As Morgan was speaking, Calder let himself lean into his father's hand on his shoulder for just a moment. Just a brief moment to pretend they had the kind of relationship they both wanted.

Once Morgan finished speaking, Calder sighed, then stiffened his shoulders, giving his father the unspoken message to remove his hand. A look of disappointment crossed his face for just a second, then he removed his hand, and Calder said, "Thank you for your help, Morgan. Slán agat." Then he extended his hand to shake.

Morgan shook his hand and replied, "Tabhair aire, a Chalder. I hope to see you again soon."

Calder gave a stiff nod and turned to leave. Morgan watched him go with a melancholy smile, then he turned and headed back to work.

Calder walked along the banks of the stream they had followed on the way to the healers. He quickly came across Lir taking a long drink. The púca lifted his head from the brook and rested it on his shoulder after a long look at his best friend. Calder wrapped his arms around Lir's neck, allowing himself a moment to soak up the compassion and sympathy Lir offered freely.

After a short time, Calder patted Lir on the neck a couple of times and said, "Come on, Lad. Let's head back to the house. We owe Croía a ride, after all." Lir's ears perked up at that. "Oh, I like her! She feeds me the best treats," Lir replied enthusiastically.

As they turned to head back to the Ó Faoláin manor, Máire suddenly stepped out from behind a tree with a pouty look. She was dressed in a skintight green dress that barely covered her assets. "Well, well, isn't Croía the lucky one?" she said. "How does one get a ride from the fabulous Calder Ó Faoláin, anyway?" Her suggestive tone left no doubt about what she meant. She took a couple of steps forward, putting her far too close to Calder for his comfort, but remembering his mother's earlier warning, he didn't dare step back.

"Oh, Máire, you know how much work our horses require. We just promised my cousin, Croía, she could help us exercise Morrígan and the others," he replied, clasping his hands behind his back so he wouldn't accidentally put them somewhere Máire definitely wanted them. There wasn't much room to maneuver since there were barely a few centimeters between them at this point. Time to call in reinforcements.

Máire leaned into Calder, putting both hands on his chest, and said, "Hmm, maybe I could come along? Surely, Lir could carry two?" She stared up at him, licking her lips and letting her hands trace circles over his chest. Calder quickly grabbed her wrists, then sandwiched her hands between his own, patting them a couple of times and dropping them, then he sidestepped her to give Lir a scratch.

"I don't know about that. If he doesn't quit gorging on strawberries, he won't be able to keep up with Morrígan much longer," he joked, breaking out their secret code. Lir snorted and replied, "Fine, you can just ride Morrígan then. I'll go find Croía." And he quickly trotted off, feigning, or maybe not, indifference.

Without Lir there as a barrier, Máire quickly closed the distance between them, but Calder was quicker, spinning around and saying over his shoulder, "Shall we take a stroll?" Then he took off as quickly as he could manage, within the bounds of politeness.

Máire followed, of course, nearly running to keep up with Calder's long strides. "Where are we going?" she asked, panting slightly as the quick pace and tight dress caused a little shortness of breath.

Calder, who was a few paces ahead of her, looked back at her and said, "We still need to meet Croía." Máire looked disappointed and said, "Oh, okay." Then she brightened a bit and said, "If Lir wants Croía to ride with him, maybe we could both ride Morrígan?"

"Well-" Calder started, slightly panicked as he tried to devise an excuse. Then he heard the sound of Lir's hooves galloping toward them, and his best friend crested the hill in front of them.

Siobhán followed on Morrígan, and Croía brought up the rear on Morrígan's dam, Fiadh. Calder breathed a silent sigh of relief as the sight of his mam caused Máire to stop in her tracks. Siobhán pinned Máire with the look of a disappointed mother.

"Máire, how unexpected! What brings you by today?" Siobhán said, her icy gaze looking Máire up and down, clearly disapproving of the outfit, and attitude, exhibited by the young woman.

Máire tugged her skirt down and her bodice up as she answered, "Oh, I was just out and about, and I happened to run into Calder."

After another pointed look from Calder's mam at the inappropriate outfit, she replied, "I see. Well, you will have to excuse us. We made plans for a ride, and we have some family business to discuss. I'm sure you understand." Siobhán's tone made it clear she really didn't care if Máire understood or not; the conversation was at an end.

Calder took that as his cue to leap on Lir's back, give Máire a half-hearted wave, and lead the way as Lir leapt forward, Morrígan and Fiadh happy to follow him on his mad dash across a meadow filled with a plethora of different flowers in all the colors of the rainbow. Bees and butterflies quickly flew out of their way, and Máire was left staring after them, wondering how things had turned out that way.

Family
is life

# ELEVEN

Máire wandered through the gardens around the World Tree, mumbling to herself as she took a stick and whacked the heads off flowers as she walked by. Granted, there were plenty of flowers to torture; it was Tír na nÓg, after all. The gardens around the World Tree were incredibly lush and extravagant. There were flowers, plants, bushes, and shrubs of every color imaginable, and maybe a few that bordered on the unimaginable.

Floating through the air were little flecks of white fluff from propagating trees that caught the late morning sunlight. Several of them caught in her strawberry blonde hair, but she was too frustrated and upset to notice. After a few more minutes of indiscriminate floricide, she flopped down on a bench, thoroughly disheartened.

"What did those flowers ever do to you?" a smooth, mellow voice asked from behind her. She quickly turned around to find Corley Devlin, an Earth Fae a few years older than her, staring at her with a smug grin.

Máire rolled her eyes and turned back around. "Feck off, Devlin. What are you after?"

"Me? Not a thing. Not one thing," he replied, strolling around the bench and sitting next to Máire, just a little too close. Máire turned some next-level side-eye on him, then flared a short burst of flame up and down her right side. Corley uttered a rather high-pitched shriek and jumped back to a more respectable distance.

"Look, I'm sorry. Let's start over," Corley said. He extended his hand and said, "Dia duit, a Mhuire." She stared at him for a long time, then shook his hand and said, "Dia is Muire duit, a Chorley."

Corley leaned back and draped his arm over the back of the bench. "So, what has you in such a snit, Máire?" His bright blue eyes showed sincere interest, despite his earlier shenanigans.

Máire looked over at him, her own pale green eyes narrowed in suspicion. "Why do you want to know?" she asked.

Corley leaned in and said, "Maybe I'm just a nice lad?" Máire just snorted. "Sure, maybe," she replied with a healthy dose of sarcasm.

"Try me," he said, wiggling his eyebrows suggestively. That made her snort with actual laughter. "I've just been trying to get to know someone, but his mother keeps interrupting. It's getting annoying," she explained.

"I see," he said. "Who's the lad?"

"Calder Ó Faoláin," she replied. Corley scowled and said, "Bloody fucking brilliant. Of course, it is." The memory of Calder's left hook clipping his jaw during a stupid fight last year left a sour taste in his mouth. Then, to make matters worse, he'd offered to help him up, pretending to care after he'd just embarrassed him. *I just need to keep my damn mouth shut,* he thought. *I know I bring it on myself, but damn it, he didn't need to rub it in with that "be the bigger man" bollocks.*

Máire watched his reaction with interest, wondering how she could use his visceral response to Calder's name to her advantage. *What if I get him to help me put a few dents in Calder's reputation? Oh, that idea has definite possibilities.*

She turned toward Corley, licking her lips and pulling her shoulders back to emphasize her cleavage. Then she tossed her hair over her shoulder, the pieces of tree fluff lending her a comical air. Corley schooled his face not to portray any mirth; he didn't need her getting all huffy again. She said in a slightly husky voice, "I have an idea."

Corley carefully replied, "Really? What's that?" She pursed her lips, then said, "What if we worked together to bring Calder down a notch?"

Corley thought about that for a moment. He'd been pining for Máire for years but had never had the courage to do more than casual flirting. This might be his chance to gain her respect. Perhaps it might also lead to something...more. Also, the thought of being able to see Calder knocked down just a bit appealed to some darker aspect of himself, and that was too much to resist. "What do you want me to do?"

Máire didn't even try to hide the smile that crossed her face at that moment. She began going over her idea, Corley adding his own thoughts as they fleshed out the details. As they plotted, she thought, *Once we've damaged Calder's reputation, he'll need someone to help pick up the pieces.*

Sitting underneath a large bush with purple, poofy flowers situated directly across from the bench the two co-conspirators were currently conspiring on was Laoise, currently in the form of a small, white squirrel. She had her fluffy tail between her paws and was nervously twisting it into a knotted mess. *Bloody hell, Corley!* she thought. *I thought for sure you'd help pull her out of this obsession with the Ó Faoláin lad and maybe give her a tumble to*

*relieve that mountain of stress she lives under. But here she's gone and pulled you over to the dark side. Now I have to go get reinforcements.*

She scurried away quietly, knowing that Saoirse would be nearby. *Where is that little vixen?* she thought, shifting into her preferred chihuahua form as she searched.

She found the red fox stalking crawdads by the brook, just a bit downstream from the World Tree gardens. As she approached, Saoirse crept a little further forward, almost ready to pounce on the unsuspecting snacks. Just then, Laoise stepped on a twig, causing it to crack and scare away the crawdads.

Saoirse let out a frustrated sigh and turned back toward Laoise, "Are you thick or what? Can't you see I'm huntin' here?"

Laoise trotted up to her and said, "What I see is you being a gobshite, leaving your Corley without the little bit of sense you might impart."

"What? He's been right as rain of late. It's that Máire of yours, isn't it?" Saoirse shook her head, a look of disgust on her face.

Laoise puffed up her chest and got right up in that fox's face. "Listen here, you little pox bottle! My Máire does the best she can with that arsehole da of hers, constantly breaking her down, making her feel worthless. I know you've seen how he treats her!"

Saoirse sighed again and replied, "Alright, little pup, don't get your tail twisted. I know he's a waste of air. So, what have our two troublemakers cooked up now?"

Laoise explained Máire's obsession with Calder and how she had hoped Corley might distract her best friend. Instead, Corley seemed to be following Máire even further down her obsessive path.

Saoirse shook her head and said, "If it had been anyone else, I'm sure he could have distracted her just fine. But Corley has a blind spot when it comes to Calder Ó Faoláin. Last year, he got completely pissed, off-his-tits drunk with a few of the other Earth Fae. He made a stupid comment about Calder's mam, saying he wished she would tuck him in at night. He's such an eejit sometimes. Well, Calder walked over to him, clocked him in the jaw, then tried to help him up. At some point, Corley realized how stupid he was acting, but he was too proud to admit it and accept Calder's hand. I know he has let it fester, and now it's become an obsession of its own."

Laoise flopped down next to Saoirse and said, "What a bloody mess our Fae have made of themselves, eh?" Saoirse just nodded. "Well, there's nothing for it then; we need a plan to straighten this lot out," the pup continued.

Saoirse looked thoughtful, then replied, "Both of them have good hearts; they just let their emotional baggage get in their way, then make the stupidest damn choices! We just need to nudge them in the direction their hearts are telling them to go." She stood up straight and extended her paw. "I'm in. How about you?"

"I was in before you knew there was a problem," Laoise responded. She shook Saoirse's paw and continued, "Let's get these knuckleheads sorted. Then maybe we can actually take a day off."

Family
is life

# TWELVE

"No, no, no!" Áine squawked, landing and stomping over to where Lir and Cara were going through the dance moves she was trying to teach them. They were currently in one of the studios, slightly bored since they'd already handled all the paperwork and were waiting for their turn to add elements to the river table Calder and Keegan were concentrating on at the moment.

"It's step-ball-change, step-ball-change, walk, walk, walk, strike a pose," she reiterated, rather crankily, walking through the sequence once again. Then she mumbled under her breath, "It'd be easier to teach that house plant the steps," as she flew back up to her perch atop the set of shelves in the corner, ostensibly because she needed a "global view."

Lir immediately sat down and said, "I heard that," and proceeded to pout. Cara had to turn around to keep from laughing at the two of them. When she had herself under control, she turned back around and said, "Alright, I think it's time for a break. What is there to eat around here?"

Lir perked up at that and said, "Oh, I know where he hides the good stuff. Follow me!" and he took off down the hall. Áine yelled, "Wait up, Goat Boy! I'm starving!" Then she launched herself off the shelf and flew off in chase.

Cara just chuckled and followed them down the hall. "You two better save some for me!"

Keegan watched intently as Calder prepared to carve a detailed section of the river table with his combined earth and water powers. He had filled the sink at one end of the studio with water, and a five-gallon bucket of sand was nearby. He brought a small thread of sand over one shoulder and an equal thread of water over the other. He twined them together around his left hand, both elements constantly moving, and he revved the speed of the combined thread up to the point a soft whirring sound could be heard. Then he grasped the thread like a pencil or a scalpel and began to carve away the bits of wood that didn't belong.

Once he really began to work, he was captivating to watch. He was carving, or sculpting really, an underwater ocean scene with a coral reef, a multitude of sea creatures, as well as every sub-aquatic plant imaginable. And the level of detail was truly breathtaking—it almost seemed as if the waves were moving back and forth, the fish and other creatures swimming around, and the plants swaying with the tides.

Occasionally, he would pull the thread of sand and water back, nodding to Keegan. While he took a couple of deep breaths, she would use a brief, controlled blast of air power to brush the excess water, sand, and wood from the table's surface. Then the carving would resume, Keegan's amazement, and her respect for his talents, growing by the minute.

After quite a while, Calder released the two threads back to their respective containers, and Keegan swept the table clean with her air. He also plucked all the excess water and sand from the floor and sent all of that to the two containers as well. Finally, he gathered all the wood chips and sawdust from the floor and sent them to their own containers, too.

The two of them looked the scene over for a moment. There was a giant octopus curled around a piece of the coral reef, each individual sucker meticulously captured. There were sea horses and dolphins, merrows, and selkies, as well as schools of fish, all depicted in exquisite detail.

"This is simply stunning," Keegan replied, words escaping her in the face of this level of craftsmanship. "I'm not sure what I can add."

Calder smiled, blushing slightly at the compliments. He said, "Why don't we start with adding some dimension? Deepen the color where shadows should be, and we'll go from there."

Keegan looked it over and said, "Okay, but I hope I don't ruin it." Calder replied, "Just don't burn it to ash. I can probably fix anything short of that."

She chose the section around the octopus to begin with, very slowly and carefully letting a trickle of fire brush against the wood, just enough to slightly darken it. As things progressed, Keegan's confidence grew, and she began taking a few more creative liberties, adding swirls and shadows among the waves.

Calder's smile continued to grow as he watched her progress. Watching someone tap into their innate artistic abilities was always satisfying, and she had more than her fair share.

When she finally seemed to be winding down, he said, "I think we've discovered another talent to add to your list. Let's see now, that would include exemplary food service work, outstanding gymnastics and parkour skills, mediocre thievery..."

Keegan sputtered as she started to defend her thieving skills, then realized how ridiculous that was. The delighted smile on Calder's face made her narrow her eyes. "Very funny," she replied, shaking her head at being drawn into that trap.

Calder gave one last chuckle and said, "Seriously, you just displayed some outstanding talent. Far better than I did on my first try. Thank goodness I had Lir destroy those first few attempts. They weren't pretty."

Keegan made a mental note to check with Lir because he seemed like the sentimental type. She would wager that a few of those first attempts might still be around somewhere.

Calder walked over to the couch in the corner of the studio, motioning for Keegan to follow. When they were both seated, he said, "I know you must be dying to hear what I discovered on my last trip home. There's good news that is also somewhat problematic. I spoke with the Chief Healer in Tír na nÓg, who said that since your mother has been away from the homeworld for so long and there's so little ambient magic on Earth, your mam has basically had her battery drained. But it's easily fixed; she just needs to spend a decade or so back in Tír na nÓg."

Keegan's excited expression became tempered somewhat at that realization. "Oh," she said, looking thoughtful. "And there's the problematic part," Calder replied. "So, in order to formulate some sort of plan, we need a little more information. Can you tell me the details of why Niamh chose to leave the homeworld and raise you on Earth?"

"Okay, so it basically all comes back to my uncle the asshat," she began, interrupted by the sharp bark of laughter Calder couldn't contain at her choosing the same colorful description his mam had used. "Sorry, please continue," he said, getting himself under control.

"So, I guess my Aunt Étaín fell for this douche nozzle named Cass. They were all lovey-dovey for a while, then Cass saw my mom and became obsessed. He started following my mom around, being a super creepy stalker dude and scaring the crap out of Mom. My aunt was basically in serious denial, so she was no help.

One day, he managed to trap my mom when my future dad walked by and put a stop to things. Mom and Dad fell in love, hooked up, and then they got sloppy. Cass caught them together and tried to blackmail them. Shortly after that, they figured out I was getting ready for my grand entrance, and it became clear that Cass would put two and two together. Things were further complicated because my dad's mother was Head of some Council and..."

"Wait, let me get this straight. Your da is Shay Ó Brien?" Calder interrupted in shock.

Keegan replied, "Yeah, that's him." Calder looked her over with this new information. "You have his eyes," he said. She smiled and said, "So I'm told." He shook his head and said, "I'm sorry, please continue."

"Okay, well, between Uncle Cass, the asshat, and Nana Ó Brien, the control freak, my parents couldn't find a way to be together, at least not with the time constraints they were under, so it was decided my mom would run—run to Earth and do her best to keep me safe and hidden."

While Keegan was speaking, Calder had been blinking back tears. He had thought his life had been burdensome, always having to hide a part of himself, never able to acknowledge or have a real relationship with his father. But she had been through far more difficulties than even he could comprehend.

"I'm so sorry you had to go through that, a chroí," he said, resting his hand gently on top of hers, giving it a slight squeeze. "But I want you to know, you won't have to figure it out alone anymore. I will do everything I can to help figure out how to bring you and your mother home. And you may not be aware, but the Ó Faoláin family sticks together. Family is life. So, what's important to me is important to all of them. Oh, and just so you know, my mam does not like to take no for an answer. So, she doesn't; she just figures out a way, and things tend to work out for her. Congratulations, Keegan, you now have an extended family who will walk through fire for you!"

Wide-eyed from the unexpectedly touching sentiment, Keegan suddenly stood and said, "I want to show you something. Can we take a break and go for a ride?" Calder said, "Sure, I can call a driver to take us wherever you'd like to go."

Keegan shook her head and said, "Nope, I'm driving. Let's go tell the hooligans we're going on an adventure, and they need to hold down the fort."

Family

is life

Keegan and Calder headed downstairs to the lobby, pausing at the door to the kitchen to poke their heads in and let their friends know where they were heading. A multitude of snacks were spread out on the table, and the three of them had obviously been sampling more than their fair share. Cara was sprawled in one of the chairs, the top button of her pants undone, moaning, "Never again!" Áine was lying flat on her back on the edge of the table, one wing hanging over the edge, belly stretched taut, snoring her way through a food coma. Only Lir seemed unaffected, eating a bit of this and a bit of that, humming as he went. Perhaps the fact that he had four stomachs had something to do with it.

Keegan just giggled at the sight while Calder's eyes bugged out of his head. "Lir, Lad, you do realize all this food was for the meeting I promised to host for the DnP board, right? There was enough to feed fifteen people. You know what, never mind. Keegan and I are going for a drive. You three dossers hold down the fort."

Lir stopped chewing long enough to respond, "'Kay!" before resuming his feast. Keegan giggled again and said, "Let's go, big boy," grabbing Calder's hand and pulling him out the door and down the stairs.

Keegan pulled her VW Bug convertible onto the highway heading east out of downtown. The top was down and the early autumn air smelled crisp and refreshing as it snarled her hair into a riotous mass of curls. Calder watched as she sang along, at the top of her lungs, to Pink's "Just Like Fire" blaring on the radio, face flushed and hair flying everywhere. The late afternoon sun moving across the sky behind them on its way to dusk backlit her curls until it seemed she was on fire. The effect took his breath away, especially when she glanced over at him, silver eyes twinkling. Her mood was so infectious he began singing along with her.

They drove for about half an hour, then Keegan got off on an exit on the edge of town and began taking country roads out to this beautiful, wooded area. Only a few trees were starting to show hints of fall color at their edges, but the setting sun bathed everything in glorious shades of scarlet and vermillion, a truly stunning sight.

Keegan parked off the side of the road behind a row of bushes near a meadow with several hawthorn trees, including a rather large one in the center. "I like to hide my car, just in case someone drives by. We're technically trespassing," she commented with a shrug. With a grin, he just shook his head, and said, "You're just a tiny criminal, aren't you?" She grinned back at him and said, "Trust me, it's worth the risk."

As she led him toward that large tree, he began to feel a strange tingling sensation. He looked at Keegan and raised an eyebrow. She just smirked at him and said, "Come on. This is my favorite place in the world." Then she pulled him forward, the tingling growing stronger the closer they got to the tree.

Finally, they stood right in front of the tree, their entire bodies vibrating with the magic emanating from the ancient hawthorn. "Cara and I found this place one summer, and it always just felt like home to us. Cara said it was a latent Faery Tree. I don't know about that, but I love how it makes me feel." She closed her eyes, held her arms out, and began slowly spinning, soaking the vibrations in.

She began humming that same Pink song again as she spun, turning her spin into a slow, sensuous dance. She began weaving her arms through the air, little fingers of flame flickering at various places around her body, slowly at first but soon picking up speed until there was always some part of her dancing with fire.

Calder stared at first, unable to tear his eyes away from her. After a few moments, he decided to add his own touch to the dance. He spied some flowers growing a few paces away, so he plucked several blossoms, periwinkle asters, and white oxeye daisies dotted with deep yellow centers, and spun them through the air, dipping and weaving in a dance of their own. He sent his floral offerings over to Keegan, threading them through the mass of her curls, which were currently splayed out around her head. He did his best to avoid her flames, but a few petals were definitely singed, paying the price for dancing with fire.

As Keegan felt the flowers being woven into her hair, she finally opened her eyes and looked at Calder. The look he returned was absolutely ravenous, immediately increasing her heart rate and bringing a flush to her cheeks.

Encouraged by his reaction, Keegan brought forth her air power, using it to levitate her several inches off the ground. Then she truly began to dance, spinning and flipping through the air like a trapeze artist without the trapeze, flames flaring from the influx of oxygen. Her gymnastic and parkour skills, combined with her innate magic, created a spectacular display that made Calder feel lightheaded. But more than that, it was the sheer delight on her face as she embraced the magic fully.

*Feck it,* Calder thought. *I'm all in.* As he watched her aerial display, he gathered a small amount of moisture from the air and sent the tiny droplets through the air, brushing against her skin with a feather-like touch. He began with her face, hearing a slight hiss as the water came into contact with her flame-kissed skin, most of it quickly evaporating. That light touch also caused her to gasp in surprise and pleasure. He gathered a bit more moisture from the air and got more daring with his exploration, sending the little trickles of water down her neck, between her breasts, and across her stomach, teasing her with the lightest of touches, living for that sizzle that sounded as the water made its way across her super-heated skin.

The water droplets continued their journey across Keegan's body, moving from her stomach and splitting up, going down to circle around her thighs, then coming around and over her ass and back up around her waist, making a complete circuit around her thighs and torso, climbing her breasts, circling her taut nipples, and up her neck to gently touch her lips.

The soft touch of Calder's magic, combined with the intensity shining from his eyes, stoked her fire even higher. She gave one more frenzied spin before using her air power to carry her over until she was floating within a few inches of him, her waist level with his chin, sliding down, teasingly moving as close as possible without actually touching. Calder's pulse and breathing had increased dramatically; he was quickly losing patience with the dance.

Once her eyes drew level with his, he raised his hands to cradle her face while her hands came up toward his. As he lowered his face to kiss her, her hands met his, and suddenly there was a sharp jolt, and a bright light erupted between their hands. Startled, they pulled back slightly, expanding the area of light between them. Unsure of what was happening, Keegan turned away and lost her balance, beginning to fall. Calder reached for her, and they both toppled through their newly created portal.

"Ooof," Calder grunted as he landed flat on his back, and Keegan promptly landed right on top of him, her butt knocking the air from his lungs. She shook her head, dislodging a few flowers, and looked around, confused by the new landscape, especially by the unusual tree they seemed to have fallen out of. Not to mention all the strangely colored plants and flowers, as well as strangely colored birds and other small animals she had definitely never seen before.

"Little help here," Calder huffed out, unable to take a full breath since Keegan was still sitting on his chest. "Oh, sorry," she replied, scooting off him to sit on the ground, unwilling to trust her legs to stand just yet.

"What the actual fuck just happened, Calder? Are we where I think we are?" she asked, her voice shaking as she realized the enormity of their situation.

Calder sat up and said, "Welcome to Tír na nÓg, Keegan. You're home."

Family

is life

# FOURTEEN

After Calder's pronouncement, he looked around to ascertain if anyone had seen their spectacular arrival. The Druids would be here soon, alerted by the disturbance caused by the portal, so he threw a quick invisibility glamour over them. Any Fae would see a sparkle, but they wouldn't know who it was. He reached for Keegan's hand, but she quickly scooted out of his reach and stood up.

"No offense, man, but the last time you touched me...shazam—brave, new world. I need to catch my breath," she said, leaning forward to rest her hands above her knees and taking a couple deep breaths.

Calder sat up and moved to one knee in front of her. "Listen, I don't know exactly what happened there, but I do know that in order for a portal to open, all four elements need to be called and combined." Then he poked her nose with his forefinger. "See? No shazam,"

That elicited a smile from her. "But until we figure out our next steps, we need to avoid notice," he continued. "I'll keep us hidden until we're in the forest, but let's stick to the shadows and make our way to my family's house, eh?"

Keegan straightened up, nodded, and gave him a hand up. "Okay, lead the way."

They began making their way through the gardens near the World Tree, taking care to move from one bush or shrub to the next quickly and quietly, sticking to the shadows as much as possible. Or at least Calder did. Keegan made a modest effort to stay quiet and unobtrusive, but her curiosity about a place she'd only ever dreamed of visiting began to overtake her caution.

She started lagging behind, investigating the strange new plants and animals that were suddenly right before her. A smile spread across her face as she delighted in her surroundings, playing with the little pieces of fluff floating around them. "Calder, what is..." she began to ask, but Calder quickly made his way back the few paces to her, shushed her, and quietly replied, "Keegan, I know you're excited and enthralled with this new place, but please, can we just get to my house? I promise I will eventually answer every question you have after we're safe and sound. Fair enough?"

Keegan acted slightly pouty, but she nodded and said, "Fine. But you better pencil me in for about a month because I have a lot of questions." Calder gave a small chuckle and, unable to resist adding a little spice, replied, "I will give you my undivided attention." The look in his eyes left no doubt exactly what kind of attention he planned to give.

Keegan shuddered as his words and expression evoked quite the reaction. "Okay, I'll cooperate. Let's go," she said, holding out her hand. Calder took it, squeezed slightly, and said, "Follow me."

They reached the end of the gardens and quickly dashed across the open area between them and the wooded area that backed up to the Ó Faoláin property, Calder dropping the invisibility glamour as soon as they were at the trees. The movement caused a small flock of purple birds with bright yellow breasts to startle and take flight. This caught the attention of a certain Earth Fae, who just happened to be loitering near the World Tree, hoping to learn something useful to Máire. Corley had almost given up and gone to get a pint, but luckily, he was a little hungover and moving slowly today; otherwise, he might've missed it. *Oh my, who is that sweet young thing?* He watched them make their way into the trees behind the World Tree Gardens.

He was now torn between following them and possibly finding out more or finding Máire right away. As they disappeared in the trees, he thought, *Feck it, I'm going to look for her. I've never been very good at staying hidden.* He turned away and went to look for his favorite Fire Fae.

As they entered the trees, Calder turned back, looking over his shoulder as the hair on the back of his neck stood up. He saw nothing amiss but couldn't shake the feeling of being watched. He stared for another moment or two and finally continued on his way. He gave Keegan's hand a quick squeeze and proceeded to lead her to his home.

Keegan's mind was racing as they wove through the trees and brush. There were so many questions that she didn't even know where to start. *How is this possible? Mom always told me the only portal to Tír na nÓg was in Ireland.* She also couldn't help but feel excited. *I'm finally home! And home is amazeballs! The colors and sounds are so over the top it's like nothing I could have imagined. It even smells amazing!* She took a deep breath, soaking in the myriad scents of all the flowers and trees in bloom. By the time they reached the meadow behind the Ó Faoláin home, she was grinning like an idiot.

Sitting on the back porch was Calder's brother, Reilly, who was taking notes on his laptop, always working on his book. He looked up at the two of them, eyes widening to a comical degree, and said, "Oh, brother, you've made a right bags of this, now, haven't you? What were you thinking, bringing her here with no warning?"

Calder scowled at him and said, "This was an unplanned trip. Who's home?"

Reilly grinned back at his scowl and said, "Can't wait to hear this tale then. The lot of us are home, Mam included, although I think she's about to take Morrígan out for a run."

Calder said, "Could you ask Croía or Colin to stop her, then gather everyone in her library for us? We obviously have a lot to sort."

Reilly stuck his head in the door and bellowed, "Croía, run and tell Mam her ride will have to wait. Calder's here, and he brought the cailín. He wants us in the library." Calder just shook his head, mumbling, "I could've done that."

It took just a few minutes for them to reach the back porch, but by then, Keegan was experiencing a bit of culture shock. The sheer magnitude of the Ó Faoláin family manor was intimidating...until Calder opened the back door and ushered her into the warmest, most homey-feeling kitchen she'd ever seen. She couldn't help but smile as she took in the large, well-worn, but gorgeously carved, kitchen table. He didn't have to tell her how many discussions had happened around it. You could feel the love of family just walking in the door.

The sound of Calder's family making their way to the library could be heard as they passed out of the kitchen and down the hall, turning the corner into the great room. Keegan was mesmerized by the various pieces of woodworking adorning the walls. It was like looking at the family's history carved into their home.

When they reached the great room, she stopped and gasped

at the sight of the mantle. "Fallon, my mam's husband and my brothers' da, carved that," Calder explained. She walked right up to it, only stopping when her face was mere inches away, so she could inspect this masterwork more closely, giving it the attention it so obviously deserved.

After a while, she looked back at Calder and said, "I know he wasn't your biological father, but he would've been so proud of you. Talent appreciates talent, and you took after him without ever meeting him." Calder looked at her, dumbfounded, eyes welling with tears, and said, "I can't think of anything you could've said that would mean more to me."

Keegan took his hand again, squeezed it tightly, and said, "Just speaking the truth." Calder wiped his eyes and gathered himself for a moment. Then he said, "Come on, let's get the questions over with." He led her out of the great room, down the hall to the right, and into the library.

Siobhán sat down at the head of the table in the library, leaning back and crossing her legs as she watched her progeny gather for a family meeting. She had been preparing to take Morrígan for a long ride; the fiery mare needed more exercise than the average horse to keep her somewhat manageable. Suddenly, Croía ran into the stable, shouting, "Wait, a hAintín Siobhán! Reilly said there's an emergency family meeting! He wants everyone to meet in the library right away. And Calder's here with a pretty girl."

Siobhán sighed, patted the mare she had been about to saddle, and said, "Hold that thought, Love. I need to sort my boys out first." Then she handed the bridle to Croía and said, "Would you take her back to her stall, dear? It looks like my ride will be postponed for a bit."

Now, as she watched her three oldest boys pester each other

while waiting for her youngest and his guest, an old fear reared its ugly head. She had worked so hard to keep her family together and united in purpose, all while keeping Calder's secret, that any time a major change happened, she was terrified they wouldn't be able to adapt, and everything would come tumbling down.

She took a couple of deep, cleansing breaths to regain her sense of calm. She was just being silly, indulging in that same old fear. She and the boys had weathered every change they had faced in the past, and they would continue to do whatever they needed to do in the future. She may have made many mistakes in her life, but she had raised some fine lads. *The Ó Faoláins stick together no matter what. Family is life.*

The door to the library swung open, causing the conversation to immediately stop as all eyes turned to see the youngest Ó Faoláin brother enter, followed by a short Fae with a mass of red curls. When the girl looked over at Siobhán with those gorgeous silver eyes, she couldn't help but let out a small gasp. *Well, that puts a new spin on things.* She'd seen those eyes before, and the implications were enormous.

Siobhán stood as they entered the library, came around the table, extended a hand to her, and said, with a smile, "Fáilte, Keegan. We're so happy to meet you." Keegan returned the firm but gentle handshake and replied, "Tá áthas orm bhualadh libh." Everyone's eyes widened a bit at her unexpected use of Irish. She looked around self-consciously and said, "Did I say it right? My mom taught me a few phrases so I wouldn't sound rude if I ever got to visit the homeworld."

Conor laughed, showing off his dimples, gave her a wink, and said, "Well done! You were perfect." Keegan smiled back at him with a grateful look in her eyes.

"Indeed," Siobhán agreed, also smiling at her. "Keegan, these are Calder's brothers, Liam, the eldest, and the twins, Conor and Reilly." Each brother nodded and smiled at her when their name was said. "Please, everyone, have a seat." Everyone took their place around the table, Siobhán pausing briefly to give her youngest a tight squeeze and whisper a welcome in his ear.

Keegan's hands were on her knees, nervously tapping a rhythm until Calder covered one of them with his, gently squeezing it and leaving it there. She gave him a quick glance, nodding her thanks for his support.

Once Siobhán was seated, she waited until all eyes were on her, then said, "So Calder, why don't you tell us what brings you both here?"

Calder cleared his throat and said, "To be honest, we're not entirely sure, Mam." He glanced at Keegan, then back to his mother, and continued, "Keegan had driven me out in the country to show me her favorite spot. Her friend, Cara..." Keegan gasped and quickly stood, crying, "Oh crap! Cara, Áine, and Lir! They're going to freak the hell out!"

Calder stood up, picked the lone surviving flower from the back of her hair, and tucked it behind her ear. He took her hand again and said, "Calm down, a chroí. As soon as we're done here, we'll send word. They'll be fine." Then he sat back down and tugged on her arm until she followed suit.

The three brothers were chomping at the bit to make a comment about Calder being affectionate with a real-life female, but a stern look and a shake of the head from their matriarch quickly quelled that notion.

"So, we were out in the country near this tree. Keegan's friend, Cara, had once told her she thought it was a latent Faery Tree. Anyway, as we got near the tree, there was this incredible tingling sensation..." Reilly snorted a laugh, which he quickly turned into a cough; the threat of mucking stalls didn't need to be voiced; a look from Siobhán was enough.

Calder rolled his eyes at him but continued, "This tingling sensation got stronger the closer we got to the tree." He paused, loath to share details of an intimate moment in front of his family. This time it was Keegan's turn to squeeze Calder's hand in encouragement, whispering, "It's okay, go ahead."

Calder cleared his throat and said, "Anyway, when we got close to the tree, we were kind of, uh, dancing as we called our elements..."

"Dancing?" Conor asked incredulously. "Come now, Lad, I'm as big a fan of euphemisms as anyone, but let's cut to the chase, shall we? You two were after eating each other's face, at least, maybe a little more, and..."

Siobhán brought her hand down on the table sharply, effectively cutting the conversation off. "Conor, that's quite enough." She looked at Calder and said, "I think we get the picture, Love. What happened then?"

He replied, "So, we were both calling both our elements, and then our hands touched, and there was this kind of jolt, and a bright light began between our fingers. As we stepped back from each other, a portal began to stretch out between our hands. It looked just like the portals the Druids call. Then we fell through it and landed at the World Tree."

Liam let out a low whistle and said, "A Dhearthráir Beag, you've outdone yourself this time." Calder narrowed his eyes and opened his mouth to respond, but his mother cut him off.

"Put that nonsense away right now!" Siobhán said tersely, then sat back in her seat. She paused for a moment, a thoughtful look on her face. Then she said, "Alright, my Loves, it's time for the Ó Faoláins to pull together once again."

She turned to Keegan and said, "Calder has shared a bit of your story, including that your mam is weakening from being off the homeworld too long. He told us that the healers said she would need to spend at least ten years in Tír na nÓg to fully regain her strength and stamina. So, we must make a plan for that to come to pass. But before we can finalize any kind of plan, we must put all our cards on the table. Is Shay Ó Brien your da?"

Keegan's eyes widened, and she replied, "Yes, he is. And I don't mind you knowing that, but how exactly did you know?" She looked at Calder, and he immediately replied, "I didn't tell her. Hell, I didn't even know until our conversation at the office, remember?"

"Then how?" she asked, looking at Siobhán. As she was about to reply, Keegan said, "Wait a minute. It's my eyes, isn't it?"

Siobhán nodded. "Yes, I'm afraid they are very distinctive, but we will manage. The easiest way to distract people from something is to introduce something unfamiliar into the situation. I'm embarrassed to say that many Aos Sí consider humans to be an inferior species. I think it's bloody ridiculous, but unfortunately, not everyone agrees. In this case, however, their bigotry works in our favor. Since you were born and raised on Earth, we will simply say that your father was human."

Liam started nodding and said, "That just might work. Mention humans around most Fae, and their eyes glaze over. There is some novelty in the pop culture of Earth, but that is the extent of the interest for most Aos Sí. It will be far easier for them to believe that silver eyes must be commonplace on Earth than that Keegan is the daughter of the Head of Council, making her a Dúb-" Siobhán turned a withering glare on her oldest, causing him to clear his throat and continue, "uh, meaning she holds dual powers."

Reilly added, "Give the people an answer that doesn't challenge their worldview, and they will jump all over it."

Keegan began to look hopeful as the conversation continued, Siobhán and the brothers filling in her back story with as much truth as possible, creating a tale that would be easy for her and Niamh to remember. Then she remembered why they ran in the first place.

"But wait," she interrupted. "There's still a problem. The major reason my mom had me on Earth is because my uncle, Cass Daugherty, was obsessed with her and found out about Mom and Shay's relationship. If she comes back, she'll be right back where she started, with Cass stalking and blackmailing her, threatening to expose them if she doesn't give him what he wants."

Siobhán didn't even hesitate before she responded, "Love, Cass Daugherty is a tiny fish in a rather large pond. You leave him to me. I'm a much bigger fish. Meaner, too, when it comes to someone threatening me and mine. And whether you like it or not, Keegan, you and your mam are now part of mine."

Keegan looked down to hide the sudden onslaught of tears Siobhán's words caused. "Thank you," she whispered with a slight sniffle. Calder squeezed her hand again, then rubbed his thumb gently along the back of her hand, letting her know he echoed his mother's sentiment.

Siobhán leaned forward, gathering her brood's undivided attention. "Alright, Calder, you take Keegan to the kitchen and get her some dinner, then you two stay in your suite until I come for you. Your brothers and I have some work to do before we can implement our plans."

Calder nodded, then looked at his mam tenderly. "Go raibh maith agatsa, a Mháthair. Thanks to all of you," he said, including his brothers as well. "You don't know how much this means to me. To us." Keegan blushed at that but kept her gaze on the family, echoing Calder's thanks.

Liam teasingly replied, "Oh, I think we have some idea, Lad." Calder smiled at his older brother, then at the rest of his family, and led Keegan from the room in search of sustenance.

# Family

is life

# FIFTEEN

Keegan sat at the kitchen table, tracing the intricately carved edge with her fingers, trying to process what had happened. Calder was rifling through the pantry, rounding up something for them to eat. He was humming while he worked, which made her smile. *I could get used to this,* she thought. *Especially since I suck at cooking.*

She looked up as he returned to the table, arms full of food, a big grin on his face. "This should tide us over for a bit," he said. She gave a little chuckle and said, "One would hope."

She stood and came around to his side, taking a few items and helping him lay everything out on the table. There was soda bread, freshly washed veggies from the garden—carrots, cucumber, and tomatoes, and some peaches picked that morning. Calder grabbed a cutting board from the counter and a knife from the block, slicing and dicing things into manageable pieces. He stopped momentarily, pointed with his knife to a shelf holding various carafes of different kinds of oil and vinegar, and asked, "Hand me the balsamic?"

Keegan found the container of balsamic vinegar and brought it over to the table. "Anything I can do to help?" she said. He shook his head and replied, "Nah, I've got it. Oh wait, there is one thing. Aoife is with Thomas on Earth at the moment, but whenever she leaves Tír na nÓg, she usually makes sure there's a platter of meat for easy sandwiches left in the fridge. Could you check and bring me whatever she left for us? And check for some cheese as well."

Keegan went to what looked similar to a refrigerator and opened the door. Inside, front and center, was a platter of thinly sliced beef and a chunk of goat cheese. She took a moment to look over the Aos Sí version of a fridge, eyes widening a bit as she noticed everything was powered by magic. When the door opened, a spell for light was triggered. And she could feel something that confused her. "So, I can tell something is siphoning off the ambient heat to create colder air. But where's it going?"

Calder stopped what he was doing and joined her at the magic fridge. He reached inside and picked up a small piece of metal, about the size of the palm of his hand, and shaped like a triquetra. About a third of the symbol was glowing red. He handed it to her and said, "This tiny bit of metal is called a teas and has been enchanted by a Fire Fae to slowly leech heat from the air and store it safely until it can be released. It will shut itself off when it gets full, and we'll replace it with a new one. The full one can then be used, kind of like a lighter, to start fires or provide warmth. It only takes a little trickle of magic, any kind of magic, to trigger the release of the heat. Pretty clever, eh?"

Keegan turned the teas over and over in her hand, fascinated by this new utilization of magic, possibilities blooming in her mind. Calder laughed and said, "I can see the wheels turning. Which makes sense, considering your cousin, Máire, created that teas. Enchanting objects is in your blood."

Keegan's eyes widened at that revelation, and said, "Wow, I had no idea magic could be used like that." Calder's voice got a bit husky as he said, "I can't wait to show you exactly what I can do with magic, hAibhleog." Keegan blushed but was intrigued enough to ask, "Aibhleog, what does that mean?" She looked up at Calder, and he gently tucked one of her unruly curls behind her ear, then traced along the side of her face and down her jaw with the back of his index finger. She bit her lip, breathing a little heavier than normal, and felt herself leaning in toward him.

Calder took a deep breath and whispered, "Ember, it means ember. You feel like a glowing ember, just waiting to burst into flame." He shook his head as if to clear his thoughts and said, "You have no idea how hard it is to think straight around you." Then he straightened and took a small step back, adding just a bit of distance between them. "Mam will have my head if I don't get you fed soon. Come, put the teas back, and bring the lamb and cheese over to the table."

Keegan sighed but did as he asked. Once Calder had everything cut up and ready to go, he piled food for the two of them onto a platter, grabbed a couple of Guinness from the fridge, and led the way to his rooms, Keegan following with a couple of glasses and some napkins.

After a few minutes, they came to a door that Keegan immediately knew must belong to Calder's rooms. The door was an intricately carved portrait of Lir in his goat form, prancing through a meadow chasing butterflies. It almost looked like it would come to life and begin moving at any moment, and it took her breath away, causing her to audibly gasp.

Now it was Calder's turn to blush. He carefully opened the door, balancing their food and drink, and motioned with his head for her to enter. Keegan walked past him and was immediately left breathless again.

Calder's walls contained floor-to-ceiling carvings of various scenes, mostly involving trees and animals, and to say they were exquisite was putting it mildly. The level of detail continued to amaze her, no matter how often she saw his talent displayed.

Calder shut the door behind him and proceeded to set their food and stout out on a table, which was also intricately carved, of course. When Keegan turned around, she saw the back side of the door, which was covered with the portrait of a huge, muscular horse, rearing up on his hind legs, pawing at the air. It was stunning, striking, and ultimately unforgettable.

She turned toward Calder, pointing at the door, and said, "This is freaking amazing!" He replied, "Oh, thanks. Lir is always fun to carve."

Keegan said, "Huh? I saw Lir on the front of the door, but who is this horse on the back?"

Calder chuckled, laying everything out and pouring the Guinness into glasses. "That's right, you've never seen Lir in Tír na nÓg. When he comes home, he typically reverts to his natural form—a púca. That giant horse is what he looks like here."

Keegan plopped down and barked out a laugh. "I can't wait to see Áine's reaction!" Calder chuckled and said, "Wait until you see Áine's true form. I have a feeling she'll be spectacular as well."

"Wait, what? Áine has a true form? What is it?" Keegan asked excitedly. He replied, "I don't know for sure, but I have my suspicions. At any rate, we'll have to wait until she can join us to find out."

She plopped down in a chair and let out a deep sigh. "So much has happened in such a short time. I feel like I'm still trying to catch up." Calder sat across from her, reached across the table, and took her hand, squeezing it. "I know. I keep forgetting this is all new to you. Eat something; this brave new world requires a lot of energy." He took a slice of soda bread, smeared a little goat cheese on it, then layered on a couple of thin slices of meat, a slice of tomato, and drizzled a little balsamic vinegar on top, making an open-faced sandwich. He offered it to Keegan, who took it and dove in with a big bite. The flavors were perfect together, and she let out a little moan, but he resolutely refused to be distracted by all the little contented sounds she made while eating, adorable though they were.

He started to make a sandwich for himself, and while he worked, he said, "There's something else I need to speak with you about. You know about Aisling's Prophecy, yeah?" Keegan nodded, her mouth too full to speak as she inhaled her sandwich. "There is a reason it's also known as the Dúbailte Curse. Aos Sí have a lot of good qualities—we are generally very creative, hardworking, and loyal, with many other positive attributes. We are also, however, stubborn, proud, and rather superstitious, I'm afraid. So, when our people have labeled something a curse, you can be sure the vast majority of Fae will view that thing in a negative light. I want you to understand how important it is to keep your air power hidden. If anyone even suspects you of having dual powers, you could be in great danger." He paused to take a bite of his sandwich, studying Keegan's expression to make sure she was taking this seriously.

Keegan finished the bite she was chewing and took a long draught of her beer. Then she looked at him and raised an eyebrow, "Look, I know that when my mom was my age, this dual power thing was a big no-no. I get that. But surely things have changed a bit since then, right? It may not be completely acceptable, but how dangerous can it really be?" She stopped to take another drink, then picked up the last bit of her sandwich to finish it off.

Calder was shaking his head before she was done speaking. "Maybe on Earth, that would be true. But Aos Sí have been around for millennia. When you live as long as we do, change happens very slowly. Far too slowly sometimes. Believe me when I say there are Fae out there who have been doing things the same way for hundreds of years. Never mind that there might be a better way now."

Keegan finished the last bite of her sandwich and washed it down with the last of her Guinness. "Even so, surely there are enough Fae out there who want to move into the twenty-first century? Maybe they just need someone to lead the way?" She picked up a slice of peach and popped it in her mouth. It was, by far, the best peach she had ever tasted. She couldn't help but let out another little moan. "Does everything taste so good here?" she asked, making short work of her share of the peach slices.

Calder stood up, ran his fingers through his hair in frustration, and began pacing. "You are not listening to me! Do not underestimate the danger you will face if your duality becomes known! Superstition and magic make very bad bedfellows. I do not want to see you get hurt."

Keegan stood up and went over to where he had stopped pacing, near the door. "I know you're worried about this, Calder. And I promise to be careful. But I still think you're overreacting just a bit. I can take care of myself, you know," she said, unable to keep a slight smirk from her face.

The smirk was a step too far. Calder let his fear overwhelm him, and he grabbed Keegan by the arms, letting out a frustrated groan, and pushed her back against the door, saying, "You don't understand! I just found you! If I lost you...I don't know what I'd do!" His adrenaline surged at the thought of losing her, making his breath come heavy and fast. He stared at those gorgeous silver eyes looking back at him, eyes that were starting to fill with desire at the realization of just how much she meant to him.

He turned away and began pacing, his emotions racing and a very real sense of panic beginning to creep over him. *Why can't I make her understand the genuine danger she is in! I don't know how to explain it so she will truly grasp what could happen. I've never felt this way about anyone before, and I'm not sure I could live without her.* He stopped pacing as that last thought's full horror hit him.

He quickly crossed the room, pushed her roughly against the door, and brought his hands up to bury themselves in her curls, the force of his grip verging on the edge of painful. She tilted her head up and looked into his deep green eyes. Those eyes were filled with fear and desire in equal measure, although desire was beginning to take over. Her eyes then moved down to his lips, licking her own in anticipation.

Calder slowly lowered his face toward hers, giving her ample opportunity to stop things if she wasn't ready for this step. Instead, she entwined her own fingers in his wavy hair and pulled him down to her.

When their lips touched, it felt like electricity radiated through both their bodies, all the way to their toes. They started slowly, reveling in the taste of each other, just enjoying the feeling of their lips moving together.

Keegan enjoyed that for a bit but quickly grew impatient and turned her head to deepen the kiss, probing tentatively with her tongue. Calder quickly responded, welcoming the intensity of her kiss and returning it in kind. After a few delightful minutes of that, Keegan began kissing her way down his jaw to his ear, nibbling as she went.

Calder took that opportunity to return the favor and kissed his way past her ear, down her neck, giving little nips all the way down to her collarbone. His hands moved from being buried in her hair down her back to cupping her buttocks. This was all the incentive Keegan needed to give a little jump and wrap her legs around his waist. Calder moaned, squeezing her butt and kissing his way back up to her mouth.

Keegan wrapped her arms around his neck and squeezed her legs tighter around his waist. She'd never felt this level of intensity before. She lost herself in the moment, feeling nothing but his hands, lips, and tongue, caressing and nipping, licking and kissing, making their way slowly but surely across her skin.

Calder was utterly enthralled with the petite Fae in his arms. He knew she didn't truly understand the dangers they both faced. But she was well and truly entrenched in his heart now. He would do anything for her. Family is life, and Keegan was most definitely family.

Family
is life

CHAPTER

# SIXTEEN

Once Calder and Keegan left for the kitchen, Siobhán collapsed into her chair, closing her eyes and pausing for a few deep breaths. Then she straightened in her seat and said to her three remaining sons, "Alright, Lads, it's time to pull together. Reilly, could you please get me some paper, an envelope, a pen, and the family seal from my desk behind you? I need to write a letter to Keegan's mam and explain the situation."

He hopped up, gathered the supplies, and brought them to his mother. She took them and then looked each of her sons in the eye in turn. "I need you lot to take this letter to Niamh. And whatever happens, make sure you impress upon her the severity of the situation. She used to live here, so she understands what this place is like."

She began writing the letter, taking care to strike just the right tone. She didn't want to panic Niamh, but she wanted to impart the correct amount of urgency. It took a bit of time, but finally, she was done. Then she folded the letter, put it in the envelope, and placed the family seal over the closure. The seal was in the shape of a wolf's head superimposed over a thick hawthorn tree. She let a tiny trickle of magic flow through the seal, and the image was transferred to the envelope in metallic forest green wax, sealing it shut. She handed the envelope to Liam and said, "Alright, grab yourself some sandwiches, pack an overnight bag, and grab some horses to make the journey back to the World Tree as quick as possible. The Druids will hold them overnight, and I'll send Colin and Croía to collect them tomorrow. Just get to Niamh, explain the situation, and bring her home. Don't forget Keegan's friends Cara and Áine, or Lir. The sooner this is sorted, the sooner we'll all be able to relax. Or the sooner we can prepare for the next crisis, whatever the case may be. Now go, Lads. I've got some more work to do here."

The brothers left the room, splitting up to accomplish all their tasks. Conor headed to the kitchen to make sandwiches, Reilly went to gather the horses, and Liam made his way to their rooms to throw a few things in a bag. Reilly wouldn't care if he brought the right stuff, so long as he grabbed his laptop. Conor would be pissed that he forgot something, no matter what. Liam shrugged and thought, *I'll just do the best I can.*

After her sons left, Siobhán sat back in her chair, enjoying a brief moment of silence. She finally got up, walked over to the bar in the corner, and poured herself a shot of whiskey. She tossed that back, then sat down with her writing supplies again. *This letter may take a little longer,* she thought. She began to write, choosing her words carefully. If this letter fell into the wrong hands, it could be disastrous, so she had to be circumspect and vague while still getting the message across. She finally finished, forgoing the seal in this case to avoid possible incriminating evidence. She picked up the letter and left the room to find Colin.

Turns out she didn't have to go far. Colin was in the great

room, on his way to who knows where. "Lad, I have a job for you," she said, waving the letter at him. "Could you take this to Muireann at the Healer's Compound, please? Your discretion is, as always, appreciated, Love."

"Of course, a hAintín Siobhán," he replied. "I'm happy to help." She smiled at him, handed him the letter, and, giving him a maternal pat on the shoulder, said, "Good Lad. Be quick, please."

Colin took the letter, tucked it in the back of his waistband, and pulled his shirt down over it. "On my way now. Be back soon," he replied and took off toward the stables.

*Now to sort out my youngest and his new cailín,* she thought with a mental sigh. She had hoped he might be spared this level of complication in his love life. *Ah, well, seems like it's never easy.* And she made her way toward Calder's suite of rooms.

When Siobhán stopped in front of Calder's door, she couldn't help but smile at the carving of Lir. That bloody goat might be the happiest creature she'd ever seen. And Calder's skill with wood-working never ceased to fill her with pride. *It's amazing how the only child of mine who was not biologically related to Fallon managed to take after him in so many ways,* she thought. *Child of his blood or not, he would have been so proud of Calder.*

She shook her head to bring herself back to the present and lifted her hand to knock on the door. About that time, she heard a throaty moan followed by a giggle. *Oh dear,* she thought. *I didn't realize things were quite this advanced. Time to inject a bit of caution.* She rapped loudly several times on the door.

It took more than a few minutes before Calder opened the door, cheeks flushed and breathing heavily. Keegan sat at the table, looking every bit as disheveled as her son. Siobhán looked back and forth between them, and all she did was raise an eyebrow and cross her arms.

Calder cleared his throat and said, "Yes, Mam, can I help you?" She walked past him and sat at the head of the table, motioning for him to sit next to Keegan. He sat, taking her hand and meeting his mother's gaze.

Siobhán took a last look at each of them and said, with a wry grin, "Well, it seems you two have been keeping yourselves entertained." Both of them blushed but refused to drop their hands or gaze. Siobhán noticed and said, "But at least you seem united. That's something."

"Now it's time for a word of advice from your mam, son. And Keegan, I don't know your mother personally, but I believe she would agree with what I'm about to say. If you two are serious about this relationship that I can see blossoming between you, I beg you to listen to me now. Be careful, my Loves! I'm sure Calder has tried to explain the situation in Tír na nÓg to you, Keegan. I would also wager that you might think he was exaggerating the danger. That, a chroí, is simply not the case. Your mother gave up her entire life here to keep you safe. Do you think she would have done that if she didn't think it was absolutely necessary? And after my husband died, I would have been delighted to pursue a relationship with Calder's father. But it just wasn't possible. So please, please, listen and take to heart what I'm saying. Protect yourselves and each other because I've already lost more than anyone should. If I lost either of you, I'm not sure my heart could stand it." As she was speaking, she stood and moved between them, putting a hand on each of their shoulders. When she was done, she gave them each a squeeze and returned to her seat.

"Now, to catch you both up on the current situation. I've written your mam a letter, Keegan, and sent Calder's brothers back to Earth to deliver it. I'm hopeful they will come home with Niamh, Cara, Áine, and Lir so that we can all work together to devise a plan that allows Niamh to stay home and heal while keeping you all safe."

She paused momentarily, tapping a finger against her pursed lips as she collected her thoughts, then continued, "It will take at least a day or two for the lads to get to Niamh, collect her and the others, hopefully, then return. In the meantime, Keegan, you can stay in Blathnaid's room, just down the hall. Croía's sister is currently at university, and I'm quite sure she wouldn't mind having a guest while she's away. Feel free to explore this wing and its interior gardens, the kitchen, great room, and library. But please don't venture anywhere else until everyone returns and we all get our stories straight." Keegan nodded her agreement, Calder giving her hand a gentle, supportive squeeze.

"Thank you, Love," Siobhán said. Then she looked at Calder and said, "Walk with me, mo bhuachaill. Keegan, I'll send Croía to show you to your room. Try to get some rest." Keegan nodded again, and Calder kissed the center of her palm, then stood up and followed his mother from the room.

Family

is life

CHAPTER

# SEVENTEEN

Siobhán spotted Croía just down the hall from Calder's rooms. She sent the cousin to show Keegan to her sister's room. Then she walked next to her son in silence for a time, trying to choose the right words. She needed him to hear and understand the magnitude of the situation with Keegan. Calder kept stealing glances at her, wondering when she was going to speak. Finally, he said, "Mam, just spit it out. If you chew on those words any longer, they won't be fit for hearing."

Siobhán chuckled and said, "Sometimes I forget how perceptive you are, Lad." Calder gave her a big smile and said, "Just part of my charm." His mam rolled her eyes and said, "Yes, you are definitely charming. Which brings me to what I've been mulling over."

She took Calder's hand and pulled him over to a couple of chairs across the great room from the carved mantel. She gave the mantel a long look, seeming to draw strength from it. Calder squeezed her hand, trying to reassure her.

"I know I've already expressed my desire for you and Keegan to be careful. But I want you to hear me now. This is a dangerous journey you are about to undertake. And while I worry for you, I worry even more for that lovely cailín. She has been through so much, Calder. I know you have suffered, too, but you had your brothers and me and a multitude of extended family on your side. Keegan has only had her mam, her friend, Cara, and her familiar to rely on. Not to mention, she was stuck on another world with a minimum of magic. She knows almost nothing about our home-world." Siobhán paused for a moment, collecting her thoughts. Calder waited patiently, instinctively understanding that it was important for her to get this out.

"I guess what I'm trying to say is you need to be absolutely sure. Be sure you are willing to finish this journey, side by side with Keegan; come what may, before you ever step foot on the path."

Calder looked at his mam, then looked down, shaking his head. Looking back up, he smiled slightly and said, "Oh, Mam, I'm afraid that while your speech is well-intentioned, it's far too late for me. I'm falling in love with her. When I think of her, my heart races. When I'm next to her, I only want to protect and make her happy. I know our relationship is dangerous, but it's a danger I'm willing to face." Then he gave a little shrug and finished with, "She's worth it. All that and more."

Siobhán covered his hand with both of hers, tears pooling in her eyes. "I was afraid that might be the case. A parent always wants their children to be happy and hopes that they might have fewer hardships along the way. Things don't always work out that way. But I am so happy you two found each other. That stupid Dúbailte Curse be damned. The Ó Faoláins will stand beside you all the way. If you love Keegan, that makes her family."

Calder reached up and wiped away a tear that was making its way across her cheek. "And family is life."

It was only a few moments after Siobhán and Calder left the room that there was a light tapping on the door. "Come in," Keegan said, feeling very strange about someone who lived here knocking and asking her permission to enter. The door opened, and Calder's cousin, Croía, stepped in. "Fáilte, a Keegan. Siobhán asked me to show you to my sister's room," she said, giving a shy smile and a nod of welcome. "Follow me, please."

Keegan followed Croía down the hall a short way until she stopped before a door embellished with carved horses, including the most adorable little foal frolicking in a meadow filled with flowers. Keegan couldn't help but run her fingers over the intricate details, yet again amazed at the skill level. "This is Calder's work, isn't it?" she asked.

Croía nodded and said, "All the Ó Faoláins have above-average skill with woodworking, but Calder is a generational talent. He almost makes the figures come alive."

Croía opened the door and led Keegan inside her sister Blathnaid's room. The room was bright and cheerful, but in a very calming sort of way. The walls were covered with more carvings, of course. There were several horses, a family of wolves with some pups romping through the grass, and a multitude of trees and flowers. It felt as if you were actually in the forest and exuded the serenity of nature.

"This may be the coolest room I've ever seen," Keegan commented. Croía looked confused for a moment. "Shall I start a fire? It will warm things up in no time," she said. Keegan giggled and said, "No, sorry, that's just a figure of speech where I'm from." Croía giggled back and said, "You'll have to teach me more about Earth. I've never been, but I really want to go."

"Oh, girl, I would be happy to teach you all the things. But first, I'm curious. Can you tell me more about the Ó Faoláins? I know a little about Calder but almost nothing about the rest of you," she replied with genuine curiosity.

"Well, I can't see any reason why not. Siobhán is the kindest, smartest Fae I know. She has a huge heart, but she's also very politically savvy. More than once, she's been able to steer the Council to do the right thing, even when some powerful Fae wanted things otherwise. We have a big family, and we're a bit spread out over the homeworld, but we make sure to get together for all the holidays, and the cousins take turns living with different relatives periodically. We don't really have servants; all the family members chip in and take turns with the different chores. A hAintín Siobhán says, 'Why in the world would we ask someone else to do something we're perfectly capable of doing for ourselves?'"

"She sounds wonderful," Keegan commented. "What about the brothers?"

Croía giggled again and said, "Oh, they're always acting the maggot, but they're good lads at heart." Keegan's forehead furrowed, and she said, "Okay, I think I lost something in translation there. Acting the maggot?"

Croía's giggle turned into a full-blown laugh. "Sorry, it's slang for getting into mischief, yeah?" Keegan nodded and laughed as well, "Yeah, I've known quite a few boys that reminded me of maggots, so that tracks."

"Liam is the oldest, and he's brilliant with the businesses. I wish he could relax a bit and enjoy himself, but I think after his da died when he was so young, he always felt like he had to pull his weight, take some of the load off his mam," Croía continued. Keegan nodded again and said, "Yep, what little I've heard of him matches that description."

"But aside from the work he does for the businesses, he also works tirelessly for his charity. And he may tease his younger brothers, but I'm quite certain he would die to keep them safe. Or any of the family, for that matter," Croía explained.

"Then there are the twins, Conor and Reilly. They're fraternal twins, but they still have that slightly creepy ability to finish each other's sentences." Keegan chuckled at that. "Conor is very charismatic and great with people when he bothers to put forth an effort. He's also a bit of a, what's the term, when someone dates a lot of different people, but nobody seriously?"

Keegan smiled wryly and said, "I think you're trying to tell me Conor is a bit of a slut." Croía blushed and giggled but said, "Yep, that's Conor. If there's a male out there he hasn't tried to charm, I don't know who it would be. But to be fair, he also has a bigger heart even than Siobhán, especially regarding animals. One time, there was a foal born prematurely. Nobody thought she would survive, but Conor was determined. He went to the healers, found out what he needed to do, and spent every moment of the next week nursing that baby back to health. He even slept in the stables. I had to bring food out to him, or he would've forgotten to eat."

Croía paused momentarily, then said, "But don't tell him I told you that story. He says he likes to keep his philandering, shallow reputation intact. Sometimes he's a bit of an eejit." She rolled her eyes for emphasis.

Keegan barked a laugh, "I know what that term means; no explanation necessary."

"Reilly lives in his head somewhat. I guess that's what makes him a good writer. He's working on a novel right now. I've no idea what it's about because he refuses to let anyone read any of it except Calder and Lir. Reilly's always trusted Calder and valued his opinion more than any other."

Keegan looked thoughtful and said, "It's because he knows Calder wouldn't hurt him. Or use anything he wrote against him, even unintentionally." Croía tilted her head, considering that, and finally, she nodded in agreement.

"He also really trusts Lir. Believe it or not, that little goat is smarter than most. And Reilly is quite the photographer, as well.

He's excellent, but I don't think he believes it when we tell him that," she continued.

"I love all the brothers. They're family, and family is life. But Calder is my favorite cousin. Don't tell the others I said that," she looked worried for a moment until Keegan reassured her, "Don't worry, I won't. But why is he your favorite?"

She thought for a minute, then replied, "It's because he really listens to you. And it doesn't matter who you are. He pays attention to what you have to say, whether you're a three-year-old showing him a flower you just picked or the Head of the Council. It doesn't matter; you get all his attention." She smiled at Keegan and said, "It makes you feel seen, and that's an amazing feeling."

Keegan considered her words, smiled back at her, and squeezed her hand, saying, "Thank you, Croía. I really appreciate your help."

Croía said, "My pleasure, Love. I just wanted you to know you picked a good Fae and a good family." She turned toward the door and said, "My sister is about your size; feel free to borrow some clothing if you'd like. The bathroom is through that door in the back. I'll be wandering around, helping with chores, so feel free to find me if you need anything." Keegan nodded, and Croía let herself out, leaving the overwhelmed Fae alone with her thoughts.

*Is this family for real?* she wondered. *Usually, when things seem too good to be true, it's time to run. But I really hope I don't have to.*

Family

is life

# EIGHTEEN

Liam and the twins rode up to the World Tree, dismounted, and waited for the Druids to appear. They tied their horses to the hitching post, knowing they would be well-taken care of, and returned to their stable after they left.

Four Druids approached the World Tree, the invisibility glamour unnecessary on the homeworld. One of them motioned for the brothers to stand before the tree, then the four Fae began to call forth their power. First, the burly Earth Fae called together a stream of rock, dirt, and flowering vines, swirling around his body, starting at his feet and moving up around his waist, over his shoulder, and twining around his upraised arm, just circling his wrist, waiting to join with the others.

Next came water, pulled out of the air to encircle the tiny blonde Water Fae from head to toe. She called the moisture to loop down around her arm, diagonally swirling across her chest, waist, and legs, then moving back up in a rather unique infinity knot.

Then the Fire Fae raised a fist, calling his element to spread from his fist down to engulf his entire body in a wave. He had always been a bit dramatic.

The final Druid, a tall, dark-haired Air Fae, slowly raised her arm, causing a mini cyclone to surround the four of them, picking up the other three elements and swirling them together. Each Fae stepped forward and brought their hands toward the center of their circle. As their hands touched, a loud buzzing energy filled the air, and a bright, shimmery light emerged from the center of their hands. Then they began stepping away from each other, pulling that light outward, the portal stretching wider until it reached an appropriate size. The Druids then flicked their wrists to flip the portal on its side.

The brothers cast a quick invisibility glamour on themselves, then wasted no time stepping through, emerging into the green landscape of Ireland. Once they were on the Earth side of the portal, it snapped shut as if it had never been there.

Liam took a look around, making sure there were no tourists nearby. Luckily, it was dark out, so the Faery Tree was deserted. They dispelled the invisibility glamour, and Liam called Thomas to arrange a flight and a ride to the airport.

Conor grinned at his brothers and said, "So, this is an interesting turn of events, no? Our quiet little brother found himself a tiny spitfire."

Reilly looked up from where he was sitting on the ground, typing on his laptop. "I like the cailín," he said. "I get the feeling she suffers no fools. Guess that means you're out of luck, Conor." His twin picked up a stick and threw it at Reilly's head, thumping him in the temple.

"Ow, you langer, that was uncalled for!" He complained, rubbing his head briefly. Then he stowed his laptop back in his bag for safekeeping.

Liam watched the twins bicker with amusement. It'd been too long since he'd spent any length of time with his brothers.

*Maybe this crisis with Calder is a blessing in disguise,* he thought. He'd missed the lads. He promised himself to delegate more at the charity he ran. He might have a lot of responsibilities, but he hired good people. They could handle things for a while.

While Liam was lost in thought, the twins' bickering had escalated from small sticks to small rocks, and now they were using their earth powers to fling sharp little pebbles back and forth at each other.

Liam rolled his eyes and said, "Give over! Can you two at least pretend like you're more mature than a couple of ten-year-olds?"

Conor and Reilly stopped pelting each other with rocks, looked over at their older brother, looked back at each other, shrugged simultaneously, and said in unison, "Nope." Then the barrage continued, even stronger than before.

Liam sighed, then used his own earth power to lift a tree limb the approximate size of a baseball bat into the air, letting it hover menacingly over the twins' heads, and said, "Let me rephrase. Give it the fuck up, or I'll join in. 'Kay?"

Conor and Reilly paused the barrage again, looked at each other, then looked at the size of the branch floating overhead. It took them a moment to internally debate the pros and cons, but they finally concluded that the bruises were probably not worth it. They both let their pebbles fall to the ground.

Just then, Thomas pulled up in the forest green BMW and rolled down the window. "Well, come on then, Lads. Aoife just made a chocolate Guinness cake, and she insisted I bring some along for you. Hop in and have a little snack while we drive."

Since Aoife's Guinness cake was legendary, the brothers didn't have to be told twice. They piled into the vehicle and started scarfing the dessert down while Thomas began the short drive to the airport.

The brothers were all asleep in their fairly comfy reclining chairs, and the pilot said, "We'll be landing in Kansas City in about twenty minutes." They all stretched and rubbed the sleep from their eyes.

Liam checked his phone and saw that it was a little after nine in the morning, Kansas City time. He paused to collect his thoughts, then dialed the number he had looked up earlier in the flight.

"Niamh anseo," a voice on the phone replied.

"Good morning, Niamh, my name is Liam Ó Faoláin," Liam began, but was interrupted with, "Ó Faoláin? Are you related to Calder Ó Faoláin?"

"Yes, he's my brother," Liam replied.

"Oh, thank goodness! I've been trying to reach my daughter and her friend, Cara, but they haven't been answering. I even tried Calder's office since that's where they were, the last I knew. Do you know where they are?" she asked, desperation apparent in her voice.

"Yes, Keegan is safe, and I believe Cara, Áine, and Lir are at Calder's office. I think Keegan said, 'They were in the midst of eating themselves into a food coma,' if I'm not mistaken. My guess is they are sleeping it off. Hopefully, Cara will answer if you try her again." Liam explained.

"Oh, that's such a relief!" Niamh replied. "But why can't I reach Keegan? Where is she?"

Liam cleared his throat and said, "Actually, that's why I'm calling. As I said, she's safe, but I'm afraid she's...home."

Niamh sounded confused when she said, "No, she's not. I'm at home." Then she gasped and asked, "Wait, you don't mean the homeworld, do you?"

"That's the place," Liam said. "Look, it's a long story. My brothers and I are about to land in Kansas City. Would it be possible to come to your house so we might explain?"

"Of course," she said. "Do you have the address?"

"Yes, I looked it up earlier. We should be there in about half an hour."

"Alright. I'll be in the garden. Come around back when you get here," Niamh replied.

The brothers pulled up to Niamh's old farmhouse in a large, rented van. They heard someone singing quietly as they made their way around to the back of the house.

*Éiníní, éiníní, codalaígí, codalaígí,*
*Éiníní, éiníní, codalaígí, codalaígí*
*Codalaígí, codalaígí*
*Cois an chlaí amuigh, cois an chlaí amuigh*
*Codalaígí, codalaígí*
*Cois an chlaí amuigh, cois an chlaí amuigh.*

The brothers paused to listen, enchanted by Niamh's sweet soprano singing an ancient Irish lullaby. When she paused momentarily, Liam cleared his throat to announce their presence.

Niamh lifted her head from where she was harvesting ripe tomatoes from her garden. She blushed at being overheard, but the brothers' expressions showed they had enjoyed the impromptu performance. "I used to sing that to the girls when they were little. Sometimes I wish we could go back to those days," she said wistfully. "But we have other matters to discuss. I find I do my best thinking when my hands are busy," she said. Conor mumbled, "You must know our mother."

Niamh smiled and said, "Sounds like I'd like her. At any rate, I have beans and cucumbers that need harvesting. You can pile them on the table."

The brothers began helping harvest Niamh's vegetables. After a few moments, Niamh said, "So tell me how my daughter and, I assume, your brother managed to find themselves in Tír na nÓg. The only portal I know of is in Ireland, and Keegan has never been."

Liam set down the few cucumbers he'd picked and replied, "Well, from what I understand, Keegan and Calder were near what we think is a latent Faery Tree just a few miles from here. They were calling their elements...and I do mean ALL their elements."

Niamh gasped at that and shook her head. "I have warned that child over and over again. I really thought she knew better than this."

Conor dropped a handful of string beans on the table and piped up with, "In their defense, I think things were getting a little hot and heavy, so they probably weren't thinking straight."

Reilly and Liam both smacked Conor on the back of the head. "You are such a gobshite," Reilly said to his twin.

Niamh lowered herself into a chair, her energy flagging with the stress of this news. Liam shooed the twins back to picking vegetables and sat down across from her.

"I'm afraid there's another piece of information I need to tell you. Calder has been researching your illness and has found that the only way for you to heal is to return to Tír na nÓg."

Niamh rested her head in her hands, a deep sigh escaping her at that news. "I was afraid something like that might be necessary. For how long?"

"I believe they said about a decade," he replied. "But here, my mam wrote a letter for you." He handed her the note. She took it, broke the seal, and quickly perused the contents.

Niamh closed her eyes, almost undone by the anxiety this situation created. She had worked so hard for so long to keep them all safe. And now it seemed like the only way for their continued safety was to return to the lion's den. Then she had the most unsettling thought...*What if this happens to Keegan, too?* The more she thought about it, the more she realized, well, of course, it would happen to Keegan eventually. There just wasn't enough ambient magic on Earth to sustain Fae long-term. Niamh lifted her head, eyes pooling with tears. "I don't know if I'm strong enough for this," she admitted.

Liam took her hand and gave it a gentle squeeze. "We'll be your strength, Niamh. Your family has officially been adopted by the Ó Faoláins. And to us, family is life."

Niamh squeezed back, then wiped the tears from her eyes. "Thank you, Lad. I hoped I was wrong, but I had a feeling this day would come eventually. It's time to face it head-on." Then she stood, and the two of them gathered the vegetables from the table. She called the twins to bring their bounty along and led them into her kitchen. It wasn't as large as their mam's, and some of the paint was beginning to peel, but it was just as warm and comforting.

"Pack everything up, Lads. No use in letting good food go to waste. There are some brown paper bags in the pantry. I need to make some arrangements and get the necessities packed up for all of us. I've no idea when we'll be back, so this will take me a bit. I'll be as quick as I can," she said, already heading to her room to begin packing while making the first of many phone calls.

Liam and the twins did as directed, packing the vegetables and other perishables they found. While they worked, Reilly said, "She and Mam will be thick as thieves. Felt for a minute like we were ten years old and back at home." Conor and Liam chuckled at the funny yet accurate observation.

Niamh reappeared with an armload of suitcases and duffel

bags, some half-filled, others still empty. She said into the phone, "Hold on a moment, please." Then she turned to the brothers and said, "Can one of you call Cara? Do you have her number?"

Liam said, "I have it. I'll ring her now."

"Thank you, Love. We need all hands on deck for this situation." Niamh resumed her conversation and headed slowly up the stairs to pack for everyone else.

Conor said, "Come on, you two. Mam would never forgive us if we let her do all the work. Let's go help." His brothers nodded their agreement and headed upstairs to lend a hand.

Family
is life

A buzzing sound startled Cara out of a deep sleep. She sat up and looked around, trying to determine where the sound was coming from. As she took in the wasteland that was once Calder's office kitchen, she mumbled, "Oh my."

The table was covered with various containers, mostly empty, several of which were overturned, leaking their sauces onto the table. Amid that mess, Áine was still lying flat on her back, one wing hanging over the table's edge, snoring like a lumberjack. Occasionally she would pause her snoring to let out an enormous belch, then continue snoring as if nothing had happened.

"Well, that's attractive," Cara commented. "Now, where is the goat?" She looked around and didn't see him anywhere. Finally, she peeked under the table and found him curled up, sleeping contentedly, with a smile on his face.

Meanwhile, the buzzing continued. It sounded like it was coming from the table, so Cara began searching through the mostly empty food containers until she found her phone. It was only slightly sticky.

She picked it up with two fingers and answered the call. "Hello?" she said.

"Cara? This is Calder's brother, Liam. We don't have a great deal of time, but you need to know that Keegan and Calder accidentally portaled themselves to the homeworld. My brothers and I have been sent to gather Niamh and you three to bring you back there as well," Liam explained.

"Wait, what?" she said. "Sorry, I thought you just said Keegan and Calder accidentally portaled themselves to Tír na nÓg."

"That's exactly what I said, I'm afraid," Liam replied. "Listen, I don't have time to get into the details, but suffice it to say that we need to get Niamh and you three to the homeworld as quickly as possible. Niamh is busy packing up your things now. I need you to wrangle Áine and Lir, so you're ready to go when we arrive. Oh, I also need you to grab the active projects file from Calder's office. He said it was on top of his inbox. I hope we'll be there in half an hour or less."

Cara shook her head, trying to clear the cobwebs from her brain. "Okay, we'll be ready," she said, hanging up the phone.

By this time, Lir had poked his head out from under the table and looked up at her. "Lir, we need to get ready. Keegan and Calder somehow portaled themselves to Tír na nÓg. The brothers are getting Niamh now, and then they're picking us up to take us to the homeworld."

He nodded, stood up, and began picking up trash from the floor, helping to clean up as much as possible without hands. Cara leaned over the sleeping parrot, wondering about the best way to wake her up. She finally decided the direct route was best, so she gently poked Áine's belly, hoping that would be enough to break her out of her slumber. All that happened was a slight hiccup in her snores. *Okay then,* Cara thought. *I guess a little more force is warranted.* She poked Áine's belly a little more forcefully. This caused Áine to sit up, let out a belch and a squawk simultaneously at a deafening volume. Unfortunately, this startled Lir, causing him to freeze up and faint. Áine looked at the goat and barked out a laugh, saying, "That never gets old!"

Cara knelt beside Lir, petting him while he recovered, and said, "Áine! We don't have time for that! Keegan and Calder portaled themselves to the Fae realm, and Niamh and the Ó Faoláin brothers will be coming soon to pick us up and take us home."

Áine shook her head and said, "I go on one little food bender, and this is what I miss! I should never have let her out of my sight. She draws trouble like a magnet."

By this time, Lir had recovered, climbing back to his feet, wobbling just a little, with Cara offering a steadying hand on his back. "Okay, now that we're all awake and aware, let's make a plan. Lir and Áine, you two get this kitchen cleaned up as best you can. I will wipe things down if you get all the trash thrown away. Meanwhile, I've got another project to get ready." Áine tilted her head, hoping for more details. "Don't worry, you'll see what I mean soon," Cara said. She left them to their work, making her way to the studio Keegan and Calder had been using before their impromptu trip off-world.

By the time Liam and company pulled up in front of Calder's office, Cara and the familiars were waiting patiently with a half-finished river table beside them. Liam and the others got out of the van, Niamh rushing over to hug Cara, Áine, and even Lir.

Liam and the twins looked over at the river table. "Uh, we weren't really expecting to take any furniture with us..." Liam began, but Cara firmly interrupted with, "I'm sorry, that's non-negotiable."

Conor laughed and said, "Alright then, I guess it's time to

rearrange the luggage." The twins quickly began working on getting the table to fit into the van with all the other items.

Cara handed Liam the file he'd requested. "Thanks, I promised to contact everyone and let them know there's been an emergency and their orders will be delayed." By then, the twins had tetrised everything into the van, so Cara nodded and climbed in, followed by the familiars.

Once everyone was loaded up, they headed to the downtown airport. The drive went pretty quickly since they had missed the morning rush hour. After they arrived, it took a few minutes to get the table and all their bags loaded onto the plane. As they all settled into their seats, Áine decided she had waited for answers long enough.

"Okay, somebody better start talking about how my Keegan managed to portal herself all the way to the homeworld. How the hell is that even possible?" she demanded.

Reilly said, "Well, the best we can tell is that they were both calling all their elements at the time. Then, when they made physical contact near the latent Faery Tree..."

"Wait, wait, wait," she interrupted. "What do you mean they were calling all their elements and then 'made physical contact'?"

Conor piped up with, "We figure they were getting ready to hook up. At the very least, they were going to be doing some serious shifting."

"Boom chicka wah wah," Áine added. Cara flicked her on the back of the head and motioned toward Niamh with her head. "That's her mom," she hissed at the parrot. "Well, if she's a mom, she's done her fair share of boom chicka wah wah herself," Áine replied smugly.

Cara facepalmed while Niamh just smiled. "Oh Áine, what would we do without you?" Áine appeared to give that question serious thought, then replied, "Probably never leave the house and live out your days in despair."

Conor and Reilly watched this exchange, their grins growing with each comment. "I like her," Conor mentioned, nodding toward Áine. "She kicks arse and takes names."

Áine nodded approvingly and said, "Finally, someone who appreciates the queen that I am." Then she flew over, landed on the arm of Conor's seat, and presented her head for scratches. Conor complied, and the two of them chatted away in their own little world.

Lir walked over to Reilly and gave him a little nudge. "Oh, Lad, I didn't forget you." He reached into his pocket and pulled out a cloth. As he opened it, the sweet smell of strawberries wafted toward him. Lir wasted no time digging into his favorite treat.

Cara was impressed by his thoughtfulness. "Do you always bring him a treat?" Reilly laughed and said, "Of course. Who could resist that face?" They looked at the goat, who was currently eating his way through the berries, making a huge mess, but Lir's face was angelic as he ate his special treat, even with strawberry juice dripping from his chin.

"Anyway," Reilly continued with their hypothesis, "when they touched while calling all four elements, they must have activated or whatever the latent Faery Tree and bam...portal." He paused to use the cloth the strawberries came in to wipe the juice off Lir's face. Lir nodded his thanks to him.

Áine let out a whistle. "Note to Keegan: No screwing around with Calder near a Faery Tree." Cara rolled her eyes but couldn't hide her smile.

"Alright then, what are we waiting for? My girl needs me. Let's go home," Áine said.

Family
is life

# TWENTY

A sprinkle of dappled sunlight danced along the pastoral scene carved across the bedroom wall. Birds were singing rather loudly, causing Keegan to turn away from the window and cover her head with a pillow. *I am so not a morning person*, she thought. *Oh well, time to get moving.* She rolled onto her back, did a huge stretch, then threw the covers back and hopped out of bed.

She wandered into the bathroom and turned on the "light," which consisted of tapping another metal Celtic knot attached to the wall. This caused the knot to glow, and the glow then spread to several knots attached to the ceiling and around the large mirrors on the opposite wall. There were even little sliders on the control knot, allowing for the dimming of the ceiling or each set of mirror lights.

Once the lights were on, she took a good look around and, frankly, was very impressed. The walls and floors were made of a light, cream-colored marble, shot through with veins of pale pink. Just as wood carvings covered many of the walls of the house, the intricacy of the marble carvings in this one bathroom did not disappoint. The forest motif, interspersed with horses, wolves, and other animals, continued in the bath, with an emphasis on willows and vining flowers. Overall, the effect gave the feeling of curtains being drawn back, allowing for a sense of privacy with just a peek here and there.

There was a tub that could easily fit six people in one corner and a small area in the opposite corner with a toilet surrounded by a privacy wall. There were two sinks and two mirrors along the far wall, and a set of shelves was along another, holding fluffy towels, washcloths, and robes, as well as all kinds of body wash, shampoo, conditioner, and any other type of grooming product imaginable.

She walked past the tub and poked her head around an open doorway. A huge, walk-in shower was hidden back there, with a long bench and several built-in shelves to hold whichever grooming products had been chosen in the other room. Overhead was a strange-looking shower head, which appeared to match a small control panel on the wall. Several different glyphs seemed to coincide with different types of shower streams, as well as a slider for water temperature. Keegan pressed one of the glyphs, then had to jump back quickly to avoid getting her borrowed pajamas soaked. She pressed it again to shut it off.

Keegan returned to the main room, chose some bathing products, grabbed a couple towels and a robe, and came back to the shower. She then spent the next half hour indulging in a steaming hot shower while going over everything that had happened in the past twenty-four hours. It was a lot. But while it was definitely an unexpected turn of events, there was also an element of excitement for her. She finally got to visit the home-world! She'd been dreaming about this for years, and it was everything she thought it would be. This world's sights, sounds, and smells were so luxurious they were almost overwhelming. But she thought she could get used to it.

She was also excited to meet her father for the first time.

Although that brought a little anxiety as well. She knew her mom had told her he wanted her, but what if that had changed? She didn't know what she would do if he rejected her.

Keegan decided it was time to face the world, so she turned off the water, tied up her hair in a towel, dried off, and put on the robe. She returned to the main room and paused to put some product on her curls. No need to get all frizzy. Then she headed into the bedroom, picked out a pale blue blouse and darker blue skirt, some underclothes, and even found a pair of tan sandals that fit.

Just as she finished dressing, there was a knock on the door. She opened it to find Calder there, dressed in a crisp white shirt and dark brown pants, both of which were tight in all the right places. He gave her a brilliant smile, which made her tingle all over, and she returned it in kind.

"Housekeeping," he said with a grin and a wink. She giggled at him and grabbed both his hands, pulling him close to her. As she breathed in his scent, a combination of cedar trees and spring rain, those tingles from earlier returned with a vengeance, and her heart started to race for good measure. She leaned toward him to breathe him in even more and let out a happy little moan.

Calder looked down into those luminous, silver eyes and felt himself wanting very much to skip breakfast so he could throw this little ember onto the bed just a few feet behind her. He would love to see how long it took to fan that ember into an inferno. But then his mother would come looking for them, and that was not a conversation he was ready for. So, he took a deep breath and, with a Herculean force of will, stepped back and said, "Mam is waiting for us in the courtyard with breakfast. As much as I have other things on my mind at the moment, we'd best not keep her waiting."

Keegan grinned at him with a twinkle in her eye and said, "Oh really? What other things might you have on your mind?"

She stepped forward and attempted to press herself against him, figuring a little torment before breakfast never hurt anybody. Or not too much, at any rate.

Unfortunately for her, he was too quick for that, and he side-stepped her, grabbed one of her hands, and began to lead her down the hall toward the courtyard. "None of that. You have no idea how much my mam hates being kept waiting. That's not a can of worms we want to open this morning."

Keegan sighed, pouting just a bit, but allowed him to lead her to breakfast.

Walking into the courtyard brought Keegan up short, caught by surprise at the opulence of the place. Flowers of every shape, size, and color seemed to grow from every available speck of greenery. Lush did not adequately describe the level of extravagance at play. And if the flora was over the top, the fauna was not to be outdone. Birds in a riot of colors flitted through the branches of trees heavy with peaches, apples, and various other familiar and exotic fruits. She saw squirrels, rabbits, foxes, and badgers, or creatures resembling those animals, in a variety of unusual colors, all playing throughout the courtyard gardens.

"This place is super extra," Keegan mumbled to herself, causing Calder to grin and respond, "Áine should feel right at home then, don't you think?" This made Keegan snort, causing Calder's mother to raise an eyebrow, but she kept any comments to herself.

Siobhán stood at the head of a small table, decorated simply with a white linen tablecloth and a few flowers, displayed in a pretty crystal vase. There was a variety of fruit, some Keegan recognized, some she didn't, as well as some eggs, bacon, sausage, tomatoes, beans, mushrooms, black and white pudding, and potatoes...a proper Irish breakfast. So, while the table was the model of classic simplicity, the breakfast was every bit as extra as the landscape.

"Fáilte. I thought it would be nice to have a bit of breakfast," Siobhán said. Keegan snorted again before she could stop herself, causing Calder's mom to raise that same eyebrow again. Keegan giggled and said, "Sorry, uh, ma'am, it just occurred to me that Americans aren't the only ones who like big breakfasts. Your understatement just added that little extra tickle for me."

Siobhán looked the breakfast table over, smiled, and said, "I suppose we do go a bit overboard, don't we?" Keegan held her thumb and forefinger close together. Calder laughed, highly amused by the interaction.

"Well, we have big families; what can I say?" Siobhán said with a shrug. "None will go to waste; I promise you that. Now dig in, you two. As Keegan pointed out, we have plenty."

The three of them filled plates and spent the next few minutes sampling the fare. Keegan could hardly keep herself from moaning her way through the meal. "Okay, I take it back. If the food on Earth tasted this good, I'd lay out a spread like this every day, too," Keegan managed between mouthfuls.

Once everyone had eaten their fill, Siobhán pushed her plate away, leaned back, and said, "Now, Keegan, I thought it might be helpful for you to have some understanding of how our homeworld works. Has your mam explained any of this to you before?"

Keegan nodded and said, "Yeah, she explained the four clans, one for each element. And how there is a Council, which resides here in Tionól, made up of the two oldest Fae from the head family of each clan. Although I think if someone doesn't want to serve, they can refuse and let someone else in the family do it. I know those families can change, but I think that happens pretty rarely. Oh, and I know there is a leader of the Council who is like king, or president, or something like that." Calder couldn't help but smile at that description.

Siobhán was also smiling. *This girl is really quite charming,* she thought. *I can see why Calder likes her.* "That's a fair description of our system of governance. We don't really have an economic system, as you understand it, but we do occasionally barter for items. Some families, however, like the idea of wealth, so they charge for their services and products and refuse to barter, requiring Earth money, which I will never understand. Almost every family has businesses on Earth as well as the homeworld, so coming up with Earth funds is rarely a problem. It is occasionally annoying, though. But I digress. I think you've got at least a basic idea of how Tír na nÓg functions. Now I'd like to discuss how Aos Sí think. You've grown up on Earth, but more importantly, in America, which is a very, very young country."

Keegan looked ready to dispute that, but Siobhán said, not unkindly, "Don't argue with me, a chroí, you'll lose. A two-hundred-and-fifty-year-old country is still in its infancy. This means that the people you grew up around have a very different worldview than people whose society has existed for millennia. Aos Sí change very, very slowly. When you live as long as we do, hurrying seems unnecessary. This also means that we can become very set in our ways. Add to that a perhaps unhealthy relationship with superstition, and you have a perfect storm of immobility. Why change when it feels like you've already discovered the best way to do something? This is how a good portion of our society views things." Siobhán paused to take a drink and gather her thoughts.

"I am telling you all of this because I want you to understand what you'll be up against. The Dúbailte Curse is taken very seriously. I know that seems incredible to you, but I assure you, it is very, very true. If it weren't for that fucking curse, well, things might be different for us. But that's not how things have gone, and we must live in what is, not what we wish it were," Siobhán sighed, then reached across the table to take them both by the hand. "I won't belabor the point any longer. But I hope you will take my words to heart. I care about you both." She squeezed their hands, then released them and stood. "Now I've got some work to do. Feel free to take some time and talk things over. I'm hopeful the brothers, your mam, and friends will return this evening. Until then, enjoy our home. If you need anything, just find a cousin and send for me. They'll be able to find me. Now to get this cleaned up."

She reached up to grasp a triquetra pendant around her neck and let a trickle of Earth magic flow into it. It started to glow a deep green color, and within a couple of minutes, Colin entered the courtyard and began clearing the table. Calder and Siobhán started to help, and Keegan hopped up to lend a hand. Siobhán told her that wasn't necessary, but Keegan said, "Nonsense. I did my share of eating; I can certainly do my share of cleaning up." Siobhán nodded in agreement, and Calder couldn't hide a proud smile. The four of them made short work of the breakfast table, and they parted ways, Siobhán and Colin back into the house while Keegan and Calder began a stroll through the courtyard gardens.

The two of them walked in silence, holding hands for a few minutes. Then Keegan turned to Calder and said, "Why didn't you tell me how over the top this place is? It's like something from a movie."

"Because it's just home," Calder replied. "I guess I sometimes forget that you didn't grow up here. This is what seems normal to me. To tell the truth, Earth seems a little barren." That elicited a laugh. "But I guess this does look a little like something you might see in a Marvel movie."

"No," she said. "Don't tell me you're a Marvel fan, Ó Faoláin!" Calder laughed and said, "I don't know if fan is the right word, but I will admit to watching a couple of the films."

Keegan looked around like she was checking for anyone nearby who might overhear, then said, "Can I tell you a secret?" Calder nodded. "I've always had a crush on...Thor!" Calder chuckled and said, "There's something you've got in common with Conor." Keegan giggled at that.

They walked in silence a bit longer, just enjoying each other's company. They both kept stealing glances, quickly looking away when the other noticed. Calder thought to himself, *I could happily lose myself in those eyes.* He took a deep breath, trying to calm his racing heart so he could think clearly.

After a few more moments, she turned to him and said, "So, I'm curious about something. How were you so easily able to keep your water power a secret?"

Calder looked at her and said, "Oh, I wouldn't call it easy. At least not at first. But after Liam almost drowned, things got easier."

Keegan just raised an eyebrow and said, "Huh?" Calder laughed and said, "Let me rephrase. When I was about nine, my brothers and I were swimming at a nearby pond. Liam broke his arm and got it lodged under some rocks. We didn't know what was happening, but I panicked and used my water power to pull the pond back and save him. After that, our whole family knew, so it didn't seem like quite as heavy a load to carry."

"Many hands make light work," Keegan said. "At least that's what my mom used to tell me, usually when trying to get me to help her with chores. I guess it's true for a well-kept secret as well."

Calder said, "Usually, I would disagree. Secrets tend not to stay secret when too many people know about them. But my family is a special case, I suppose." Just then, they turned a corner, which was out of sight of the windows. Calder looked at Keegan, and that overwhelming feeling that all was right with the world so long as he was with her washed over him again. He didn't know exactly why, but he wanted nothing more than to protect her and make her happy.

So, he took this opportunity to pull her close, sliding his hand around to the small of her back. "Have I told you today how absolutely brilliant you are, my dear?" She giggled and replied, "No, I don't think you have."

"Well, let me rectify that horrible oversight right now," he said, running the back of his hand down the side of her cheek, down her neck, and around to cradle the back of her head, entangling his fingers in her mass of curls. "You, my beautiful, funny, fiery Fae, are the most brilliant cailín I have ever laid eyes on. And I would happily tell you that every day for the rest of our very, very long lives."

His words left her breathless, but then he clenched the hand caught in her hair into a fist and tilted her head back, giving his hungry mouth access to nibble, lick, and kiss his way from the hollow of her throat all the way to the tip of her pointed Fae ear. She started to turn her head toward him, wanting to reciprocate, but he tightened his fist even more, causing just a bit of pain, and said, "Uh, uh, I'm not done yet. Wait your turn, Love."

Then he proceeded to devote his full attention, and a seriously talented set of lips, tongue, and teeth, to making Keegan squirm. He took his time, searching out every sensitive area from her collarbone upward, teasing her relentlessly, drawing out the pleasure until it bordered on pain.

Just when she was about to scream in frustration, they heard the doors open, and Colin called out, "Calder? Your mam asked me to fetch you to help in the stables. She wants you to give me a hand since all your brothers are gone."

Calder slowly loosened his hand in her hair, giving her back the full range of motion. Then he leaned close to her ear and whispered, "Remember this position, Love. I'm only getting started." After which, he gave her a very sedate peck on the lips, came around the corner they were hidden behind, and followed Colin to the stables.

Family
is life

# TWENTY-ONE

Máire wiped her forehead on the sleeve of her shirt, too engrossed in her work to stop and find a towel. *Just a tiny bit more,* she thought, smoothing the last rough edge from her latest design. She turned the intricate knotwork over and over in her hand, allowing herself these few moments of pride in her craftsmanship. *This is almost as good as Mam's,* she thought. *Maybe even a little better.*

She set the artifact on a shelf with several others, each waiting to be enchanted. She ran her fingertips along the other pieces, feeling their inherent qualities—strengths and weaknesses at the molecular level. Máire looked over to where Laoise, in her favored chihuahua form, lounged on a dog bed in the corner and began explaining, "Mam always talks about the enchanting process, like imbuing the artifact with magic is the only important part. But learning how to shape it so that the power flows in such a way that a loop is created, that requires true artistry! It maximizes efficiency and allows me to accomplish the same output with half the magical expenditure."

Laoise just nodded and smiled, happy to see Máire relaxed and excited about anything. As her best friend continued to chat about the finer points of enchanting objects, the pup noticed a familiar bushy tail sticking out from behind some shelves along the workshop's wall.

When Máire paused a moment in her speech, Laoise hopped up and said, "Time for a potty break. Be back shortly." She made her way out of the doggie door Máire had installed just for her, followed quickly by a reddish ball of fluff.

As soon as said fluffball made it outside, Laoise was in the vixen's face, asking, "What's the craic, Saoirse? Why are you here?"

"Corley is on his way here, and he has some news that may make our current situation worse," Saoirse said. She quickly explained what Corley had seen, and they discussed the ramifications.

"Bloody hell," Laoise concluded after their talk. "I think I hear him coming now. Alright, just do your best to limit the damage afterwards." She watched as Saoirse headed down the path to stall him. "Bloody hell," she whispered again.

Laoise came in through the doggie door, walked over to Máire, and propped her front legs against her Fae's shins. Máire picked her up and put her on her shoulder, then returned to preparing the artifact for enchanting.

There was a light knock on the door. Máire immediately stiffened, afraid it was her da at the door. Laoise whispered, "When has Cass ever knocked?" Máire gave an awkward chuckle and replied, "True." She walked over and opened the door to find Corley leaning against the door frame.

"Look what the cat, er fox dragged in. Saoirse," Máire greeted Corley's familiar with a nod and put Laoise on the floor before turning some side eye on the Earth Fae. The dog and fox hopped into the dog bed together to watch the show.

"Now, now, I promise you are going to want to hear what I have to say," Corley said with a wry grin. "I'll be the judge of that. What's the craic?" she replied, still standing in the doorway.

Corley turned toward Máire, leaning close to her ear and whispering, "Your lover..." Máire interrupted him with, "He's not..." Corley shushed her by placing a finger over her lips. "Tsk, tsk. Let me finish." He gently ran that finger down her lips, chin, and neck to the hollow of her throat. He leaned in by her ear and whispered, "Your uh, friend, Calder, has a secret."

He leaned back to look her in the eye, but his finger still rested lightly in the hollow of her throat. She gave him a smile, then flared her fire just where his fingertip touched her. "Ow!" he exclaimed, sucking on his finger for relief. "That was completely unnecessary!"

"So was touching me," she pointed out. "Now, what are you on about? A secret?"

"Yes, well, I was hanging around the World Tree Gardens when I heard the portal open. No big deal; people go back and forth all the time. I expected whoever used it to stroll out of the gardens, maybe grab a couple of horses, and ride off. But no, all of a sudden, I see this flock of birds take off, and I notice your buddy, Calder, sneaking into the woods behind his family's home. And he wasn't alone." Corley paused for dramatic tension.

Máire just raised an eyebrow and said, "So? He's got a house full of brothers and more cousins than he knows what to do with. Why do I care if he's sneaking through the woods with one of them?"

"Because it wasn't one of them, that's what I've been trying to tell you," Corley replied. "So, who was it?" Máire asked, her curiosity finally piqued. "That is the million-dollar question, isn't it? All I know is she was a tiny little thing who looked like the mass of red curls on her head was trying to swallow her whole."

Máire looked thoughtful for a moment. "And you're sure you've never seen her before?" she said. "Oh, I would've remembered this cailín," Corley responded with a chuckle. Máire narrowed her eyes and began pacing back and forth, thinking over what this might mean.

Corley followed her inside the workshop, closing the door behind him. Even though the majority of décor was primarily functional, he did notice a few things Máire had added purely for enjoyment. Several potted plants were scattered throughout the room, as well as a couch and a couple of armchairs with soft blankets and pillows piled on them, all in shades of blue and green. Not to mention Laoise's dog bed and several soft rugs scattered around the floor. All of these soft touches were well away from her work area, out of reach of any stray sparks that could ignite the fabric.

He strolled around, lightly touching the artifacts on the shelves. Some were waiting to be enchanted, some were finished and waiting to be delivered. He could feel the energy humming inside the finished pieces. He'd always been fascinated by the art of enchanting artifacts, and it was indeed an art. Depending on the skill level of the enchanter, an artifact could be created to do almost anything. They could be used for simple things like lighting a room or keeping the icebox cold. With a higher level of skill, they could be enchanted to do more complex tasks. They could also be used for very destructive purposes if the need arose. Aos Sí had become increasingly reliant on artifacts to make their lives easier, so Máire's talents were already in demand. The Fire Fae might be young, but she was already quite an advanced enchanter. Her mother had taught her well.

"I'd forgotten how good the Daugherty family is at enchanting objects," Corley said.

"Doran," Máire corrected, pausing her pacing to look over the artifacts she and her mother had created. "Wait, I thought your last name was Daugherty?" Corley asked, confused.

"It is, but my enchanting skills come from my mam's side," Máire explained. "Da has about the same level of skill with enchanting as you do. Which is to say, none."

Corley laughed and said, "Hey, you don't know! I might be the best enchanter ever!" Máire just pursed her lips and lifted one eyebrow. "Okay, no, I'd be shite at that," he admitted, laughing again. His laughter was a bit infectious, causing Máire to crack a smile.

Once his laughter died, he continued, "I might not be worth a damn as an enchanter, but I could build you a place of your very own. A workshop with built-in shelves and plenty of space so you can create whatever new artifacts your brilliant little mind can devise. I'd even replicate this cute little doggie door so Laoise can come and go as she pleases. And perhaps Saoirse could come to visit now and then. I might even tag along if that's alright with you?" He kept his eyes down as he talked, but when he reached the question at the end, he looked up, meeting Máire's eyes.

A look of such longing passed over Máire's features for just a moment; it made Laoise ache for her. "Oh, my sweet girl," she whispered. "Do you see how important this is?" she quietly asked Saoirse. "I see, my friend. I'll help however I can," the fox replied.

By this time, Máire had once again mastered her expression. "Yes, well, there's no point thinking about what might come to pass. Right now, we need to figure out who this new player is."

Corley looked down to hide the flash of disappointment that crossed his face. "Of course. That's why I came over immediately to tell you what I'd learned. What did you have in mind?"

Máire resumed her pacing and replied, "We have to gather more information. I will see if Mam knows anything. I need you to stake out the Ó Faoláin manor."

"Oh boy, more skulking," he replied under his breath. In a louder voice, he said, "Of course. Happy to help."

Once Corley agreed, Máire's face lit up. "Thank you, Corley. This means a lot to me."

"Like I said, I'm happy to help. I will report back once I know more," he replied, daring to squeeze her shoulder.

"Come on, Saoirse," he called to his familiar. Before jumping, she whispered to Laoise, "I will try to keep him on the right path. You do the same." The dog nodded, then the fox followed her Earth Fae out the door.

Once Corley and Saoirse had gone, Máire picked up her familiar and continued pacing, petting the dog as she went for comfort. She'd only made a few trips back and forth across the workshop when a throbbing burst of agony slammed into her skull, causing her to stumble to her knees. Laoise landed on her feet, growling and spinning around to try and find the danger. Máire pressed the palms of her hands against her temples, feeling like that was the only thing keeping her head from exploding.

"What? What is it? I don't see anything!" The chihuahua was growing frantic, unable to figure out what was hurting Máire. She shifted into a white wolverine, ready to tear into whatever was causing the danger, provided she could find it.

Máire suddenly heard a tritone voice inside her mind, saying, "Poor, poor Máire. Always trying so hard, never quite good enough."

She was on her knees, still trying to hold her head together with her hands. "Who are you, and what the fuck do you want?" she cried.

"We just want to help poor Máire. There are ways for you to

get all you desire if you're willing to do what it takes," the voice explained.

"What do I have to do?" she asked, breathing hard to manage the immense pain.

"Just a future favor," the voice replied. "Your promise is all that's required."

Máire did her best to think through the situation, but the pain grew by the minute. "Fine!" she agreed. "I promise!"

The pain left so quickly that it took her breath away. She collapsed to the floor, trying to understand what had just happened. Laoise, still in wolverine form, growled and backed up, trying to protect Máire from whatever the danger might be, even if she still hadn't identified the threat.

"It's okay, it's gone now," the Fire Fae reassured her familiar. "You can shift back." Laoise shifted back to a chihuahua and climbed into Máire's lap, thoroughly licking her face. "What just happened?" the familiar asked.

"I'm not entirely sure. I heard a really strange voice in my head, and it felt like someone stuck a red-hot poker into my head and scrambled things around a bit," she explained.

"A voice? What did it say?" the dog asked, trying to piece together what was happening.

"Basically, it told me I could have what I want if I was willing to do what it takes," she said.

"Oh, really? And what does that cost?" Laoise asked. "A future favor is all it asked for," Máire replied. "All? I'd say that could turn out to be quite a steep price. One which you've already promised to pay," the familiar reminded her.

"Well, since my brains were being scrambled at the time, I'd say that qualifies as some extenuating circumstances," Máire stated. "I'll just have to cross that bridge when we come to it."

Family
is life

# TWENTY-TWO

The flight to Ireland was uneventful, save for the volume of Áine's snores. They reached a point where Conor downloaded a decibel meter app to his phone, and he and Reilly were placing bets on exactly how loud she would get. Conor eventually won when she reached one hundred decibels, roughly the same level as an approaching subway train. After that, Niamh picked her up and carried her to the rear of the plane, providing some level of relief from the noise.

Finally, they landed near Dublin and piled into the waiting BMW driven by Thomas. As they made their way to the Faery Tree, Liam called ahead, letting the Druids know their party was on the way.

When they arrived, the four Fae were waiting for them. With minimal flair, they quickly called their elements and flipped the portal sideways for them to enter. The brothers went first, wasting no time. Next came Niamh and finally Cara, who said, "Okay, everyone, she insists we stand back and 'make way for her grand entrance,' or some nonsense like that. Trust me, it's faster and easier to do what she wants."

Liam and the twins stood with Niamh and Cara a few feet

away from the World Tree portal, surrounding the river table they weren't allowed to leave behind. Looking into the portal, Lir could be seen in his goat form running toward them. As soon as he crossed the portal, he shifted into his púca form. He pawed the air and let out an ear-shattering neigh.

"Nicely done, Lad!" Conor said, giving him a round of applause. Reilly let out a shrill whistle and clapped a few times for him. Even Liam gave him a few polite claps. Niamh and Cara didn't have to fake their enthusiastic applause. "Woo hoo!" Cara exclaimed. "Yay, Lir!" Niamh happily applauded the goat-turned-púca.

Lir bowed to the crowd, enjoying the attention for a few moments. Then he turned around and, in his best announcer voice, said, "Ladies and gentlemen, Fae of all stations! I present to you, home for the first time in more than twenty years, Áine the Magnificent!"

On the Earth side, Áine hovered in front of the portal, savoring the moment briefly. She took a deep breath, whispered, "Finally," to herself, and made a big loop to gather some speed before bursting through the portal. As she crossed over to the Tír na nÓg side, she dipped toward the ground, then swooped back over herself, completing a beautiful and dramatic flip. Perhaps even more gorgeous was the sight of all Áine's feathers simultaneously bursting into flame the second she crossed into the homeworld, giving way to her natural form of a phoenix. She finished her flip with a few twists and turns for good measure—she was nothing if not an entertainer.

Everyone burst into applause—Áine the Magnificent, indeed!

As she hovered above them all, Niamh stepped forward and held out her arm. Áine settled on the proffered arm, wrapping her flaming wings around Niamh's head, for once quiet in the face of all the praise and applause. "I'd forgotten exactly how magnificent you are, Love. Thank you for all you've sacrificed to help me keep my baby girl safe."

"Sacrifice? There was no sacrifice. She's my baby girl, too. I wouldn't have had it any other way." Then she launched into the air, skimming right over Lir's head, saying, "Come on, Goat Boy! Everyone follow us; we know the way!" The two highly excitable familiars took off toward the Ó Faoláin manor at full speed.

Conor said, "They realize it's our house, right? We know the way home."

Cara said, "Let them have their fun. They'll figure it out eventually."

Liam had gathered some horses from the Druids' stable and began handing them out to everyone. "I arranged for the river table to be delivered to the manor tomorrow. Everyone okay with riding back to the house?"

Niamh and Cara mounted their horses with minimal effort. They might not have had a lot of money while living on Earth, but Niamh had ensured both Keegan and Cara knew how to ride and ride well. Niamh replied, "I will assume, with all the excitement, you didn't realize you were asking two Aos Sí Fae whether or not they could ride a horse and refrain from taking offense. This time."

Conor and Reilly, who were also mounted, looked at each other, then at their older brother, and said, together, "You're on your own." Then they wheeled their horses around and took off after the familiars.

Liam turned his best smile toward the two females and said, "Please forgive me; I momentarily lost my head. It won't happen again."

Niamh gave him a prim look and replied, "See that it doesn't, Lad." Then they clicked their tongues at their mounts and took off after the twins.

Liam shook his head after Keegan's mother and friend,

mounted his horse, and mumbled, "Why do I get the feeling the excitement is just beginning?" He turned his mare toward the manor, let her have her head, and they began the short ride home.

Siobhán was on the back porch, sipping on a cuppa, staring at the tree line, lost in thought. Her son's unusual romantic situation made her think about her love life. *Could it really be possible?* She didn't want to get her hopes up, but oh, if only it could be true for her. She couldn't help but keep a tiny flame of hope alive, even if she never said the words out loud.

Even though the light was fading from the sky, painting it in glorious shades of scarlet and gold with reddish-purple edges, there was enough light for her to notice movement at the tree line. She thought she recognized Lir in his púca form, running full speed toward the house. There were also a few other horses and riders a way back, but keeping pace with Lir was a glowing reddish blur. *Is that what I think it is?* she thought.

She approached the door and called into the kitchen, "Keegan, Calder, I think you're going to want to see this."

The couple came out onto the porch, hand in hand, and Calder said, "See what?" Keegan pulled him to the edge of the porch, squinting at the movement in the distance. "Wait, what? Does visiting the homeworld come with a complimentary stroke? Somebody explain what I'm seeing here," she said, thoroughly confused.

Calder finally noticed the commotion and put two and two together. "Ah, yes. An Banríon indeed," he commented quietly to himself. He stepped behind Keegan and wrapped his arms around her, resting his chin on top of her head. "Well, you see that glorious black horse running toward us? That is Lir in his púca form." Keegan gasped and replied, "He's amazeballs! Those glowing gold eyes are stunning."

"Yes, he's a pretty boy, that's for certain. And you can pick out the rest of the group a bit further back riding mere mortal horses." Keegan nodded, then said, "Yeah, I see them. But what's..." Calder chuckled and interrupted, saying, "And that glowing, sparkling, flaming red and gold blur? That, Love, is Áine in her natural form of...a phoenix."

By this point, her familiar had gotten close enough for Keegan to make out the details as Áine was obviously showing off with her aerial display. Her friend was absolutely glorious! The flames surrounding her ranged from deep scarlet to a bright vermillion to a rich golden color, with hints of blue sparking at the edges. "I guess you were right...she is spectacular!" she finally commented. And if anyone knew Áine, it was Keegan, so she began applauding and screaming praise, encouraging everyone else to join in, including Colin, Croía, and a couple of newly arrived cousins who had no idea why they were cheering. Even Siobhán was coaxed into a few congratulatory whistles. *She'll love this reception,* Keegan thought.

Finally, Áine decided she had shared her magnificence long enough. She made a graceful landing on the porch railing, sinking into a curtsey in front of her adoring fans.

Keegan rushed over and picked Áine up, spinning her around, heedless of the flames as only a Fire Fae could be. "You. Kicked. Ass!" she gushed, fully willing to feed Áine's ego in this instance. "I know, right?" Áine replied. "You have no idea how long I've been waiting to show you that!"

Calder walked up, giving her a slow round of applause. "Truly breathtaking, a Bhanríon," he said, making Áine stutter a bit as she replied, "Yes, well, I tried to tell you that from the beginning." Then she turned to Keegan and, in a very loud aside, said, "Are we sure he's not a little slow?" Keegan couldn't help a slight giggle, causing Calder to give her a look that said, "Really?"

Lir had gotten bored and started grazing, but the rest of the group was finally arriving, so he made his way back over to the porch. Cara was the first to nearly tackle Keegan in a full-body hug, followed closely by Niamh. Áine folded her flaming wings around the group hug, giving them a moment of semi-privacy.

Keegan finally pulled back and said, "Mom...Áine...she's stunning! Why didn't you tell me?" Niamh laughed and said, "And risk the wrath of the queen? She's been planning her big reveal to you for years now. It'd take a braver soul than I to steal her thunder!"

That elicited a laugh from all of them, Áine included. Siobhán approached, causing Niamh to remember her manners. "Oh, a Bhean Ó Faoláin...," Niamh began, but Siobhán interrupted her, saying, "Please, call me Siobhán. May I call you Niamh?" Niamh replied, "Of course!" Siobhán nodded, shook hands with Niamh, and said, "Brilliant. Fáilte, a Niamh and a Cara. And, of course, fáilte to you as well, Áine. May I say that you treated us to a stunning aerial display?"

"It was nothing major, but thank you, Siobhán," Áine replied, obviously pleased at the praise. Keegan leaned over to Cara and whispered, "She knows who to suck up to, doesn't she?" Cara snorted, earning her the infamous raised eyebrow. "You did that on purpose!" Cara hissed at Keegan once Siobhán had moved her attention back to the entire group. Keegan gave a low chuckle and said, "I just didn't want to be the only one on the receiving end of that eyebrow."

Calder was near enough to overhear and said, "No chance of that. I believe Conor is the current record holder, but Reilly wasn't far behind. It will take you two decades to even get close."

Siobhán took that opportunity to get things moving. "Colin, Croía, would you please take the horses to the stables? We'll return them to the Druids in the morning." The two cousins gathered the mounts' leads and took them to the stables for a good rub down and a snack.

"Excellent, thank you. If the rest of you will follow me, we'll head to the library to discuss the situation and form a plan," she said, leading the way into the house.

"Lir, you coming?" Calder called to his familiar. Lir considered for a moment, then shifted to his goat form and trotted over.

"Care to give me a lift, Goat Boy?" Áine asked, not really waiting for an answer. She settled herself on Lir's back, and they followed Siobhán into the house. Keegan's group and the brothers brought up the rear.

The newcomers slowed in front of the great room mantel, but Keegan hustled them along, promising they could peruse at their leisure later. Once everyone made it to the library, Siobhán bade them all sit down. Then she began the conversation with, "I think it's obvious we have much to discuss. If you don't mind, I'll begin. Everyone in this room knows Keegan and Calder share an extraordinary circumstance."

Conor piped up with, "Yeah, they're both Dúb-..." Reilly clapped his hand over his twin's mouth. "Really, Lad? Mam has only lost her shit every time one of us has used that word since forever."

Áine leaned over and stage-whispered to Keegan, "See? Slow runs in the family." Keegan and Cara couldn't keep it together after that, laughing so hard they cried. Siobhán and Niamh shook their heads, wondering how things had gone off the rails so quickly.

"Yes, well, regardless of how I feel about that stupid curse, both Keegan and Calder have dual powers," Siobhán continued. "But since Niamh's medical issue necessitated their return to the homeworld, we now need a back story. I've been thinking about this situation and think I have an idea. Let me explain, and then we can go over any possible issues that might arise."

Siobhán looked at Niamh and continued, "If you want to distract people from something, it's best to give them something else to focus on. And if that something is in some way salacious or otherwise gossip-worthy, even better. So, instead of a certain prominent Air Fae, we need to introduce someone else as Keegan's father." Niamh gasped at that last bit, realizing Siobhán knew the identity of Keegan's biological father.

"Don't worry, Love, your secret is safe with us. And while I'm not proud of it, the fact is Aos Sí have our share of prejudicial attitudes. That damn Dúbailte Curse is the most prominent example, but another area some Fae have issues with is interbreeding with humans," Siobhán continued. Cara looked at the ground, unable to shake the unwarranted but familiar feeling of shame that the mention of her mixed blood brought up.

Áine hopped onto Cara's shoulder and lifted her chin with a wingtip. "None of that. You are amazing, and don't you forget it! You know my motto...chin up, tits out!" Cara rolled her eyes at Áine's antics but couldn't help the smile they elicited.

Siobhán's eyes widened slightly, but she recovered quickly. "Yes, well, you can't argue with that. And just so you know, Cara, none in the Ó Faoláin family believes in that backward way of thinking. There's absolutely no truth to the idea that you are somehow weaker, magically or otherwise, just because you're half-human. In fact, in the case of you and Keegan, you two are probably more powerful than most of us full-blooded Fae."

Keegan perked up at that and said, "Huh? Why would we be more powerful?" Siobhán replied, "Well, because of Earth's lack of ambient magic. Calder, didn't you explain this to her?"

Calder looked slightly abashed and said, "Sorry, Mam, I hadn't gotten to that yet." Then he turned to Keegan and said,

"Since there's less ambient magic on Earth, you've had to work much harder to do even the simplest acts of magic while you were there. You've built up your magical muscles, in other words. Try it out if you'd like. Just take it slow, please. I'd like Mam's house to still stand when you're done."

Keegan and Cara shared a look and nodded to each other. Áine chuckled and said, "Three, two, one...lift off!" Both Fae attempted to gently lift themselves up with their air power. Because of the extra strength they both had, however, the two of them shot into the air, just barely stopping before concussing themselves on the ceiling of the library.

"Well, that could come in handy," Liam commented dryly. Siobhán agreed, "Quite. I'm just glad Keegan chose to try out her air power first. The house might not be quite ready for a Keegan-shaped flame thrower."

The two Fae enjoyed zipping around the room near the ceiling, giggling. "A Chailíní, there will be time for that later. Would you take your seats, please?" Siobhán asked. The females complied, somewhat regretfully.

"So, even though it's a nasty prejudice, in this case, it works in our favor. If we say that Niamh fell in love with a human, got pregnant with Keegan, and the three of them lived together on Earth, most Fae won't look past their distaste for humans to examine the story more closely," Siobhán explained.

Niamh looked thoughtful, then said, "That all sounds great, except for one thing. Cass Daugherty. My asshat of a brother-in-law..." Siobhán turned to Calder and said, "I told you that was an appropriate term." He just rolled his eyes and grinned. Niamh looked slightly confused but continued, "So, Cass knows Shay and I had a relationship. If he accuses Shay of being Keegan's da, one look at her eyes, and it won't be a hard story for people to believe."

Siobhán indulged in a smug smile and replied, "Cass may have been up and coming in our society when you left, Niamh, but he is barely tolerated now. Leave him to me. It will be my pleasure."

Family
is life

# TWENTY-THREE

Áine hovered in the air at eye-level with Lir, wearing a scowl on her face. He was currently in his púca form, but she chose to ignore that and said, "Goat Boy, I'm beginning to think the Ó Faoláin slowness has rubbed off on you! This choreography is not that difficult."

Lir huffed and replied, "You're trying to teach me steps meant for two legs. I have four."

Áine considered that for a moment, then said, "I assumed you would just do the same steps with your front and back legs. But the hooves do complicate things a bit. Can you shift to something with two legs?"

Lir thought about it and said, "I could, but I really like having four legs. How about this?" He shifted into an inky black wolf, still with his signature glowing golden eyes, then stood up on his hind legs. "Will this work?"

"That'll do, wolf. That'll do," she replied. "Okay, let's take it from the top." She nodded at Cara, who was sitting on a bench nearby, to start the song over. Cara sighed and hit play on Áine's iPod. *I knew I should've chosen rock!* she thought. *Keegan is doing DJ duty next time. No more rock, paper, scissors to choose who has to help Áine with her music. I always lose.*

Snoop Dogg's "The Next Episode" began playing through the Bluetooth speaker beside Cara on the bench. "Ba-Ba, Ba-Ba-Ba, Ba-Ba-Ba, Ba-Ba-Ba-Ba-Ba," Áine sang along to the background music. "Okay, and five, six, seven, eight."

Áine hovered in front of Lir, demonstrating the steps. The two of them managed to stay mostly together through a couple of verses. "Not terrible, but we can do better," she commented as the song ended.

Keegan and Calder walked across the courtyard toward the group, hand in hand, and Keegan asked, "Áine, are you teaching Lir how to crip walk?"

"Well, duh. Gangsta rap is my jam. And he's led a sheltered life; somebody needs to broaden his horizons," she replied.

"Of course. Silly me," Keegan said, shaking her head. The familiars continued working on the choreography while Keegan and Calder sat on the bench next to Cara.

Just then, Colin walked into the courtyard with a crystal vase and scissors. Calder called him over, "Hey Lad, come here for a bit, please." Colin came over, and Calder continued, "What are you after? Did Mam send you out here?" Colin nodded and said, "She asked me to gather some fresh flowers for the breakfast table. And Croía asked me to tell you all that breakfast will be ready in twenty minutes or so."

Calder said, "Outstanding. Do you think you could gather the flowers over that way and occasionally hit play on Áine's iPod?" He nodded to Cara, and she showed Colin what to do.

He shrugged and said, "Sure, why not?" He picked up the iPod and speaker and walked a bit further away. The familiars followed, continuing their dance party.

Cara turned to Calder and said, "Oh, thank goodness. I needed a break." He smiled and said, "My pleasure. I was also hoping the three of us could speak for a bit. If your family is going to be living in Tionól and functioning in the homeworld society, I wanted to go over a few things that might be helpful. And a few other things that might keep us all from being persecuted and banished." He spoke lightly, but the seriousness of the situation was palpable.

"I know that you, Keegan, understand that you cannot use your air power in public. But I want to make sure you know you cannot use it while in Tír na nÓg at all. Ever. Not even in the privacy of your own home," he explained. Keegan gave a little derisive laugh and said, "Well, that shouldn't be a problem since we don't have a home."

Calder hooked a finger under her chin and raised her head until he could look into her eyes. "You will always have a home here, mo chroí. But I understand your family needs their own place. We are working on that, but it may take a little time. We need to bring you before the Council and get you all formally recognized. That gives you standing you just don't have right now," he said.

"I understand. My head is just still spinning. It's hard to think straight," she explained.

He pulled her back against him and wrapped his arms around her, offering support and comfort. "I think that's to be expected. You'll adjust, I promise. And I am happy to help in any way I can."

He paused for a moment, then said, "There's something else I wanted to speak to you about. How much do you know about your family here on the homeworld?"

She said, "Well, there's Uncle Cass, the asshat. And Aunt Étaín, who apparently is so obsessed with her husband she turned her back on her own sister." Saying these things out loud was more challenging than she thought it would be. How her family had managed to get so fucked up was beyond her. She took a deep breath and continued, "And I know I have another cousin, Máire, but I don't know much about her. I'm kind of excited to meet her, though."

Calder and Cara shared a look, and Keegan said, "What? Is there something I don't know?" Calder said, "Well, yes. I'm afraid Máire has taken after her father. According to Mam, she's become a bit obsessed with me." He looked down, a bit embarrassed by the situation. Keegan gave a small, mirthless chuckle and said, "Of course. I've been hoping she might be someone who could become a friend, so of course, she'd be an obsessive nightmare."

Cara added, "Well, not to defend her or anything, but from what I've gathered on the few trips to see my mom, her father has really jacked her up. She is definitely a hot mess, but I don't think she's irredeemable. But Calder is right; she is a few beers short of a six-pack. At least she was last summer. Probably best for now to put her on the back burner and worry about her later."

Calder said, "I just wanted you to be aware of the situation. I don't know how far her obsession goes, but if she knows you're important to me, she could be dangerous." His forehead wrinkled as worry overtook him at the thought of anything happening to her.

Keegan's eyes narrowed; she held out her hand and released what she thought was a small burst of flame. With her strength, however, she singed the tree branch about eight feet above them. She cringed and said, "Sorry. But that makes my point for me. She doesn't know the meaning of dangerous. I don't know if we can ever have a good relationship, but I will not pull any punches. She's the one who needs to watch out for me. I'm done playing."

Calder, worry lines still in place but slightly more relaxed, planted a light kiss on her cheek and said, "That's my girl. But I have a question. What do you mean by 'another cousin?' Is there someone I haven't met yet? How do they fit in the equation?"

Keegan blushed a bit and said, "No, you've met her." Cara held up a hand and said, "My mam is Spéir Ó Brien, Shay's sister."

Calder let out a low whistle. "Alright then. Yes, that's something else that can't ever be mentioned." Keegan nodded and replied, "I know. I'll be more careful."

Colin, along with Áine and Lir, walked over and said, "I think we're all done. Breakfast should be almost ready, so don't wait too long to head to the kitchen." He headed back toward the main house, a simple bouquet of gloriously colorful flowers in the vase.

As he left the courtyard, Niamh entered and made her way toward the group. Calder nodded to Lir and said, "Nice shape, Lad. Why don't we go help set the table and see if Croía needs anything?" Lir nodded, then stood on his hind legs, singing, "Ba-Ba, Ba-Ba-Ba, Ba-Ba-Ba, Ba-Ba-Ba-Ba-Ba," as he crip walked his way out of the courtyard. Calder just followed behind him, at a loss for words.

Niamh reached the bench, looked back at the wolf, and said, "Let me guess—Áine?" The girls just nodded. "Ah, well, she is a force of nature, that's for sure," Niamh replied.

"So, how are you three doing? A lot has happened in the past few days. Is everyone coping alright? This manor has more rooms than they know what to do with. I'm pretty sure we could find a room and do some primal screaming if that would help?" she said with a smile.

"We're okay, Mom," Keegan said. "The important thing is you already seem a lot better since we got here. All of this will take some getting used to, but it's pretty exciting, too. I've waited for this my whole life."

Niamh reached out to both Keegan and Cara, putting a hand on each Fae's cheek. "I know you have, a stór," she said. "I know both of you have wanted this for a long time. And I'm glad to be home. I already feel so much better; it's unbelievable. But it's hard for me to see you two in danger. Please promise me you'll both be careful."

They both nodded, and Niamh continued, "Good. I also

wanted to tell you that we're in this together, whatever happens. And with the Ó Faoláins' help, perhaps we can build a good life here. I'm certainly willing to try."

Both girls nodded again and said, in unison, "Us, too." Áine took that as her cue to gather them all in a group hug. After a moment, she said, "Okay. Time for breakfast," and led the way toward the kitchen.

Family
is life

# TWENTY-FOUR

Calder tried to keep his mind on the task at hand, which was rinsing the dishes before loading them into the Fae version of a dishwasher. But a certain Fae was bent over the kitchen table, wiping it off, and he was having a hard time keeping his eyes off her butt. Everything was round and curvy and more than a little distracting. *Okay, now she's doing it on purpose. That is completely unacceptable.*

He put the last dish in the washer, dried off his hands, and turned around, leaning back against the counter with a grin. Keegan had been rubbing a dishrag over the same portion of the table for at least the last three minutes. He walked over behind her, pressed himself against that delightfully round ass, and leaned over, putting one hand on either side of her waist, blocking her in. She started to stand up but could only get part of the way, running into a rather firm, nicely chiseled chest.

She turned back to look at him, a mischievous gleam in her eye. "Took you long enough," she said, tilting her face toward his, inviting a kiss. Calder gave her a whisper-soft kiss near her ear and whispered, "Feeling salty, are we? I can work with that." Then his tone changed slightly, and he said, "I need you to know if I do anything you're uncomfortable with, you should tell me. Right away, yes?"

Keegan gave a low chuckle, held up a finger, and said, "Lover, I am many, many things. Helpless is not one of them." She let a trickle of her fire magic bloom on the tip of her finger. It was still a ten-inch flame. "I promise, if you annoy me, you will know."

Calder gathered a tiny cloud of moisture from the air and doused her flaming finger. "Fair enough, my little Aibhleog. Why don't you stay down there for a bit, eh?" Then he put a hand between her shoulder blades and gently but firmly pushed her back down on the table. He began running his hands all over her back, kneading and massaging, occasionally gripping her waist as he kept grinding his hips against her firm backside. Then he moved his hands up to her shoulders, leaning forward a bit, pulling back on her, pushing her harder against him.

Keegan leaned into Calder, pressing against his hardness, doing her best to tease and entice him. *Fuck this,* she thought. *I need to take him to bed. Enough teasing!* She tried to turn over, but the aroused Earth Fae snaked one arm around her waist while twisting his other hand around in her hair, gathering it in his fist and using it to pull her upper body back against him.

As soon as her back hit his chest, he tilted her head to the side and devoured her neck, hungrily kissing, biting, and licking from her ear down to her shoulder. His passion surprised her, eliciting a moan from her before she knew what was happening. She could feel him smiling against her throat when he heard that.

As he continued lavishing attention on her neck, his other hand moved up her stomach to her breast, kneading and squeezing, tweaking her nipples through her shirt, causing them to stand at attention. He was rewarded with more moans, each a little louder than the next.

*She's not going to be quiet. Hmm, I like that,* he thought, feeling himself grow even harder, a feat that didn't seem possible.

All at once, Keegan felt him take a step back, breaking all bodily contact except for his hand in her hair. He somehow managed to flip her over and lift her up onto the edge of the table, one-handed, all while keeping a tight grip on her hair. The second her ass landed on the table, he was back between her legs, pushing them apart a little wider so he could nestle himself tightly against her.

He went back to licking and nipping her neck, inhaling her intoxicating scent. *She smells like honeysuckle and rosemary,* he thought. *I can't get enough of this cailín.* As he was kissing and sucking along her collarbone, she actually whimpered. He couldn't hold back a low chuckle.

Keegan had finally had enough foreplay. She wrapped her legs around his waist, using the strength in her athletic thighs to pull herself tightly against him. Then she grabbed his face and pulled it up so she could stare into his green eyes, glazed with desire. "Enough playing," she said to him, practically growling. Then she planted a kiss on him that nearly stopped his breath. He happily returned her passion, their lips and tongues weaving and dancing together.

As they kissed, she began running her hands over his body, unable to get enough of him. He let go of her hair and started running both hands along the outside of her thighs, working his way up to cup the cheeks of her butt, squeezing and kneading, his fingers dancing closer and closer to the heat at her core.

She began grinding against him harder and faster, feeling warmth building inside her. Now it was Calder's turn to moan, unable to help himself.

"Calder, I'm..." Conor walked into the kitchen, then stopped short at seeing his brother and Keegan grinding on the kitchen table. "Oops, didn't mean to walk in on that." Keegan and Calder quickly stopped kissing and held each other, breathing heavily. "Damn, kids, you realize there are like ten unused bedrooms in this place, right? But no, you two decided, 'Hey, let's get busy on the kitchen table! That would be a great idea.' You know we eat here, right?"

Calder lifted his head, looked over his shoulder at his brother, and said, "I swear, Conor, if you don't get the fuck out of here, you will live to regret it."

Conor's laughter rang out loudly. "I'm leaving, Loverboy. But you should be thanking me. Niamh asked me to find Keegan and remind her that they are supposed to be meeting with Mam to discuss being presented to the Council. If I hadn't been nice enough to find her, you might very well have had her mother walk in on the two of you dry-humping. On our kitchen table." He shook his head and shivered. "Sorry, that really gives me the willies. Anyway, you'd best straighten yourself up and head to the library. And you, a Dheartháir Beag, had best go take a cold shower. Trust me, it helps."

Calder gave her one more tender kiss, then picked her up, swung her around off the table, and set her on the ground. She ran over to the sink, splashed a little cold water on her face, straightened her clothing, and hurried past Conor toward the library.

Conor gave his little brother one last side eye, chuckled, and sauntered back the way he came, humming under his breath, tickled by the situation.

Calder leaned against the kitchen table, taking deep breaths, willing his body to calm down. After a moment, he pushed upright and headed toward the stables, looking for Lir.

He found his familiar hiding from Áine in one of the stalls in the stable. "What's going on, buddy?" he asked. Lir finished the apple he was chewing on, sighed, and said, "I just needed a little break.

Áine is great, but she can be a little extra." Calder laughed, saying, "Truer words have never been spoken, Lad. How about a good run?" Lir perked up and said, "Great idea!"

Lir trotted out of the stall, stopped to let Calder hop on his back, then trotted the rest of the way until they were out of the stable. They passed Colin on the way out, and Calder said, "If anyone asks, we're headed to Lir's pond." Colin lifted a hand in acknowledgment and continued into the stables to feed the horses. Once they were past him, Lir put on a burst of speed a regular horse would be incapable of matching.

Calder held on tight, laughing madly, letting his frustrations, sexual and otherwise, bubble out of him with the laughter. Lir darted into the woods, dodging around trees and under branches, making Calder keep his head on a swivel. Luckily, he was used to the púca's antics and had no trouble keeping his seat.

After several minutes of breakneck speed, they burst out of the trees into a clearing around Lir's favorite pond. The familiar stopped momentarily, then gave a whinny and turned the speed back on, heading straight for the water. "I thought we talked about this, Lir!" he yelled, holding on for dear life as the púca plowed into the pond.

Calder found himself treading water as his best friend pranced around, laughing and splashing. "You talked about it," Lir commented. "I agreed to nothing!" Calder splashed him with some water, but couldn't help but laugh.

Since they were already wet, they decided to take a bit of a swim. Summer was quickly winding down, but it was still very warm, so the water felt great. Lir found it hilarious to dive under the water, sneak up on him, then jump out of the water to surprise him. Calder let him have fun, content to float on his back, thinking about his little Aibhleog. As he floated there, he closed his eyes, picturing Keegan, and began creating her likeness from the water around him. He imagined her floating in the air just above him, her wild hair flying around her face, those gorgeous eyes opened wide, and a huge smile on her face. Her arms were stretched wide, and her breasts were mere inches from his chest. He opened his eyes then to admire his work, running his fingers through her curls, along her cheek, over her lips, down her neck, and across her shoulder. Then he let her form dissipate, splashing over him and back into the pond.

Suddenly, he heard a faint, "Goat Boy!" echo across the clearing. He rolled over and began swimming toward the edge of the pond. Lir responded, "Over here!" and also began swimming toward the pond's edge. Calder turned toward him and said, "I thought you needed a break?" Lir responded, "I got one. Now I'm ready for more Áine. She's pretty entertaining." Calder laughed and said, "Yes, Lad, she is indeed." They both climbed out of the pond, and Calder used his water power one last time, wicking the moisture from the two of them, instantly drying their hair and his clothes.

Áine pulled up to hover in front of them and said, "I've been looking everywhere for you!" Lir replied, "We just needed a little ride, and then we decided to take a swim. But we're done now. Wanna go teach some of the other familiars how to crip walk?"

Áine's eyes widened, and she said, "Well, of course I do! You're lucky I have my iPod and speaker with me." She patted the strap of the small bag that ran diagonally across her chest. Cara had gotten it for her so she could take her music with her. "Why didn't you suggest this before? I could've been sharing my talent all this time! Let's go, Goat Boy!" She waited impatiently until Lir led the way, then followed him, asking all kinds of questions about who might want to learn the choreography. "Oh, and we need to find someone with thumbs who can work the iPod," she said as they headed off through the woods. Lir replied, "There's a raccoon in the group; she can probably do it."

Calder shook his head and started walking back to the house.

High Druid Deirdre suddenly felt a vision coming on. Luckily, she was one of the few Ovates who always remembered their visions. After the scenes finished playing through her mind, she said, "Things are moving quickly now. I must be quicker." Then she wrote a message, sealed it, her seal imprinting a metallic gold five-fold symbol consisting of a central ring surrounded by four others, then found a novitiate to deliver it to the only person who could help.

Once he was alone, Corley stepped out from behind the huge tree he'd been hiding behind. He could hardly believe his luck! He'd been hanging out in the woods near the Ó Faoláin stables when he overheard Calder call out that they were headed to Lir's pond. Luckily, he knew which pond that was, so he followed along behind them.

*Never did I expect to see something this momentous, though. Máire will be beside herself!* He took off at a trot, hoping to catch her at her workshop.

After a quick jog, he came over the last hill and saw smoke coming from her workshop's chimney. He slowed down, trying to catch his breath, and after a moment, he knocked on the door.

Máire opened the door, soot and sweat streaking her face. She'd obviously been working on her artifacts. Corley grinned at her and wiped a rather large smudge from her cheek. "Hard at work, eh?"

Máire rolled her eyes, crossed her arms over her chest, and said, "Obviously. What are you after, Devlin?"

Corley replied, "Now, now. I just came upon some information you will definitely want to hear."

Máire waited for a moment, but Corley seemed happy to drag this out forever. "Oh, for feck's sake, Lad, spit it out already!"

He laughed and said, "Fine, but I should really come inside. And trust me, you want to hear this." She sighed but stepped aside and motioned for him to enter, shutting the door behind him. "Happy now? Or can I make you some tea?"

He said, "Actually, it's almost lunchtime..." Máire slapped her hand down on the worktable and said, "Get on with it already!"

"Alright, alright. You have no patience at all. Anyway, I just saw Calder Ó Faoláin down at Lir's pond with his familiar. They were swimming and horsing around. Then, suddenly, I see all this water swirl up above Calder and take the form of this gorgeous little cailín floating above him."

Máire's eyes widened, and she said, "Wait, what? Are you sure about this?" Corley nodded and said, "Sure as we're standing here." She tapped her forefinger against her soot-smudged chin, lost in thought for a moment. "And you're absolutely positive there was no one else around? No other Water Fae somewhere nearby?"

"No, there was nobody. I made sure," he reassured her.

Máire began pacing, considering all the angles. She didn't even know where to start! There were so many possibilities. After she'd made a few passes back and forth across the workroom, she suddenly stumbled mid-stride as an agonizing pain felt like it was about to split her head down the middle. Corley watched her with a look of concern, obviously gathering that something was wrong.

Máire quickly turned and walked over to her icebox, pulled out a drink, and began drinking, fighting her way through the pain. That now familiar tri-tone voice echoed throughout her mind, saying, "Your path forward is clear if you want to win the attention of this Fae." The voice then explained exactly what would be needed to implement their plan.

Corley watched Máire carefully, certain that something was going on but unsure exactly what it was. After a few moments, she turned back to him and seemed to be her usual self. She said, "Alright, here's what we're going to do." Then she outlined the plan she'd just received from the agonizing voice.

Corley wasn't sure how he felt about the situation; something didn't feel right. But he decided to go along for now. He would reserve judgment for the moment.

Family
is life

# TWENTY-FIVE

Keegan kept fidgeting with her clothes and hair, unable to contain her nervousness. She was finally going to meet her dad! Even though neither of them could admit their relationship, she was still incredibly excited and nervous. What if he wanted nothing to do with her? She didn't think she could stand being rejected by him. Her mom put a hand on her back, rubbing in a circle, and whispering, "It's alright, a stór, just breathe. We are together, we have friends, and we have a plan. We're going to be fine."

The two Doran females, along with Cara, Calder, both familiars, and Conor, were all in the waiting area of the Council Hall. Siobhán was already inside, along with her sister, Fiona, both of whom sat on the Council as representatives of the Nolan family. Liam and Reilly were there as well, sitting for the Ó Faoláins. Being the slightly older twin, Conor could have had the seat, but he swore he would die of boredom if he had to sit on the Council, so Reilly took the seat instead.

The Aos Sí Council consisted of seventeen Fae, with each clan having four representatives, plus the Taoiseach, who was voted into office and could be from any family and clan. The Taoiseach typically kept things moving, acted as a mediator during disputes among the Council representatives, and was the tie-breaking vote when needed.

The clan representatives were chosen from the top two families, two per family, as voted by each clan at the Feis, held once every decade. Feiseanna could be called in times of distress or emergency, but that hadn't happened in centuries. Occasionally, the families for each clan would change, but with a folk as long-lived as Aos Sí, change often took quite a while. The eldest members of each family typically held the seats, but Fae who weren't interested, or didn't feel well-suited, often abdicated their seat to younger relatives. So, it was quite fortunate for Niamh's family that the Nolans and Ó Faoláins were the Earth Clan representatives. Having a few representatives on your side from the beginning never hurt.

The waiting area was decorated with a plethora of Celtic knotwork, with a giant tree of life carved above the doors to the Council Chamber. Triskeles, Dara knots, triquetras, and Celtic crosses could also be found, carved into furniture as well as free-standing sculptures. The different elements were also represented, and not just within the knotwork. There were waterfalls where the water flowed through the shapes of knots, then circled back to the top to start the journey again. Fire sculptures shaped like triskeles and triquetras were self-sustaining, and a continuous light breeze made wind chimes in the shape of Dara knots and Celtic crosses emit a delicate tinkling sound.

The colors were rich and varied but tasteful. Beautiful tapestries also adorned the walls, adding texture and more color. The general atmosphere was calm and serene, which was helpful since being brought before the Council could be a somewhat stressful experience.

Keegan attempted to calm her mind and slow her breathing, but was having limited success. Calder took her hand and led her to a couch to sit. Then he turned her hand over and began massaging and kneading the muscles and tendons, working the anxiety out through her fingers. After a few minutes, he switched and did the same for the other hand. When he was finished, she shook her hands and said, "Wow. I had no idea I had that much tension in my hands. That felt amazing, thank you!" He ran a finger down the side of her cheek and said, "My pleasure."

The doors to the Council chambers opened, and Reilly poked his head out and said, "We're ready for you. Follow me." Then he led them through the doors and up the center aisle to the front of the chambers. The Council representatives were arrayed in a horseshoe shape, with the opening toward the doors and the Taoiseach seated in the center of the semi-circle. A few chairs were located on either side of the aisle, cutting through the middle, since most Council meetings were open to anyone. Corley and a few other Fae watched the proceedings.

Each Council member had a torque tattooed around their neck, consisting of intertwined, twisted knotwork capped at the end with triquetras. Amongst the knotwork, there were also little symbols of that Fae's element—the Fire Clan had flames, the Water Clan had waves, the Air Clan had swirls of wind, and the Earth Clan had vining leaves and flowers.

Keegan took all that in quickly, then turned her eyes to the front and found her own eyes looking back at her. Her father, Shay Ó Brien, smiled gently at the daughter he had not claimed, trying to apologize for two decades of missed opportunities in that one smile. It was an impossible task, but his attempt left her feeling hopeful.

Keegan could feel her eyes welling up as she was finally able to lay eyes on her father. She had waited for this moment her whole life. She took a couple of deep breaths and attempted to blink them back. Calder moved a little closer to her, letting his arm brush against hers, offering what support he could under the circumstances. Likewise, Áine, who was perched on Keegan's shoulder, nuzzled her hair, whispering soothing nonsense in her ear.

Shay moved his eyes to Niamh's, again trying to impart some kind of support wordlessly. She looked back at him with no rancor in her eyes and nodded, encouraging him to do his job.

He gathered himself and said, "The Aos Sí Council would like to welcome Niamh Doran and her daughter, Keegan, before us today. The Dorans have been living on Earth for more than twenty years, but have decided they would like to return to Tír na nÓg. They have been staying with the Ó Faoláin family, who have also agreed to vouch for them.

"Does anyone want to bring forth discussion on the matter?"

There was some whispered debate between Étaín and her daughter, Máire, but eventually, the daughter backed down from whatever she had suggested. Étaín raised her hand and was recognized, then she said, "I would like to know why I, as Niamh's sister, am only learning about this now?"

Niamh turned toward her sister and replied in a clipped tone, "We've only been here a few days. And since my last correspondence to you went unanswered, I felt pretty confident that I knew your stance on our homecoming."

Étaín opened and shut her mouth several times, but eventually, she just said, "I have no further questions," and seemed to sink further into her seat. Máire rolled her eyes and crossed her arms in disgust.

An Air Fae raised her hand, and Shay called to her, "Yes, Éabha Regan, Air Clan, you have the floor."

The dark-haired Fae, with piercing blue eyes, locked her gaze onto Niamh and Keegan. "So, personally, I would like to know a little more about this family's history. I remember when Niamh's parents were killed, but shortly after that, she just disappeared. Where have they been? Why haven't they come back before now? Not to be nosey, but I think the Council has a duty to make sure they aren't running from something or preparing to bring danger to our community."

Liam raised his hand and said, "Shay, may I say something before they answer Éabha's questions?" The Taoiseach nodded at him. Liam turned toward the Air Fae and said, "With all due respect, it's frankly none of our business where Niamh and Keegan have been or why they haven't been back before now. They are undeniably Aos Sí and therefore deserve a place in our society. The fact that they are even required to present themselves before us for some arbitrary stamp of approval is, in my opinion, a remnant of antiquated thinking that does our society a disservice. We should seriously consider abolishing the practice.

"But since the practice has not been abolished at this time, I would also like to say that I have gotten to know Niamh and Keegan recently. They are both genuine, kind, and, in my estimation, trustworthy. I think I speak for my brother and the rest of our family as well when I say the Ó Faoláins support their acceptance into our society." Reilly, Conor, Calder, and Siobhán nodded their approval as well.

Éabha started to defend her questions, referencing their duty to their fellow Fae not to allow just anyone to be a part of their homeworld. Reilly interrupted her with, "Éabha, we're Fae, for crying out loud. Do you really think the lot of us can't defend ourselves and protect the others in our society from two Fire Fae? If that's the case, I'd suggest our society has become so decrepit it's not worth saving."

That caused a few gasps from some visitors and Council members as well. Shay raised his voice and said, "Calm down, everyone. We all have the right to our opinions here. But even though I think the Ó Faoláin brothers made some good points, our current policies require you to answer Council Member Regan's questions."

Niamh smiled and said, "Of course, we have nothing to hide. More than twenty years ago, I took a trip to Earth. I was curious and decided to explore the other world. While there, I met and fell in love with a human. He convinced me to stay with him, and shortly after that, Keegan was born. We've been on Earth ever since. Keegan's father recently passed away." Shay winced slightly at that but covered with a slight cough, hoping nobody had noticed. "I also had recently begun feeling weak, and after some research, we discovered that the way for me to regain my strength was to return to the homeworld. So that's what we decided to do, and here we are."

Éabha looked around at her fellow Council members, but no one seemed willing to continue the discussion, Niamh's explanation seemingly sufficient for them. So, she gave a small smile, looked at Shay, and said, "I suppose that's good enough for me, then. I have no further questions."

Shay nodded and said, "Very well, if there are no other questions, I propose we take a vote. All in favor..." Just then, there was a knock on the door. "Enter," called Shay. A messenger walked through the doors and came to Shay's side, whispered in his ear, and handed him a note. Shay thanked him and sent him on his way. As the messenger headed out, Corley slipped out the door behind him. Máire's eyes narrowed, and a scowl settled over her face as she watched him go.

Then he opened the note and read it. His eyes widened immediately, and he cleared his throat several times. "Well, I'm afraid there's been a development. I've just received an anonymous note with quite an accusation. It seems ridiculous, but its seriousness demands an investigation."

Siobhán raised her hand, and Shay said, "Yes, Siobhán?" She clasped her hands in front of her, smiled, and said, "Perhaps we could get to the bottom of things if we knew what the accusation was?"

Shay sighed and said, "Well, it's fitting you should ask since the matter concerns your family." There were several gasps around the room. The Ó Faoláins were well-respected and had been for centuries.

Siobhán's eyes widened slightly, but she maintained a mask of calm despite the tumultuous feelings overtaking her. "And what might that matter be?" she asked.

Shay looked at her, a hint of compassion in his gaze. "According to the note I received, there is an accusation that your son, Calder Ó Faoláin, is Dúbailte."

Chaos ensued at those words. Fae began talking and arguing, the volume level steadily increasing, until Shay had to break out a gavel to bring things back under control.

"Okay, we obviously have a lot to investigate. I think it would be wise, given the circumstances, if Calder would agree to stay in the custody of the Druids until we sort this all out." Calder nodded, his face a mask to match his mother's, and replied, "Of course, I've got nothing to hide."

Shay nodded his thanks and continued, "Just so there is no hint of impropriety, I believe it would also be wise for Niamh and Keegan to remain with the Druids as well. I'm sure our investigation won't take long, and the inconvenience will hopefully be short." Niamh and Keegan glanced at Siobhán, who nodded, and then they nodded as well, and Niamh replied, "Of course, whatever we need to do."

Shay says, "Thank you for your cooperation. I promise you, we will get to the bottom of this accusation with all speed. I need to finish the meeting and get the investigation underway. If you three don't mind reporting to the Druid's Enclave, I will be in contact as soon as I can."

Niamh, Keegan, and their assorted familiars and family

members exited the Council chambers together, headed for the Druids. As the doors drifted closed, Áine said, rather loudly, "Somebody should show them how to run a meeting. There was no food, no drink, and now they're locking us up. Zero out of ten, would not recommend."

Family

is life

CHAPTER

# TWENTY-SIX

As the group approached the Druid's Enclave, they were met at the entrance to the gardens by a Fae with blonde hair and piercing blue eyes. "Welcome," she said. "I am Deirdre, the High Druid. We have much to discuss, but I'd like to wait for the others before we begin. I foresaw what happened in Council today and sent a message to the pertinent parties to facilitate this meeting. It shouldn't take long for them to arrive. If you follow me, we'll have a cuppa while we wait."

She led them into the Druid's mound, which contained a series of tunnels and rooms that led underground. They followed her to a large room with several couches and chairs, all very comfortable and cheerful. A sideboard had a tea service set out and plenty of fruit and pastries. "Please help yourself," Deirdre said.

Áine flew up and down above the sideboard, inspecting the fare. "This is more like it," she said. "Keegan, Cara, somebody come make me a plate. This looks yummo. And somebody take notes for the Council. Their hospitality sucked donkey balls." She landed on a big comfy chair and waited for her food. Cara rolled her eyes and went to get some goodies for Miss Demanding.

The others all got some tea and snacks, then sat to refresh themselves while waiting for the rest of the group. Áine and Lir dug in, making themselves right at home.

Before long, a novitiate came in and whispered something to Deirdre. She nodded and stood up, saying, "It looks as though the rest of our group has arrived. Once they've had a chance for some food and drink, we'll begin."

The other group entered with Siobhán in the lead, followed by Liam and Reilly, Shay, and Morgan and Muireann Ó Loingsigh.

Keegan and Calder sat together on a small sofa, his arm around her shoulders. The entrance of Morgan caused him to stiffen. She raised her hand to cover his, giving a gentle squeeze of support.

Morgan and Muireann each looked at Calder, seemingly unsure why they were there. Calder wasn't entirely sure, so he gave a slight shrug.

Deirdre told the new arrivals, "Please help yourself to some tea and food. Then we can get started."

Siobhán made a beeline for Calder, knelt before him, and, putting her hand on his knee, said, "I'm so sorry, mo bhuachaill. We will fix this. It will all get sorted; you'll see." He covered her small hand with his much larger one. "I know we will, Mam. But I am a little confused by the group gathered here now. Surely, keeping me far from the Ó Loingsigh family is safer. So why are they here?"

"I don't know, Love, but I plan to find out," she said. Then she stood and went to speak to Deirdre to get to the bottom of things. The High Druid held her hand up as Siobhán approached, recognizing the look in the matriarch's eyes, and said, "Bean Ó Faoláin, I must ask for your continued patience just a bit longer. Please, have some tea and perhaps a snack. I am almost ready to begin."

Siobhán narrowed her eyes at the Druid but said, "Very well. Thank you for your hospitality. And please, call me Siobhán."

Deirdre replied, "Thank you, Siobhán." She looked the group over and, raising her voice slightly, said, "If everyone could please gather whatever food and drink you would like and find a seat, I'd appreciate it."

Everyone quickly finished selecting their food and sat down. Even Áine and Lir seemed to be paying attention. Deirdre began, "Thank you, everyone, for your presence here. This meeting has been a very long time coming, and I am glad it is finally here.

"I suppose I should start at the beginning. I assume everyone is familiar with Aisling's Prophecy or the Dúbailte Curse, as it is also known?" The Ó Faoláin brothers all winced at that term, and Deirdre said, "And yes, Siobhán, I know why you hate that term so much. I'm afraid I'm the reason you have call to hate it."

Siobhán's eyes widened, and she replied, "I fail to see how that could possibly be true." But Deirdre said, "And yet it is. Let me explain. I was there when Aisling's Prophecy was given. I was an ovate-in-training, and one of my responsibilities was to help Aisling with whatever she might need. One day, she asked for my help in triggering a vision, along with the Birds of Rhiannon, who often help seers reach new heights of foretelling." Several of the Fae let out a gasp at that. "I see you're aware of just how dangerous that is. But Aisling had been having incomplete and foggy visions for weeks, and she was sure we were missing something. Turns out she was right. There is an evil coming for which we are woefully unprepared."

Niamh said, "But wait, Aisling's Prophecy doesn't deal with an enemy; it talks about dual powers bringing about chaos and pain. I'm not sure how; that part was always unclear."

Deirdre nodded and continued, "When the Fae with dual powers are discovered, they will force Aos Sí to confront their stagnant ways. Prejudice, in several forms, will have to be examined and overcome in order for us to defeat the evil that is even now plotting against us."

Keegan sat on the edge of her seat and asked, "But wait, how does that make you responsible for the Dúbailte Curse? It wasn't your prophecy."

Deirdre said, "In a way, it was. I recorded the prophecy as Aisling gave it. She could never remember her prophecies, so she always had a novitiate nearby to record them. The prophecy I presented to her was incomplete. There was a final line only I am aware of." She paused for a moment to take a drink. She then continued, saying, "I had reason to believe our enemy would have moved against us immediately had they discovered the full prophecy. I needed to give us time to plan for a better outcome."

Calder spoke up and said, "Well, what is the missing line? And why would it have made the enemy attack sooner?"

Deirdre reached into the bodice of her dress and pulled out a small scroll. She unrolled it and said, "Here is the complete prophecy.

*Radiance blinds the masked peacock.*
*The hawk protects the luster, feeding the fire.*
*Dúbailte.*
*The charming wolf keens her loss, drowns her sorrows, and life*
*springs forth.*
*Dúbailte.*
*The hidden seeks out likewise, unknowing.*
*When anamchara relent, Aos Sí undergoes athrú.*
*Dúbailte, Dúbailte bring forth athrú and anord.*
*Embrace them, and na páistí will bring forth an Domhan*
*Nua.*"

Everyone's mind was racing as they tried to decipher what this new line might mean. They began whispering amongst themselves, trying to work it out. After a few moments, Calder turned a few shades paler than usual, and he stood and began pacing.

Keegan looked around, still confused, and said, "Wait a minute, my Irish still needs some work. What do the terms anamchara and páistí mean?" Áine replied, "Roughly 'soulmates' and 'children.'"

Keegan's eyes widened, and she said, with some anxiety in her voice, "So are you saying this prophecy is talking about Calder and me? And our children? And we're supposed to cause chaos and pain. And our kids will bring forth a new world? Seriously? Am I the only one who thinks this is a load of horse shit?"

Deirdre smiled sadly and replied, "I'm afraid it doesn't matter if you believe in the prophecy. The vast majority of Aos Sí do believe. Which means the chaos and pain are coming."

Calder suddenly stopped and, keeping his gaze on the ground, said, "Not necessarily. We still have free will. If we refuse to participate, the prophecy can't come true."

Keegan turned to him and said, "Wait, what do you mean by 'if we refuse to participate'?" Calder slowly raised his eyes to Keegan's and said sadly, "What do you think I mean?"

Keegan gasped, covering her mouth with her hand, then her eyes narrowed. "How fucking dare you! How dare you convince me to trust you and then turn your back on me, on us, at the first opportunity!" Tears streamed down her cheeks, quickly turning to steam against her superheated skin. She was very close to igniting. She took several deep breaths and whispered, "You're a fucking coward." Then she turned and ran from the room.

Áine glared daggers at Calder and said, "I bloody well knew it! Slow, slow, slow!" Then she brought a burning wing down on Lir's rump, not bothering to dampen the flames. "Talk to your eejit, Goat Boy. Otherwise, I'll have to handle him my way, and nobody wants that. It's such a bother to hide the body. Oh, wait!

I'm a phoenix...there wouldn't be any body left." With that, she flew after her girl, ready to offer comfort as only she could.

# Family

## is life

# TWENTY-SEVEN

Keegan wandered into the gardens surrounding the Druids' Enclave, her tears making it difficult to see where she was going. *I'm so fucking stupid! I know better than to let my guard down. I thought he was different, but letting people in always ends badly.*

She finally found a bench in a relatively secluded spot and dropped into it. She let herself sob for a bit, needing the release. It wasn't long before she heard, "Keegan, Keegan," and then what sounded like several kissing noises, "Mwa, mwa, mwa, mwa." When the sounds grew near, she finally said, "Áine. I'm not a cat."

Her phoenix friend turned the corner and flew over to perch on the back of the bench next to Keegan. "Cara! She's over here!" Áine bellowed. Keegan shook her head, pinching the bridge of her nose, and said, "Fuck my life. Again."

By then, Cara had found them, and she sat on the other end of the bench, putting her hand on Keegan's knee and giving it a squeeze. "I'm so sorry, Keeg. I never should've told you to trust him. He's a bloody moron!"

"It's not your fault. He made his own choices. I should've

known better than to let him get close in the first place," Keegan replied.

Áine snorted and said, "None of this is your fault, Love. You have every right to let someone get close. Just maybe not Mud Boy."

Cara said, "I know I'll regret this, but I have to ask...Mud Boy?" Áine rolled her eyes, "Isn't it obvious? Earth, water...mud." Cara shook her head and said, "Silly me, what was I thinking?"

Keegan still had tears streaming down her cheeks, but their antics did manage to drag a small smile out of her. Áine looked back and forth between them and said, "So, what's the plan?"

Keegan said, "Plan? There is no plan. There's just survival, same as always." Cara looked at Áine. "Well, that will just not do. Nobody hurts our girl and walks away unscathed."

"What do you think? Waterboarding? The rack? Splinters under his nails?" Áine listed off a few methods of torture she felt were appropriate responses to Calder's assholery. "What am I saying? I'm a firebird. I'll set his nipples on fire!"

Keegan's sniffles and tears had slowed down, and that last comment even elicited a small giggle. "Thank you, girlfriend, but I don't want to hurt him. At least not physically." Cara laughed diabolically, saying, "We need to show him exactly what he's missing." Áine said, "Ooh, I like the way you think! Leave the details to me. This may take a little planning, but I promise he will be sorry he ever thought about hurting our girl."

Keegan said, "Do I get any say in this?" Cara and Áine replied, in unison, "Nope." Keegan responded, "Alright then. The inmates are running the asylum."

"Damn straight," Áine said, causing them both to giggle again.

Niamh poked her head around the corner and said, "I came to see how you were doing. I should've known these two would cheer you up."

Keegan nodded and said, "That's why I keep them around after all."

"I beg your pardon!" Áine said, feigning indignation. "You know you keep me around for my outstanding vocals and hip choreography skills." She proceeded to moonwalk along the back of the bench for emphasis.

Keegan rolled her eyes and said, "Something like that." Niamh came up behind Keegan and ran her hands through her daughter's curls, something she had always loved. Keegan sighed in contentment and said, "Thanks, Mom. It's been quite a day."

"I know, Love. And I know Calder did not react the way you hoped he would. Sometimes people do that, unfortunately, especially when they're scared. Do you think that may be why he did that?"

Keegan looked over her shoulder at her mom and said, "Maybe. But that just makes him a coward." Niamh wrapped her arms around her neck, rested her head on Keegan's, and said, "That's not what I meant, a stór. He doesn't strike me as cowardly. I think perhaps he was afraid for you. Maybe? Just something to think about, a stór." Then she kissed the crown of her head, patted her on the shoulder, and walked back toward the enclave.

Keegan looked thoughtful, considering what her mother said. Áine watched Niamh leave, then said, "I love Niamh, but I still vote for showing him what he's missing. And if that doesn't work, nipple burning it is!"

As soon as Keegan and her group left the room, Liam, Conor, and Reilly all stood up, grabbed hold of Calder, who seemed a bit dazed, and began dragging him out of the room, followed closely by Lir. "Come on, Lad, time for a talk!" Conor said. Deirdre opened an unnoticed door behind her and said, "Feel free to use my office."

They hustled him inside and pushed him down onto a couch. Reilly sat beside him while Liam and Conor pulled chairs up to sit across from them. Lir lay down at his feet, offering the comfort of his presence. Conor leaned back in his chair, sighed, and said, "Damn, son. That was perhaps the most spectacular fuck up with a woman I've ever seen. Granted, I'm not usually dealing with women in this situation, but still. You flamed out gloriously!"

Calder lifted his head, showing tired, tear-filled eyes, and said, "Is this supposed to be helping?"

"No, not really. Just felt like that needed to be said. It was almost impressive if it hadn't been so soul-crushing."

Reilly kicked his twin and said, "For the love of Pete, man, shut it! He knows he's a gobshite; you don't have to rub it in." Calder looked sideways at Reilly and said, "Thanks, I think."

Liam just looked intensely at him for a moment. Finally, he commented, "You're about as sharp as a beach ball, aren't you, a Dheartháir Beag? Why would you hurt the cailín like that? I never thought of you as a coward, but now I don't know what to think."

When Lir heard Liam call him a coward, he stiffened, then slowly stood up. He took a couple of steps toward him and brought his face right up next to Liam's. Then he said, calmly and quietly, "Calder may not have handled that very well, but call him a coward again, and you and I will have a problem. A Dheartháir Mór." He stared at Liam with those glowing golden eyes until the oldest brother looked away. "I'm sorry, Lir. But it's tough to watch someone you love make the biggest mistake of their life and not understand why. What other conclusion am I supposed to reach?" Having made his position clear, Lir sank back down at Calder's feet.

"I might know the answer to that question," Siobhán said, entering the room and closing the door quietly behind her. "I let you boys have a few moments, but this feels like something I might be able to help with." She motioned for Reilly to give her his seat, so he stood and pulled another chair over to join his brothers.

"Do you remember when you all were small, and I decided to keep Calder's duality a secret from you three? I was terrified then and let my fear rule me for a long while. Until one day, my boys came to me, and my oldest, with a broken arm no less, told me in no uncertain terms that we are a family and we take care of each other. We don't keep secrets." She looked at her youngest then, and continued, "And we also don't push people we love away simply because we're afraid they might get hurt. Eh, mo bhuachaill?"

"But Mam, I'd rather have her hate me than see her get hurt," he said, the tears finally spilling down his cheeks. "Lad, you're the one hurting her. I know you think you're trying to keep her safe, but this isn't the way. Trust her. She and her family have taken care of themselves for a long time. They are strong. And so are we. Did you think we'd desert her when things got rough? She's our family, too, now."

Calder quietly replied, "And family is life." He dropped his head into his hands and said, "She's never going to speak to me again. I really am an eejit."

Siobhán rubbed his back briefly and said, "Well, she probably won't talk to you today. But give it a little time. And some serious, I believe on Earth they call it 'sucking up,' would not be out of line. I'll leave you to figure out the best way to go about that. But I have faith you'll manage." Then she stood up and began walking toward the door. Before she left, she said, "Oh, and keep in mind, you'll have to win Áine over as well. Frankly, I'd be more worried about that." And she went to rejoin the others, closing the door behind her.

Lir looked up at Calder and said, "Don't worry, I'll help with

Áine. She's not as tough as she seems." Conor barked a laugh and said, "If you say so. Me, I'll make sure to be far, far away when he tries mending that bridge. Áine's likely to burn it, and him, to the ground." Calder sighed and dropped his head back into his hands.

# Family

# is life

# TWENTY-EIGHT

Calder and his brothers had just taken seats back in the main meeting room when Niamh came in from outside, followed soon after by Keegan, Cara, and Áine. Calder couldn't help but try to catch Keegan's eye, even though he knew it couldn't end well. She looked him dead in the eye as she came in, then pointedly looked away, letting him know exactly where he stood.

Lir started to come over to talk to Áine, but she said to him, "Nope, not yet, Goat Boy. I'm not sure I could be my usual friendly self to you right now." Cara whispered to Keegan, "That was her being nice to him?"

Lir visibly deflated and moped back over to Calder. Áine saw his reaction and flew over near him. "Oh, don't go all Eeyore on me. I know it's not your fault. Just give me until tomorrow, and then we can go do something fun." Lir perked up at that and went to the food table to graze.

Then she turned to Calder, pointed a burning wing at him, and said, "But you are on my shit list, Mud Boy! Be grateful my girl is more kindhearted than I am. I voted to burn your nipples off, but I got overruled!" Calder gulped at that but wisely chose not to speak. Áine just gave a snort of disgust and flew back over to Keegan.

Deirdre stood and said, "I've been speaking with Shay and the other Council members. We think we have enough members in our corner to put this accusation to rest pretty easily. The Council will reconvene in three days. If any proof against Calder is offered, the various members will belittle and dismiss it. Niamh's story will be accepted, and she and Keegan will be formally recognized at the upcoming Samhain Ball.

"In the meantime, Niamh and her group will stay with the Fire Fae in the enclave, provided that's acceptable to you, Cara? I know you're an Air Fae, but I thought you would want to stay with the others." Cara nodded, "I'd prefer that, yes."

"Very well. As for you, Calder, you will stay in the Earth Clan portion of the enclave. I assume that's acceptable?" He nodded.

Deirdre looked intently at the group and said, "I know things are unsettled and uncomfortable right now. I promise you that will pass in time. For now, please stick to your own areas, under-stood?" Both Keegan and Calder nodded.

"Excellent. These novitiates will show you the way." Two Fae entered the room, one gestured at Niamh's group to follow her, and the other waved at Calder to follow him. Niamh and her girls left first. Calder and Lir stood when they were gone, but Deirdre stopped him and said quietly, "Keep your chin up, Lad. Things aren't as dire as they seem." Calder nodded and gave her a small smile, reaching down to run his fingers through Lir's silky black goat hair. Then they followed the novitiate out of the room.

Saoirse nearly purred as Corley brushed her silky red coat, humming under his breath as he worked. They were lounging on a living bench, one he had grown himself, nice and fluffy with the greenery creating a natural cushion. This little corner of the gardens near the World Tree was one of his favorite places. It was quiet and peaceful, a place he could hear himself think.

The sound of someone stomping through the gardens reached him, and he sighed deeply. *So much for quiet and peaceful,* he thought. He'd been waiting for this confrontation since he had ducked out of the Council meeting yesterday. *Ah, well, better get it over with.*

Máire turned the corner, saw Corley, put her hands on her hips, and said, with exasperation, "Finally! I've been looking for your sorry hide over half of Tionól, Devlin. Care to explain yourself!"

Laoise poked her little chihuahua head out of the bag slung over Máire's shoulder, but the Fire Fae gripped the bag too tightly for her to wiggle out. She sighed and settled down to wait until she could find an opportunity to escape.

Corley leaned back on his bench, intertwining his hands behind his head, and replied, "I never promised you anything. In fact, I'm beginning to regret ever sharing Calder's secret with you."

"What? That's certainly not the tune you were singing before," she snapped, her irritation apparent.

Corley gently moved Saoirse out of the way, stood up, and walked over to Máire. He looked her in the eyes and said, "Why are you trying to destroy Ó Faoláin? I may think he's a pretentious wanker, but that doesn't mean I'm willing to fuck up his entire life. So why are you?"

Máire looked uncomfortable and glanced away. "I don't have to explain myself to the likes of you," she said and turned to stomp away.

Having learned from getting burned before, Corley quickly trapped her with vines and said, "Please don't set the garden on fire! I just want to talk."

She scowled fiercely at him but held her fire at bay for the moment. He took that as a positive sign and quickly continued, "Listen, I just want to understand. Why are you willing to ruin his life?"

She looked away again but said, "I just thought, if I could make things fall apart for him, he might..." Corley started laughing and said, "Oh, that's brilliant. You were using me to destroy him, all so you could help him pick up the pieces? That's it, isn't it?"

Máire looked increasingly uncomfortable, but she didn't deny his accusation. Corley finally quit chuckling and said, "You know what? I don't even care. I know I probably should, but I don't." He released her from the vines, then, with one fingertip, lifted her chin until he could look into those pale green eyes. His own bright blue eyes were intense as he said, "I know I'm not perfect. And quite obviously, neither are you. But I like you, Máire. I've liked you for a very long time, but I've always been too afraid to say anything. I'd like to be more than just an acquaintance you occasionally take advantage of. If you'd let me in, just a little, I think we could be outstanding together." She began looking around, the beginnings of panic showing on her face. He took a step back and raised his hands by his sides. "It's up to you, fireball. You can choose to obsess about someone who doesn't even see you, or you can appreciate someone who sees only you. But either way, I'm not helping you destroy a Fae who has done nothing to harm you. I'll leave the choice of how to proceed to you." Then he turned, walked back to the bench, sat, and continued brushing Saoirse.

Máire stood there for a moment, breathing heavily, confusion and panic warring for dominance in her brain. Laoise took that moment of confusion to slip out of the bag, shifting briefly to a white squirrel to better shimmy down the vines and branches to reach the ground. Finally, Máire turned and ran from the garden, unable to stand still any longer.

Laoise quickly scurried over to the area underneath Saoirse's section of the bench. She stood on her hind legs and whispered, "You've done fabulous with Corley. I'm still working on Máire."

The fox replied, "I've barely spoken to him; he's just a good lad. I hope you can get through to Máire. Believe it or not, I think they'd be good for each other. But it's up to her."

Laoise said, "She's a good cailín, too; she's just lost her way. I'll do my best to bring her back to the path." Then she shifted back to her chihuahua form.

Saoirse replied, "Good luck, pup. I wish you well." Laoise said, "Thanks, I'll need all the good luck I can get." And she took off after her girl.

Family
is life

CHAPTER

# TWENTY-NINE

Three days after the initial Council meeting, the same group found themselves waiting outside the Council Hall once again. Áine was on good terms with Lir again, but that was the only change. She was still giving Calder some major stink eye. He had been wracking his brain for ways to approach Keegan and try to mend their relationship, but so far, he had come up empty.

Conor had decided to go in early and find a seat with the other guests. He was only in there a few moments before he came back out and pulled Niamh aside. "I thought you would like to know; I spotted your asshat brother-in-law in there. He seemed excited about something, which I'm guessing is the opportunity to pick up where he left off with the stalking. I just wanted you to know so you could be prepared. I know that things are pretty rocky between our families at the moment, but please know that we will help you however we can. And Earth Fae are very good at hiding bodies. Just sayin'."

Niamh smiled grimly and said, "I appreciate that, Lad. But Fire Fae don't leave any bodies." That made Conor chuckle and say, "Point taken."

Reilly opened the door to the Council Hall and said, "We're ready if you'll follow me, please." He led them inside, Keegan making sure to stay as far from Calder as possible. Áine was still a little worked up, so she tried to fly over to him and give him another piece of her mind, but Cara caught her foot as she flew by and redirected her to Keegan's shoulder. The phoenix shot her a dirty look, which the Air Fae returned, whispering, "You're not helping!" That finally seemed to get through because Áine settled onto Keegan's shoulder and contented herself with glaring and mumbling, fairly loudly, "Stupid Mud Boy."

As they walked down the center aisle, Niamh was not surprised to see Cass sitting in the gallery, right next to the aisle, hoping to make her walk close to him. Reilly took the opportunity to offer her his arm, placing himself between the two. It was more formal than necessary, but it nicely solved her problem. She took his arm and gave him a grateful smile, refusing to give the asshat any notice at all. Thankfully, she could not see him leering at her once she passed him.

Reilly led the group to the front of the room, then sat with the other Council members. Shay gave them an encouraging smile, then began, "Welcome back. At our last meeting, a serious charge was leveled against Calder Ó Faoláin, claiming he had both earth and water powers, making him Dúbailte. The charge was brought anonymously and without substantiation.

"Since then, an investigation has been conducted, at least as much of one as possible, given the lack of credible evidence available. Does anyone have any new information to present?"

He paused and looked around at the other Council members, giving them one last opportunity to speak their mind. A few of them looked like they wanted to say something, but nobody summoned the bravery to stand alone and accuse the young Fae without proof. Máire just sat there, alternating between scowling at Calder, giving her mother looks of disgust, and shooting confused looks toward her father, unsure why he was there but afraid it involved some failing on her part. Cass's eyes never left Niamh.

After a long moment, he finally said, "In that case, I formally drop the investigation and hereby determine the matter to be closed." Calder and the rest of his family let out a sigh of relief at disaster being averted.

"Now, on to other matters. Since the Ó Faoláins have been cleared of any wrongdoing, their vouching for the Doran family is accepted and appreciated. Niamh and Keegan, you are officially welcomed back to the Aos Sí. There will be a Samhain Ball in a few weeks, and you will be formally introduced to the public then.

"There is just one final matter then before we adjourn. The Doran family currently holds two seats on this Council. As the elder sister, Niamh, it is your right to claim one of those seats if you so wish."

Máire leapt to her feet and shouted, "No! That's not fair! This seat is mine!" Her panicked remarks caused quite a stir among the Council members and guests alike. She looked at her mother for support, but was unsurprised when her mam just looked at the ground. She even looked to her da, hoping he might at least be annoyed at the perceived slight to his family. He hadn't even noticed; he was so obsessed with his sister-in-law. Shay needed a few minutes and some serious gavel pounding before he regained control of the room.

Niamh turned to face Máire and, with more than a little sympathy for the young Fae, she said, "I'm truly sorry, but I have to retake my Council seat. You will still have a seat eventually, but I'm afraid you'll have to wait a bit." Máire's panic subsided and was replaced with a widespread numbness. Her eyes were glassy as she retook her seat, looking at the ground in defeat.

Then Niamh turned back to Shay and said, "Yes, I do wish to

reclaim my seat on the Council." He nodded and replied, "Very well." He stood and moved in front of Niamh, then turned to Máire and said, "Please join us." She stood up and moved over to face Niamh, with Shay between them. He pulled a small artifact from his pocket, marked all over with fire glyphs. He placed it on the torque around Máire's neck, near her collarbone. He then let a trickle of his power flow into the artifact and watched as the artifact seemed to suck the torque right off her neck. She gasped as it happened; the process wasn't painful, but it was definitely intense. He then thanked Máire for her service on the Council and asked her to take a seat in the gallery. Rather than endure any more, she just left the building.

Shay then moved the artifact to approximately the same location on Niamh's neck. He again let a trickle of his power run through the piece, and when he was done, he removed it to see a brand-new tattooed torque, complete with little flames throughout the design, surrounding her graceful neck. He couldn't help but let his fingers graze his former lover's collarbone, causing a slight gasp to escape her lips, but only he and his daughter were close enough to hear.

Keegan quickly looked down to hide the slight smile caused by Shay's flirtation with her mom. She really hoped they could find a way to be together. Dúbailte Curse be damned.

Shay pulled himself together and took a step back. "Please welcome our newest Council Member, Niamh Doran, Fire Clan." Polite applause greeted the pronouncement, and Niamh smiled and gave a small wave.

"Alright then, off with the lot of you. Don't forget your assignments for the Samhain Ball. It will take all of us to pull off the spectacle we have planned for this year. Get your costumes sorted, and remember—this year's theme is Happy Halloween, so you'll need a costume from Earth culture and one from Tuatha Dé Danann history. We're adjourned."

Laoise was snuggled next to Máire in her bedroom, spooning with her and singing a lullaby as she quietly cried. *My poor girl. She goes about things arse backward and then suffers terribly when they don't work out. I wish I could get her to just calm down and stop forcing things. I swear, if I ever encounter her bastard of a father when nobody's around, I will shift into something capable of eviscerating him. Everyone would be better off.*

She finally calmed a bit, so Laoise said, "Feeling a little better?" Máire sniffed but said, "A little, I suppose. I still can't believe they humiliated me that way, though." Laoise shook her little dog head and said, "I think you're looking at this the wrong way."

"What do you mean?" Laoise continued, "So you had to give up your Council seat because your aunt came home. So what? You have centuries to be stuck in a stuffy Council Hall. Eventually, the seat will be yours, so why not enjoy yourself while you have the freedom to do so?"

Máire looked thoughtful for a moment. "I suppose I hadn't thought of it like that. Maybe I could design some new artifacts..." Laoise snorted and said, "I said fun, Love, not work." Máire shrugged and said, "I like my work. And I'm good at it." Her familiar nodded and said, "I know you like it, and yes, you are incredibly good at it. But there is plenty of time for work as well. Do you even know how to have fun?"

"I guess it's been a while," she admitted. Laoise paused momentarily, then said, as casually as she could manage, "Maybe you could spend some time with that Devlin lad? He definitely seems like someone who knows how to have a good time. What would be the harm?"

Máire scowled slightly and replied, "He let me down. I hardly think I should reward that."

*Time for a little tough love.* Laoise sat up and said, "Again, I think you're looking at things the wrong way. You were using the lad, and he was willing to overlook that. He just refused to ruin another Fae's life simply so you could take advantage of him. It sounds to me like he saved you from making a big mistake rather than letting you down."

That was as direct a rebuke as Máire had ever heard from her familiar, and it brought her up short. After a minute, she said, "I'll think about it." Laoise leaned in, giving her a sloppy dog kiss on the nose. "That's all I ask."

Family
is life

# THIRTY

Keegan let her mind wander as her horse walked along the path toward the house her mom wanted to look at. She was still in awe over the sights and sounds of Tír na nÓg, but she'd gotten used to the flamboyance and spectacle enough to focus on other things when needed. So, while some part of her was absolutely astounded by the field of wildflowers they were passing, the bright, rich colors and opulent textures far beyond what she'd ever seen before, most of her attention was focused on her love life. Or lack thereof.

*I just don't understand how he turned his emotions off like that. Things seemed to be going so well! Did I do something to make him change his mind?* Keegan mulled those thoughts over in her mind as she watched a group of gorgeous, sparkling butterflies flit from flower to flower near the side of the path. They were roughly the size of her hand and came in so many different colors she wasn't sure she had names for all of them. As they fluttered their wings, tiny sparkles in those same colors floated in their wake. It was truly magnificent to see.

Áine, who had been flying overhead, settled onto Keegan's shoulder and, looking over at the butterflies, commented, "Amateurs." Cara was riding her horse at Keegan's side, and she snorted and said, "Not everything is a competition, Áine." The phoenix just looked at the Air Fae and said, "What? Of course, it is. What a silly thing to say." Then she launched back into the air and performed some impressive aerial acrobatics just above where the butterflies flew, obviously determined to outdo the oblivious insects.

The young Fae crested a small hill, and below them, the wildflowers gradually merged with a slightly more cultivated, but just as colorful, garden, with plenty of trees to shade the winding paths, as well as the seats and benches grown among the florae. Further up the subsequent rise was a gorgeous house with a stable and numerous outbuildings. It wasn't as large as the Ó Faoláin manor, but it was far larger and grander than any place Keegan had ever lived before.

"This is where we're going to live?" she asked incredulously. Niamh, who was just a bit ahead of the girls, turned in her saddle and replied, "Well, we need to check out the house and grounds to make sure we like it, but yes, if it works for us, this is where we'll live." Keegan just stared at the house and gardens, unable to find words. Niamh chuckled and said, "I guess there are some perks to living on the homeworld, eh?" Keegan nodded and replied, "Uh, yeah. I'd say so."

"Aos Sí are definitely not perfect, but our form of society has some benefits," Niamh said. "It will take a little getting used to, but I'm confident you're up to the challenge." Keegan laughed and said, "I could get used to this kind of challenge. Come on, let's go see the house!" All three Fae urged their horses into a short gallop, leaving the butterfly-trouncing Áine behind in the wildflower meadow. When the sound of the galloping horses reached her, she exclaimed, "Hey, wait for me!" and took off after them. As they pulled up next to a hitching post, Áine landed on a nearby tree branch and said, "You tried to pull a fast one on me, and I still beat you here. I'm beginning to think you'll never learn." She launched into the air and performed a few loop-de-loops for emphasis as she said, "Áine. Always. Wins!"

The other three tied up their horses, and Keegan turned to Áine, put her hands on her hips, and said, "Fine. Áine always wins. Can we go inside now, please?"

Niamh was already at the front doors, letting a trickle of her power flow into a small artifact before passing it over the engraved door handles. It was the Fae version of a key and lock, which intrigued Keegan. She was excited to explore artifact enchanting; hopefully, her mother could start teaching her the basics soon.

The elder Fae opened the front doors wide and said, "Let's see what we have, shall we?" Áine swooped overhead, entered the home's foyer, and landed on the simple but graceful chandelier above them. She looked around at the warm, polished woodwork and the dusky peach-colored walls and said, "This room's okay, but it's kinda empty."

Cara did a facepalm and said, "It's just the entryway, dork. Let's see what else there is." There was a curving wooden staircase to their right and an open doorway to the left, so she led the way to the left, the rest following behind.

They entered a spacious sitting room with various chairs and couches in shades of green with a few hints of peach, surrounding a huge fireplace. The colors of the furniture and other décor were warm and inviting, making everyone feel immediately at ease. The mantle's pale ivory marble and warm mahogany were carved with knotwork intertwined amongst the four elemental symbols. It wasn't nearly as intricate as the woodwork at the Ó Faoláin manor, but it was undoubtedly beautiful.

Keegan lightly ran her fingers across the various textures—satiny pillows, fuzzy throw blankets, beaded fringe on a lampshade—just the right combination to create a cozy atmosphere.

The room was not ostentatious, but there was an undeniable richness to the furnishings.

"This room is lovely," she said, "but we'd better check the kitchen. Mom will not be happy if it's not up to par." She went through another doorway and entered a vast kitchen decorated in shades of blue, from dark and smoky to a light, creamy hue. There was a mosaic behind the counters featuring a variety of birds, tiny hummingbirds sipping nectar from flowers, hawks circling overhead against an azure sky, and songbirds perched on the flowering branches of a tree.

Áine flew into the room and landed in the middle of a large kitchen table, turning in a full circle to take in the entire view. "Hmm. I suppose this will do. It is exquisitely decorated, so that's a plus."

Cara plopped down in one of the chairs around the kitchen table and said, "This place is awesome." Niamh just wandered around the kitchen, lightly touching things, her face exuding happiness. "So far, I think it's perfect," she said quietly.

Suddenly, there was a loud knock on the front door. Everyone looked around, startled and surprised someone would call on them when they hadn't even decided they were moving in.

"Maybe it's the current owner's representative. We don't really have realtors here, but the family who owns the house moved to another settlement, so they have someone here to help with the transaction," Niamh reasoned, returning to the front doors as she spoke.

She opened the door and was surprised to see her sister, wearing a particularly nasty expression, tapping her foot on the front porch. "Étaín, what in the world are you doing here?" Niamh asked, genuinely perplexed.

Étaín pushed past her into the foyer, saying, "I think it's time we got a few things straight since you're obviously serious about staying on the homeworld." Niamh followed, closing the doors behind her with a sigh and stopping opposite her younger sister. Keegan, Cara, and Áine watched shamelessly from the doorway to the sitting room.

"Alright, Étaín, speak your mind since it's obviously important to you," Niamh began, resigning herself to a dose of the drama that always surrounded her sister. Étaín leaned in and hissed, "I just want you to know I know why you're back, and it won't work. You've always been jealous of my relationship with Cass, but he loves me, not you! You think you'll be able to lure him away from me just because you show up here. But it won't work, so you might as well give up now." She had worked herself into a frightful state, her face flushed and her breathing erratic.

Niamh pinched the bridge of her nose, took a deep breath, and said placatingly, "Fine. You've given me a piece of your mind. Don't worry; I won't chase Cass. Your marriage is certainly safe from me." Then she held still, hoping her sister would accept that and move on.

But her words only served to enrage Étaín more. "Don't condescend to me, you hoor! I will fight to protect my family!" She was clenching her fists and shaking.

Cara had had enough. She quickly took the hoops out of her ears and said, "Áine, hold these for me." The phoenix, who was settled on Keegan's shoulders, stuck her feet out, one at a time, letting Cara slip the earrings on the bird like a couple of ankle bracelets. "My pleasure, Love," Áine replied. "Looks like it's time for an ass whoopin'!" She launched herself into the air, flying figure eights above all their heads.

Keegan and Cara entered the foyer—Keegan with fire dancing around her arms like her very own living jewelry and Cara with mini-tornadoes encircling her wrists, ready to be loosed if needed.

Niamh turned toward the girls and said, "Stand down, a chailíní. We will not mar our new home with violence, even if it is deserved. Especially not against family, such as it is." Then she turned back to her sister and said, "Sometimes the depth of your stupidity amazes me. We used to be so close, Étaín; this truly breaks my heart. You want to know what happened all those years ago? I tried to tell you then, and you refused to believe me. Your precious Cass tried to rape me. I don't fucking care what he told you; he's a lying bag of donkey shit. He became obsessed with me, and from what I can tell, he still is. Believe me or not, I really could not care less. But you will kindly take your dramatic, idiot-worshiping arse off my property. Now!"

Étaín's eyes were wide as saucers by this point, and she tried to stammer a reply, but Niamh was over it. "I said now, and I meant it. Perhaps someday we can remember how to be civil to one another, but that day is not today. Off with you, now!" She pointed forcefully toward the doors, and her sister finally stomped to the exit, opening the door. Just before she left, Niamh twisted the knife with a final revelation.

"Oh, and one last thing. I'm entitled to half of our parents' estate. I don't care about the house; you can keep that. But I will be taking my half of whatever the estate was worth when I left. Immediately." The color drained from Étaín's face, and she looked dangerously close to passing out. However, Niamh was beyond caring and said, "Now leave. If you're going to pass out, kindly do it somewhere else." And she shut the door in her sister's face.

Once it was closed, she leaned against it, taking deep breaths, unable to stop the tears from finally spilling over and running down her cheeks. She looked at the two girls and gestured them over to her. They came together in a group hug, supporting Niamh as she released the pain and stress of the altercation with her sister. Áine landed with one foot on each of the young Fae's shoulders and enveloped the three of them with her wings.

After a few minutes, they dried their eyes, and Niamh said,

"Enough of that. She's a problem for another day. Shall we take a look at the rest of our new house?" Keegan and Cara nodded enthusiastically, but Áine just launched herself up the stairs and called out, "I get first choice of rooms!" The rest laughed and followed her upstairs, ready to begin their new life in their new home.

# Family

## is life

"Hola, chicas!" echoed across the room as Niamh and her girls opened the door of the Fae salon, Fae Glam. They looked at each other questioningly, unaccustomed to hearing Spanish in Tír na nÓg.

"Hi, everyone! That's Ramona; she specializes in wild and edgy looks," a short Fae with long auburn hair said. "I'm Mikey, and I love Film Noir and Art Deco looks. I'm also very precise, so I handle those types of styles. Beckie is our resident color expert; she's a miracle worker with vivid hues. Franchesca is also fabulous with color, especially blondes, so it's a really good hair day if they team up. Carly and Kelsey do an amazing job with holistic makeovers; they're good at just about everything. And Dana manages to make every Fae she helps feel absolutely fabulous, especially those with curly hair. She's crazy good at taming the wildest of waves. Madi is the smiling Fae at the front desk who keeps us all on task and helps wherever she's needed. So, if someone can tell me what you all had in mind, we will get started."

Niamh stepped over to chat with Mikey and explain what they had decided for their costumes. Keegan and Cara were flipping through a book of photos on the coffee table in the entry area, their eyes widening with each turn of a page. "Wow," Keegan said. "This place is a bit different than a salon on Earth, huh?"

Cara giggled and said, "Yes and no. This place can create an entire look—hair, makeup, nails, clothing—and they use whatever tool works best, blending the magical and the mundane. But one thing that feels the same is the atmosphere. Walking in here felt just as relaxing as walking into our favorite salon on Earth."

Keegan thought about that and said, "Yeah, I guess that's universal. I do love that feeling."

"Me, too. Another thing I think is really cool is their use of glamours. They can assemble an entire look, stuff it into a tiny artifact, and voilà—you can activate it whenever you want. That is especially handy for events like the Samhain Ball since we have to switch from our Earth costumes to our Fae costumes at midnight. Gotta keep up that spooky reputation back on Earth, so once the costumes switch over, a bunch of Fae cross over to Earth and wreak a little havoc until dawn."

Keegan just shook her head and said, "It may take me a while to get used to just how extra this place is. But I'm not complaining." Cara looked over to where Áine was perched on the edge of the reception desk, pointedly not looking at Keegan. "Speaking of complaining, how long do you think she'll pout?"

Keegan looked over at her familiar and said, "Not much longer. I'm about to go bribe her." She approached the desk, and Cara quickly followed, saying, "I'm not about to miss this."

When they reached the phoenix, she turned away from them, still obviously upset. "Okay, Áine, how about this? If you forego your preferred Earth costume of a gangsta rapper and agree to help me with my pirate costume, I will ensure you have as much bling as you want for your Fae costume of, what was it again?"

"Macha Mong Ruad, she is the only queen on the list of High

Kings of Ireland, and she was a supreme badass!" Áine replied excitedly, momentarily forgetting she was mad.

"Okay then, Queen Macha it is," Keegan agreed. "We will gaudy you up until even these over-the-top Fae can't take it!" That made Áine positively beam with happiness.

"Cailíní, we're ready to get started. Keegan, Ramona will be working with you." The curvy, vivacious Fire Fae called out, "Come here, mija, and let me look at you." Keegan walked back to Ramona's station, which was decorated with brightly colored flowers and positive affirmations. The stylist, who was rocking a short dark pixie cut with dark red streaks throughout, looked her over with a critical eye and finally said, "Niamh filled me in on your costume choices. We are gonna make you a showstopper! Have a seat." Keegan sat down and let the effusive Fae fawn over her, content to let her create her masterpiece. Ramona began holding up different swatches of fabric, pulling Keegan's hair up into different arrangements, and trying different shades of makeup, all while chattering away in a combination of Spanish and English that was surprisingly soothing.

Keegan was enjoying herself immensely, but something was bothering her. "So, Ramona, can I ask about your background? I was a little surprised to hear Spanish on the homeworld."

"Oh, that," the stylist replied. "My papi was a Fae, but Mama was Latina. I spent most of my childhood with her on Earth. I was a hairstylist there for a couple of years, but then Mama died, so I decided to learn more about the homeworld. Once I got here and discovered how much more I could do in a salon like this, there was really no going back."

"That's kind of the same story as my friend, Cara," Keegan replied, pointing to her friend at the station across from them, where Beckie, a Water Fae, was busy changing Cara's hair to different shades of pink. Once they found the shade they wanted, she worked on pulling it all into an updo, which was no small feat given the sheer volume of hair she had to work with.

"She's a half-breed, too, huh? You tell her she should stop by if she ever needs someone to talk to. It's not always easy being one of us." Keegan nodded and continued looking around the salon.

Mikey had begun to turn Niamh into a starlet from the silver screen. Dramatic makeup and loose waves were just the beginning of this transformation. Niamh, always a massive fan of old Earth movies, looked like she was having the time of her life.

Just then, Dana walked past with Áine on a portable perch, stopping when she reached a brightly lit station on the other side of Beckie's. Áine, who was giving Dana her ideas for her Queen Macha costume, suddenly stopped when she noticed a small sticker on the mirror at Beckie's station. "Chin up, tits out! That's my favorite saying. You go, girlfriend!" she commented excitedly.

Beckie laughed and said, "A female after my own heart. You take good care of that one, Dana!"

"Happily," Dana replied. "Now you were saying about the jewelry..." Áine dove back into her thoughts about the bling required to make her costume truly stunning.

The front door chimed as it opened, and Siobhán and Croía entered the salon. "I hope you all don't mind if we join the party?" the Ó Faoláin matriarch asked. Being careful not to move her head and mess up Mikey's work, Niamh smiled and said, "Please, we'd love for you to join us."

Keegan had stiffened slightly at their entrance, but Ramona noticed and said, "Ah, chica, I don't know what that tension is about, but I promise you, she's one of the good ones." Keegan consciously relaxed and replied, "I know she is. It's her son that's the asshole."

Ramona barked a laugh and said, "Most males are at one point or another. I tried a few of them for a while, then I took a wife instead." She shrugged and went back to work.

Carly took Croía to her station and began working on her costume. Siobhán and Kelsey made their way to the station next to Keegan, where Francesca joined them. "Good morning, Keegan," Siobhán said. "How are you enjoying Ramona's talents?"

Keegan smiled and said, "She's awesome. I feel like I've known her my whole life." Ramona said, "Aww, thank you, mija. You're my kind of people."

Siobhán smiled and replied, "I understand. It's one of the reasons I love coming here. All the stylists are amazing and incredibly talented. And it just feels like coming home." Keegan nodded in agreement. Then they fell into the kind of easy silence that comes from being among trusted family and friends.

As everyone worked with the stylists on their costumes, the stress and tension they had all been experiencing recently began to slowly ebb away. There was a lot of laughter and a bit of child-like wonder as the extent of the stylists' talents quickly became apparent.

After a while, Siobhán said, "Keegan, I wanted to talk to you about something. Would that be alright?" Keegan replied, "Sure."

Siobhán paused a moment, then said, "I wanted to talk to you about Calder." Keegan immediately tensed up again, but Siobhán quickly continued, "Now hear me out, please. I'm well aware of exactly how idiotic his response was. But there's a reason, Keegan. My youngest has always had the biggest heart. And he has given that heart to you, regardless of what nonsense came out of his mouth."

Keegan couldn't hold back any longer. "I'm sorry, Siobhán,

but I really don't know how you can think that. He made it incredibly obvious that he does not return my feelings."

"Oh, my dear, it's because of what he said that I know he, in fact, does return your feelings. When Deirdre explained the prophecy, the danger became very real for him. He panicked and thought he could keep you safe if he broke things off. He's used to looking out for others. He's always been a protector, and those instincts just went into overdrive, I'm afraid."

Keegan gave her a skeptical look and replied, "I wish I could believe that, but I'm just not sure I can afford to."

Siobhán said, "I understand, Love, I really do. All I ask is that you think about it. Keep an open mind. Give him a chance to make amends."

Keegan thought about the request for a few moments. "I suppose I can consider it. But I make no promises."

Siobhán nodded and said, "Fair enough. I also want you to know that no matter what happens with my son, you will always have the support of the Ó Faoláin family. I've come to think of you as part of my kin. And, as I'm sure you've heard, family is life." Keegan's eyes welled up at that, and she blinked back tears as she nodded gratefully.

Siobhán gave her a brilliant smile and said, "Now, let's get back to enjoying ourselves. I've been looking forward to this for weeks."

Family

is life

# THIRTY-TWO

onor led the brothers, Colin, and Lir, through the door of the Fae Glam salon. "Dana, we're here! Call in the cavalry!" he said as they piled inside. Lir shifted to his goat form since they were going inside, and he was so excited his feet were tippy tapping. Samhain was his favorite festival, and he couldn't wait!

Dana walked over to them from the reception desk, her brown curls bouncing as she went. "Fáilte, a Lads. Has everyone decided on their costumes?" Everyone nodded, and she continued, "Fabulous. Conor, you can fill me in, and we'll get everyone assigned."

Conor followed her to the reception desk, where they chatted with Madi and decided who would do what. Calder crouched down so he was eye-level with Lir, stoking the silky hair behind his ears, and said, "How are you doing, buddy? Feeling good about your costume?"

Lir nodded, a few more tippy taps sneaking out. Calder laughed and said, "I'm glad you're having fun." He stood up just as Dana walked back over. She said, "Conor is already heading to Mikey's station. Franchesca will help her turn him even blonder.

Colin, the tiny cailín with the curly auburn hair, is Carly. She's an outstanding choice to bring out your inner flower child." Carly smiled and held up two fingers in a peace sign.

"Reilly, you'll go to Kelsey's station. If anyone can turn you into our friendly neighborhood superhero, it would be her." Kelsey, a cute, curvy girl with blonde hair and a killer smile, waved and said, "I'm so excited; let's get started!"

"Liam, you'll be with me. Can I assume that, based on your costume choice, we should start with shades of purple fabric?" Liam smiled and replied, "Yes, that would be a good guess."

"Excellent. Now then, that leaves Calder with Beckie to work her magic on him for both costumes. It'll be a challenge..." A Water Fae with a short blonde bob, Beckie grinned and chimed in with, "Or just another Tuesday." Calder chuckled and said, "Sounds like I'm in good hands."

"Perfect. That leaves Lir with Ramona. I know she's excited to work with you, Love." Ramona practically shouted, "Papi! It's been too long! Get over here, chico, and let me look at you." Lir gave a happy little goat bleat and trotted over to his favorite stylist. The dark-haired Fire Fae leaned over and repeatedly ran her long, sharp nails across his back, giving him a thorough scratching. He sighed in contentment and leaned into her, urging her to continue. She happily complied, lavishing attention on him.

Once she finally stopped scratching, she said, "Alright, are you ready for us to turn you into a monster?" His little feet started tippy-tapping yet again, and he said, "Yes! I can't wait!"

Over at Beckie's station, Calder was trying out life as a blonde. She had applied a glamour to change his hair length and color, and now they were narrowing down the right shade and style for both of his costume choices.

Conor was well on his way to proving blondes really do have more fun. Although his costume was going in a decidedly different direction than Calder's, Conor had always marched to the beat of his own, somewhat flamboyant, drum.

Liam was sitting at Dana's station, grinning like an idiot, covered from the neck down in what seemed like a hundred different shades of purple, each a different texture, from the finest silk to crisp linen. Dana was currently working his wavy dark hair into tighter curls and arranging them just so.

Colin had already had his hair lengthened by Carly, and she was currently tying a colorful headband around his long locks. They had already painted a peace sign on his cheek, and it appeared his wardrobe would be tackled next, based on the variety of vintage 1960s clothing scattered around her station.

Suddenly, something white and stringy flew past Conor's face, narrowly missing his eye. "What the feck was that?" he exclaimed, looking around for the culprit.

"Sorry," Reilly and Kelsey said in unison. "We're still working out the kinks," Kelsey continued. Reilly added, "I can't believe you can make fully functioning gloves like that. This is going to be fan-fecking-tastic! You're amazing!" Kelsey said, "You're welcome, Love. Now sit still and let me adjust them so we don't take out anyone's eye."

"Thank you!" Conor, Mikey, and Francesca said in unison, which made everyone laugh. Liam added dryly, "It appears that weird speaking in unison twin thing has now spread to the public. Looks like nobody is safe." That elicited another laugh, which slowly died down to a comfortable silence.

Calder decided now was an appropriate time to ask for some help with his current predicament. "Alright, everyone, I have a favor to ask." He paused to gather his thoughts, then continued, "I made a right mess of my relationship with Keegan. I know I was stupid, and I'm working on a few ways to make it up to her and hopefully get her to talk to me. Hell, I'd settle for her staying in the same room as me right now."

"All things in good time, grasshopper," Conor interjected. Everyone just stared at him, the reference flying well over their heads. Conor sighed and said, "Sorry, old Earth show. But my point is, I've had the most experience with relationships..."

"One-night stands do not count, ya himbo," Reilly said. "You are hardly the Fae to be giving him advice on his love life."

Liam spoke up then, saying, "Maybe we should ask na cailíní? I'm sure they know more about this kind of thing than the lot of us. Or you could take advice from your gay brother, whose longest relationship lasted, what was it, five weeks?"

Conor scowled at him and said, "Six. Arse." Liam just gave him a huge grin.

"When you put it like that, cailíní it is. So, ladies, what do you say? Will you help a poor, inept Fae out?" Calder asked.

"Wait a minute, mijo," Ramona said. "Something makes more sense now, I think. When we were working with Keegan's group yesterday, Áine kept mumbling something about somebody being slow and wanting to burn his nipples off. I take it that was you?" Calder winced and nodded, "I'm afraid so." Ramona laughed and said, "Oh, papi, you have got your work cut out for you! Even if you manage to win back Keegan, you'll have to do something seriously spectacular to get back into Áine's good graces."

Calder grinned and said, "But at least I know how to begin with Áine. Lir overheard her talking about wanting to be Queen Macha, so I took a little walk and gathered a few things she might like. Who is working on her costume?"

Dana paused from working on Liam's costume and said, "That'd be me." Calder turned to Beckie and asked, "Can we pause for a moment?" She nodded and said, "Sure." Then he hopped up, walked over to Dana, pulled out a small, lumpy velvet bag, and opened it, letting her take a peek inside. Her eyes widened, and she broke into a big grin, saying, "Those will be spectacular, Lad. I know just what to do with them. And I've been working on a resizing enchantment; I think that will be perfect for this situation, too. She is going to be speechless, and with Áine, that's an accomplishment."

Mikey took that moment to ask a clarifying question, "So, exactly how did you piss off Keegan in the first place? That might help us know what kind of advice would be best."

Calder explained how he was trying to protect her by breaking things off, but he did it in such a way that she took it as a rejection. "Well, yeah. She took it as a rejection because it was. Did you not consider that she's a Fire Fae and, from what I gathered yesterday, more than a little powerful? I'm quite sure she can take care of herself very well. Why is it that males always assume we're helpless? It's just condescending," Mikey continued, serving up some unvarnished truth.

Calder started to try and explain himself, but thought better of it, took a deep breath, and said, "You're right. I made a right mess of things. But I'm sorry and would really appreciate your help. I'm making a bit of an overture with my Earth costume choice, but I could really use some more ideas."

Beckie chimed in with, "It's pretty simple, in my opinion. You fucked up, and you need to own that. Tell her you're an eejit, say you're sorry, and beg for forgiveness."

Kelsey added, "An apology goes a long way, but then you need to ensure you don't do it again. If you're protective of her, it might be easy to try to save her from danger again."

"But that has to be her choice. If she needs help, I'm pretty sure she'll ask for it. Otherwise, it's just trying to control her, whether you intend it that way or not. I can tell you're a protector and that you want to keep her safe. But, Love, she needs someone who will stand beside her, not in front of her," Mikey said.

Calder absorbed everything they were saying, stunned that

he hadn't considered it from that perspective before. *I've got a lot more work to do on myself than I thought.*

"Also, don't forget to bring her a gift. It's not the most important part, but it can soothe hurt feelings. But it would need to be thoughtful; I don't think she's the kind of cailín who just wants shiny bits," Carly added her opinion.

"Oh, that's a good point. It needs to be heartfelt. And if you could make her something, that would be even better," Dana said.

Ramona had been uncharacteristically quiet throughout the exchange. Calder turned to her and said, "And your thoughts?" She narrowed her eyes at him and said, with a fair amount of intensity, "Whatever you do, mijo, bring the passion inside and outside the bedroom. Fire Fae, especially, are a very passionate group. Make her toes curl until she screams your name. But show her the same level of intensity when you're doing the dishes together or going for a walk. Just be present in the moment. Always. Otherwise, no matter how much she might love you, she will eventually get bored. Don't do that to her. Make the effort, papi. You won't regret it."

Calder looked thoughtful for a moment, then he said, "Thank you, everyone. Your help means a great deal to me. Now let's see if I can fan that little ember into a wildfire."

Family

is life

# THIRTY-THREE

Keegan stood in front of the full-length mirror in her room and played with the dark red ringlets framing her face. The majority of her hair was tied back with a red cloth, showing off the big gold hoops in her ears. A white ruffled, very low-cut blouse was also tied off with a red cloth belt, and everything was lightly covered in sparkles. *Not sure why a pirate would wear sparkly clothes, but this is Aos Sí we're talking about.* There was even a sheath for her cutlass. It was actually sharp, too, which made her a little nervous. *I don't know what the point of that was,* she thought, *but oh well. I'll just have to make sure not to cut anything off.*

She also wore tight black leggings and thigh-high black boots that were so shiny she could see her reflection. Just then, Áine flew into her room and looked her over with a critical eye. "What do you think?" Keegan asked, holding her arms out to her sides for inspection. "Hmm," the phoenix replied. "It looks good, but you're missing something? Oh, right...me!"

She swooped around the room several times, then did a barrel roll while transforming to her parrot form, ending with a gentle landing on Keegan's shoulder. Watching from the doorway to their shared balcony, Cara gave a round of applause and said, "Lovely aerial work, Áine. And you absolutely make Keegan's costume. You are definitely the centerpiece." Áine positively preened under that praise.

"Talk about centerpieces; look at you, Miss Thang!" Keegan said to Cara, who responded by holding her arms out and twirling around. She was dressed in a skimpy purple trapeze artist costume with her bright pink hair in an updo. "I love *The Greatest Showman*! And Anne Wheeler was my favorite character. You look so good!"

"Thank you, Love, so do you!" Cara replied. "Can you imagine if we had that salon back on Earth? The Halloween costume contests we could've dominated? That would've been badass!"

A knock sounded at the front doors, and Áine shouted, "I got it!" and flew down the stairs. "What's she gonna do?" Keegan said. "She doesn't have hands." She and Cara followed at a more sedate pace.

Áine hovered in front of the peephole, shouting, "Who is it?" Keegan quickly moved to open the door, mumbling, "Oh, for fuck's sake." On the front porch were Colin and Croía with the river table she had been working on with Calder. Except it appeared as though it was now finished.

Keegan tried to be indifferent to the table, but it was so damn gorgeous she couldn't help but kneel down next to it and run her fingers gently along the top. "This is amazing," she whispered, awed by the intricacy of details, even though she had already seen it in an earlier form.

Calder had outdone himself with the intricacy of the details. She had been impressed before but was utterly amazed at the final product. She could count the scales on the fish swimming around the coral reef. And the sea grass and other flora seemed to sway in the water. It was simply stunning.

She opened both doors, and Cara lifted the table with her air power and floated it upstairs to Keegan's room.

Then Keegan noticed the costumes the two Earth Fae were wearing, and she said, "Look at you two! Croía, you make a gorgeous Wonder Woman! And Colin, you might be the cutest little flower child I've ever seen!" They grinned ear to ear, and Colin gave her his best peace sign.

Croía then remembered she was supposed to deliver a message. "Calder said to tell you that he hopes you will accept this gift as a token of his admiration. No strings attached."

Keegan gave her a small smile and said, "Please tell him thank you, Croía. I love it."

The Earth Fae nodded, and Croía replied, "We'll tell him. See you at the ball!"

Laoise was perched on her dog bed at the foot of Máire's bed, watching her Fire Fae finish getting ready for the ball. She was currently pulling her strawberry blonde hair up into two pigtails high on the sides of her head. She cast the glamour she'd gotten from Fae Glam and watched it transform her. On one side, the tips of her hair, eye shadow, and tiny shorts all turned red. On the other side, everything was blue. Her torn t-shirt read "Daddy's Lil Monster," and she wore fishnets, a studded belt, multiple tattoos, and high-heeled boots. There was a baseball bat with the words "Good Night" written down the side to complete the ensemble.

"This is amazing," she whispered, smiling at how well her costume had turned out. Laoise held out hope that perhaps Máire could start down a new path tonight.

Suddenly, she let out a pain-filled yelp and gripped the sides of her head, squeezing her eyes shut against the agony. A tritone voice exploded through her mind, saying, "Your favor is being called in, little one. Tonight, when the time is right, you must act. I will let you know when to proceed. In order to set the proper events into motion, here is what you must do." The voice went on to explain exactly what had to happen. Then just as suddenly as it came, it was gone, along with the pain.

Laoise hopped down from her fluffy pink bed and went over to Máire. The familiar yipped at her girl and was picked up and set in Máire's lap. "What did it say, a stór? And don't lie to me. I can't help you if I don't know what's happening."

Máire looked at the pup and said, "They just gave me some information that might make all the difference." Her mind was racing with the possibilities of what she had just learned.

Laoise put her little paws on Máire's cheeks, forcing her to focus. "Who is it? What do they want? This could be so dangerous!"

Máire gave her a few pets and said, "I'm not sure who they are, but the information they've given me could be very helpful."

Laoise slapped her lightly on the cheek, "Promise me you'll be careful! Please!"

Máire looked her in the eyes and said, "I promise, Love. But I am going to see where this information takes me."

She put Laoise back in her dog bed, picked up the baseball bat, rested it against her shoulder, and took one last look in the mirror. Then she leaned in and put two fingers against her lips, pulling them down to smudge the bright red lipstick in the corner of her mouth. She gave herself one last smile and left for the ball.

The gorgeous golden light of the magic hour was just beginning as Keegan, Cara, and Áine approached the outskirts of the World Tree Gardens. Faery lights, the actual magical kind, floated through the air, lending an ethereal element to the landscape.

While the Samhain Ball is held during harvest time, with bales of hay, pumpkins, and various other gourds used as traditional autumn decorations, Aos Sí were anything but minimalistic. In addition to the autumn decorations, there was also a profusion of flowers, flowering vines, and trees in every imaginable color, adding their beauty to the environment. A multitude of Earth Fae had spent the afternoon calling forth the various types of flora, color-coordinating each different area of the gardens.

Benches had been grown from tree limbs, bushes, and vines, with flowers and grasses covered in broad leaves creating comfortable, cushiony seats. The designers of the garden decorations had also chosen to create little secluded nooks to provide the attendees with areas of privacy throughout.

The other three clans had also added to the festive atmosphere. Multiple water features were located throughout the gardens, where the water moved against gravity, dipping and weaving, creating spectacular works of art. The Fire Clan had created lights and torches in intricate designs that continually morphed and changed, throwing mesmerizing shadows which contrasted with the last of the sunlight. In addition to the gentle breeze that kept the Fire Clan's faery lights in motion, the Air Clan had also created sections of the gardens where flowers and vines were propelled through the air in beautiful aerial maneuvers. The small songbirds greatly favored these areas, providing an entertaining visual spectacle. It was entrancing to watch them dive and soar, swooping around on the air currents, obviously enjoying themselves.

Even Áine seemed to enjoy watching the antics of the brightly colored little birds. "I suppose they are kinda cute," she admitted begrudgingly. "Much better than those goofy little butterflies. They just had no style at all." Keegan just shook her head and ignored the familiar's grousing.

A silver tray covered in hors d'oeuvres floated slowly past the group. "Oh, snacks!" Áine exclaimed. "Wait!" she called out to the tray, which obligingly paused for her to select something. She launched herself off of Keegan's shoulder and hovered over the floating tray. She looked over the choices critically. "Hmm, what are these little balls?" she asked Keegan, who replied, with an admirably straight face, "Well, they look a little like those ice cream dots."

Áine's little parrot face lit up, and she said, "I love those! Let me have some of that." Keegan took a cracker from the tray and scooped up a big glop of caviar. Áine quickly began chomping on it, but she was only a couple of chews in when her eyes bugged out, and she spit the roe out, sputtering and saying, "What the actual fuck is that! You're trying to kill me!"

Keegan and Cara looked at each other and completely lost it, cackling until tears streamed down their cheeks. Áine continued coughing and choking, never one to let a perfectly good opportunity to make a scene go to waste. Finally, Keegan said, "Alright, drama queen, I'm sorry. But damn, that was funny!"

"I can't believe you did that. A cut-and-dried case of attempted murder if I've ever seen one!" Áine continued complaining. "Oh, give me a break; you eat live crickets! A few fish eggs shouldn't bother you at all," Keegan said, putting her hands on her hips for emphasis.

The feud was saved from escalation by the arrival of Marilyn Monroe, wearing the trademark white, deep V halter dress, accompanied by a ripped Spiderman, and the artist formerly known as Prince, complete with the white frilly shirt, purple studded jacket, dark curly hair, and a left-handed guitar. Or, as they were also known, Conor, Reilly, and Liam.

Keegan just stared, looking from one to the other, left totally speechless by both the subject matter of the costumes as well as the level of artistry apparent in their execution. Cara summed it up with, "Just wow."

Conor was more than happy to accept the barest hint of a compliment. "Thank you. I'm rather proud of this one." Liam snorted and said, "I don't know why. The stylists at Fae Glam did all the work."

"Maybe so, but I still have to sell it," Conor replied, adjusting his rather voluptuous breasts and pursing his lips for emphasis.

Keegan looked at him with a wry grin and said, "Uh-huh. You look fabulous, Darling, but I'd really love to know the story behind Mr. Purple Rain over here." She nodded toward Liam, waiting to hear the story behind his costume choice.

"It's not that strange. He was the most talented musician of his century, easily. And I really like purple," he replied with a shrug.

"Me, too," Cara replied, giving a little curtsy to show off her purple costume. Conor seemed to notice her costume for the first time. He barked out a laugh and said, "Reilly! You chose the wrong Zendaya boyfriend!"

Cara gave Reilly a shy smile, then looked at Conor and said, "No, I don't think he did." Then she lifted her arms and let her air power lift her into the air, spinning as she went. She began duplicating some of the aerial feats showcased in *The Greatest Showman*, but without the ropes. She twirled, flipped, and spun through the air, her face beaming as she was finally able to show off her powers without fear of exposure. Her grace and beauty were breathtaking as she went gliding through the air.

Reilly had pulled his mask up to see her better. He took it completely off and tucked it into a hidden pocket. Cara swooped down near Reilly and beckoned to him with one finger, a playful grin on her face. He launched a web from his fully functional web-shooting gloves. It wrapped around a tree limb, and he ran and jumped into the air, shooting webs at different branches to alter his course as needed. Cara immediately surrounded him with her air power, letting him guide his movements but supporting his weight to make things easier. He seemed to be floating around Cara as she performed her routine, taking care not to get in her way, just emphasizing the elegance of her movements. Multiple times, they came swirling toward each other, only to spin away at the last second, fingertips grazing but never fully touching the other. Both of their faces were alight with the joy of the moment as they teased and flirted with each other in full view of anyone who might look up.

Áine, her earlier irritation forgotten, fluttered to Keegan's shoulder and whispered, "Well, isn't this interesting?" Keegan shushed her, gave a little wave to the other two retreating Ó Faoláin brothers, and quietly wandered off, giving the air-dancing Fae a bit of privacy.

Keegan spent a few moments just wandering, taking in all the sights and sounds of this lush, extravagant ball. Áine flew slightly above everyone, loudly calling out any Fae whose costume she found lacking. Keegan grinned at her familiar; life was never dull with Áine around.

As she looked around, she was again amazed at the level of intricacy and sheer awesomeness apparent in all the Fae costumes. She saw Earth movie stars, fictional characters, and rock idols. A little ahead of her, she saw the back of someone in a gorgeous J Lo costume. When the faux J Lo turned toward her, she was stunned to see it was Siobhán! *Ho-Ly Shit!* she thought, taking in the famous green dress with the severely plunging neckline. *Calder's mom is a hottie!*

Out of the corner of her eye, she saw Áine flying back to her, somewhat faster than usual. The parrot pulled up at the last moment and landed gently on Keegan's shoulder. "Incoming, ten o'clock," she said.

Keegan turned her head slightly to the left and saw some-thing she never would've expected—an amazingly detailed Thor, complete with bulging muscles, long flowing blond hair, and a big ass hammer. The only thing that separated this Thor from the one on the big screen was that this one came with Calder's face. Incredibly, that was not the biggest surprise. Next to Calder/Thor was a seven-foot-tall gooey black monster with multitudes of humungous spiky teeth, the character otherwise known as Venom.

"Wait, is that...?" Keegan began. Áine shrugged her little parrot wings and said, "I don't know, but I would guess so. Goat Boy turned into an actual monster. That's absolutely fabulous!" She launched herself into the air and quickly made her way over to hover in front of the Venom costume, pointedly turning her back on Calder, just in case he had any doubt about her current feelings toward him.

She got very close to the Venom costume's face and said, "Goat Boy, are you in there?" Venom gave her a big, sloppy lick all over her face with his enormously long tongue, then the costume's head split down the middle and rolled back to show Lir's little goat head inside, grinning like an idiot. "Yep, it's me. Isn't this costume great?" he asked excitedly.

Áine shook her head and wiped her face against her wing to try and dry it off. "Blech! Yes, the costume is great, but I could do with a little less slobber next time."

Lir nodded, then the Venom head closed back up. Áine settled on his shoulder and looked back at Keegan, who had turned into a small nook with a little more privacy. Calder was making a beeline for her, so the familiar said, "Come on, let's go make fun of the other costumes. I can't believe how many people have access to these amazing costumes, and they do something dumb. I saw a lightbulb earlier. What the hell? Why would you waste all the talent at Fae Glam on a damn lightbulb costume?"

Áine continued chattering in Lir's ear as he wandered into the crowd.

Keegan waited for Calder in one of the little garden nooks, her back to the entrance, unsure of how she felt. She took a few deep breaths and tried to calm her nerves. She heard leaves rustling as he stepped into the nook, but she wasn't ready to turn around yet.

He just stood there quietly, waiting for her. When she was as calm as she was going to get, she finally turned around. He was looking at her with such a gentle expression on his face, and it just fucking infuriated her.

"How dare you!" she hissed at him. "How dare you stand there looking at me like that when just a few weeks ago you ripped my heart out and stomped on it for good measure!" Her chest rose and fell rapidly as her anger was finally released.

Calder waited a moment, then opened his mouth to speak, but Keegan said, "I'm not finished, Mud Boy! Do you know what it took for me to trust you? To open up to you? How could you just betray all of that in one fell swoop?" She had her hands on her hips, and there was actual smoke wafting from her as her temper made her control a little shaky.

Calder looked at her carefully, unsure if he was supposed to answer any of her questions or not. Finally, Keegan said, "Well? Are you going to answer me?" He just shook his head and stepped closer to her, hands held slightly extended out to the sides. "Listen, I intend to apologize soundly, pay whatever form of penance you might enjoy, and spend a great deal of time making up for my stupidity. If you would just take a seat, I will start doing all three of those things."

That mollified her slightly, enough for her to sit on the garden bench. Calder knelt down in front of her and said, "Keegan, I am so, so sorry. All I can say is that in my thick skull, I thought I was protecting you. The idea of you being in danger terrifies me. But I should have trusted you more. You are incredibly powerful in your own right, and I should have offered to stand with you against our enemies, not tried to scare you away in the misguided hope I could save you from pain."

Keegan relaxed a bit more at his words, laying her hands in her lap. He may have acted like an idiot, but he seemed genuinely sorry for the pain he caused her. Calder slowly moved his hand toward hers, giving her ample time to object. When she didn't, he covered her hand with his and gave a gentle squeeze.

She looked intently at him and said, "You still have a long way to go to get back in my good graces, you know." He nodded and said, "I know, hAibhleog, I know. I'm sure it won't be the last time I have to make something up to you. But I promise I will try to trust you more. I know you're brilliant and strong, and I will stand with you whenever you need me."

Keegan nodded and said, "That's a good start. I'll think about what else you can do." Calder started to chuckle, but the look in her eye said she wasn't kidding. He swallowed the laughter and said, "Alright then. Would it be okay for me to stand up?"

She replied, "Yes! I wanna see this costume anyway. You know I love me some Thor action." He stood and spun around so she could get a good look at him. "I feel a little like a piece of meat," he said, only half joking. She chuckled and wiggled her eyebrows, saying, "And a very juicy piece of meat you are!" Calder sighed and dramatically said, "The life of a piece of arm candy is rough."

Then he gave her a look and said, "By the way, Áine is setting a bad example for you. Mud Boy?" She giggled and said, "You have to admit, it's a pretty good zinger."

He rolled his eyes, then held out a hand to help her to her feet. "I'll admit no such thing," he replied primly. She stood up and took his proffered arm. "Come on, hero. Let's go see the sights and maybe get a snack." And they wandered off into the crowd.

Shay straightened the navy-blue double-breasted jacket for what felt like the hundredth time. He hadn't been this nervous in a very long time. The cailíní at the Fae Glam studio had told him this was the perfect costume to impress Niamh. He knew nothing about Earth movies, especially old movies, but apparently, Niamh was a big fan.

The rest of his costume consisted of a blue mariner's cap, a white dress shirt, white slacks, and shoes. He was supposed to look like an actor named Humphrey Bogart from the 1940s. *Ah well,* he thought, *I'd wear anything she wants me to if I get to spend time with her.*

He began pacing around one of the water features, finding the sound of the flowing water soothing. He'd sent a message to Niamh asking her to meet him there. Hopefully, she would show up.

"Ahem." The sound of someone clearing their throat made him quickly turn around. When he saw Niamh standing there in a midriff-baring black silk dress, complete with black high heels and slightly wavy hair, he had a hard time catching his breath. She was the most gorgeous thing he had ever seen. And he had missed her so damn much while she was gone.

"Good evening, Ms. Bacall; I believe it is?" he said, making at least an attempt at smoothness. She smiled and said, "And you must be Mr. Bogart?" He smiled back and said, "Indeed." Then he held out a hand, which she immediately took in her own, and said, "Shall we take a walk? I'd love to reacquaint you with the sights and sounds of your home." Her eyes welled slightly, and she replied, "I'd like that very much."

They began walking, hand in hand, just enjoying each other's company as they looked at all the sights and sounds of the Samhain Ball.

After walking for a bit, they found a floating tray of hors d'oeuvres and helped themselves to some food. They also found some wine floating nearby, and each took a glass. As they were eating and drinking, suddenly, Niamh went rigid, and her eyes widened. Shay turned toward where she was looking, and his heart fell a bit as he saw the Daugherty family strolling along the gardens, Cass and Étaín dressed as Shakespeare's Romeo and Juliet, followed by a rather annoyed-looking Máire dressed as Harley Quinn.

He moved to block her view of Cass and said, "Niamh, I promise you, I will not let him hurt you again." She focused her attention on Shay, took a couple of deep breaths, and narrowed her eyes before replying, "I appreciate that, Shay, but I'm the one who won't let him hurt me again. He took advantage of me when I was a young Fae, still grieving the loss of my parents. Now I'm the parent, and he will find out exactly how dangerous I can be if he comes after me or my family again." Shay nodded at that, then the two squared their shoulders and continued strolling along the gardens, intent on ignoring Captain Asshat.

Meanwhile, Étaín was chattering at Cass, her hands grasping his arm as she pointed out costumes she liked or food she wanted to try. Cass was tolerating her presence, but just barely. His eyes were squinting as if he were in pain and irritated beyond belief. As he was scanning the crowd, his face suddenly perked up noticeably. Étaín got even bubblier, thinking perhaps he was interested in what she was saying. But he looked beyond his wife as his former, and now current, obsession entered his field of view. Once that happened, his eyes glazed over; he shook his wife off his arm and began following Niamh and Shay, staying in sight of them but far enough away to avoid an outright confrontation.

Étaín just stood there with her mouth open in dismay until,

finally, something snapped inside her. *Fine,* she thought. *Fucking fine! He's a bloody pox bottle, and I'm better off without him!* Then she stomped off in the opposite direction, grabbing the first glass of wine she could find.

Máire was far enough behind her parents that she missed most of what had just happened. She was only with them because her mother wanted them to be together as a family when they entered the ball. *It's all a joke anyway,* she thought. *We haven't been a real family, well, ever.* She shook her head to clear her thoughts. *I need to be sharp tonight. Things are going to get wild before the night is through.*

"Oh, Darlin'," said a voice behind her. "You are a sight for sore eyes." She turned around to see Corley, shirtless with a long purple crocodile coat, multiple tattoos covering his chest and abdomen, and his green hair slicked back. He carried a purple cane, and as he smiled at her, she noticed he had a silver grill.

She rested her baseball bat against her shoulder, put a hand on her hip, and replied, "That is an outstanding costume, Devlin. Let's take a stroll." Then she led the way into the crowd. Corley wasted no time catching up to her, just happy to seemingly be making progress with her.

Under one of the nearby garden benches were Laoise and Saoirse, the chihuahua and red fox familiars, having watched the entire scene play out. The dog shook her head and said, "It's time to gather the other familiars, bonded and unbonded alike. There's going to be trouble tonight, and we may need all the help we can get." They split up to gather the others, hoping it would be enough.

Keegan and Calder were busy sampling some of the delicacies available. All of the food and drink were Earth-themed for the first part of the evening, but there were still a few things unfamiliar to the Fire Fae. Specialties from various countries were offered, and the couple enjoyed tasting the different treats. This included a variety of different cocktails and mocktails to wash it all down.

She was finally beginning to relax and have some hope that things with Calder might be salvageable. She wasn't prepared to fully believe it yet, but she was cautiously optimistic.

As they were talking and eating, suddenly, they heard a squawk and a loud "There's my girl! See, Goat Boy, I told you we'd find her!" They turned toward the sound and saw Lir, still dressed as Venom, but with the face open to show his little goat face inside, and parrot-shaped Áine perched on his shoulder, beginning to sway just slightly.

Keegan took all of this in, shook her head, and said, "Firstly, Lir, that costume is freaking amazing but also somewhat disturbing with your cute little goat head sticking out. Secondly, Áine, are you drunk? How did you even manage that in parrot form? And you know what happened last time. I thought we had an agreement about this."

Áine said, "Psshaw! As far as last time, it's not my fault that the Kansas City police don't have a sense of humor. And you had an agreement; I agreed to nothing! Besides, I'm not drunk; I'm barely tipsy. And it's Halloween! Or Samhain, I guess, since we're in Tír na nÓg now. Loosen up, sparkle tits!"

Calder nearly spewed his cocktail out of his nose at that last comment, and even Keegan couldn't hold back a smile. "Oh, for crying out loud, fine! You're such a little shit; you're gonna do what you want at any rate."

Áine just stared her in the eye, still swaying slightly, and said, "I think you mispronounced queen." Calder barked a laugh, and Keegan just rolled her eyes. Then Áine said, "Wait a minute, what is J Lo doing here? Wait! Calder, that's your mom! She's a MILF!

Well, not to me 'cause that's not how I swing, but you get my meaning." Keegan facepalmed and said, "Áine, would you please shut up!"

"Okay, but now I'm seeing Ben Affleck, too. Maybe I have had too much to drink. Oh, and there's Ariel from *The Little Mermaid!* Look how she has a little self-contained wave of water to hold her up; that's so cool! And her tail is gorgeous. Lir, take me over there so I can touch her tail. Look, there's Ula, and she's dressed like Rocket from *The Guardians of the Galaxy*." Lir replied, "Well, that makes sense; she is a raccoon, after all." Then he turned and headed over to where Morgan and Muireann Ó Loingsigh, and of course, Ula the raccoon, had just joined the party.

As they slowly followed, Calder told Keegan, "I think this is the strangest Samhain Ball I've ever attended." Keegan looked at the motley crew assembled and had to smile. "I've said it before, we may not be what polite society deems acceptable, but we are never boring." Calder reached for her hand and gave it a squeeze. "Polite society is overrated," he said.

They reached the group just as Áine was running her wing up and down a very patient Muireann's mermaid tail. "Oh, shiny," she said, fascinated by the iridescent shimmering of the scales.

"Oh, for fuck's sake," Keegan mumbled under her breath for the second time that day regarding Áine. Unfortunately, twice didn't come anywhere near the record.

"Áine, leave the poor girl alone! She doesn't want you petting her like she's a cat," Keegan said with exasperation. She looked at Ula and said, "I love that costume, by the way. Rocket is one of my favorite Marvel characters." Ula beamed and said, "Thanks!" Then Keegan turned to Calder and said, "Do the Fae have anything to sober up a drunk parrot?" He said, "Wow. There's a sentence you don't hear every day. Coffee and more food might help. He walked over to a nearby floating tray, spoke to it briefly, and watched it zip off to do his bidding.

"I sent for some coffee and donuts. That should help," he said when he returned. Lir said, "Come on, Áine, hop back up here, and we'll go wait for your coffee on that bench over there. Ula, you can come, too." Áine paused in her fondling of Muireann's tail and said, "Coffee? Is it hazelnut? I love hazelnut." Then she flew back up to Lir/Venom's shoulder and said, "Mush, Goat Boy! Coffee awaits!" Ula joined them, and they headed over to the bench where Lir had a seat, his better-than-seven-foot-tall frame occupying the vast majority of it, leaving just enough room for the raccoon. Áine perched on the back of the bench, and as she saw Siobhán approach, she proceeded to do a somewhat shaky little dance and sing, far too loudly, "Jenny from the Block."

As Siobhán arrived at the group, she paused and looked over at the intoxicated bird, then said, "Looks like Áine has a head start on this evening's festivities." Keegan grimaced and said, "Yeah, sorry about that. She can't hold her liquor." Siobhán laughed and replied, "Don't worry about it, Love. It is a party, after all."

Morgan, currently disguised as a very hot Ben Affleck, gave Calder a brief smile, then turned his attention to the lad's mother and said, "Siobhán, you look amazing tonight."

Siobhán blushed and said, "You're not looking so bad your-self, Morgan." Then she noticed the mermaid in the room and said, "And that is one amazing costume, Muireann! I love how you incorporated the water, and your tail is absolutely stunning!" The Water Fae smiled brightly and said, "Thank you, Bean Ó Faoláin, but most of the credit goes to the cailíní at the Fae Glam studio. They are amazing!"

Siobhán replied, "That they are, dear, but please, call me Siobhán." Muireann nodded and said, "Of course." Then Morgan said, "Siobhán, would you care to take a walk with me? We could look at all the costumes and maybe talk a bit? We've got some time until midnight."

Siobhán nodded, smiling shyly, and said, "I'd love to, Morgan." Then she turned to Calder and Keegan, noticed their clasped hands, and said, "Well, that's certainly good to see." To Keegan she said, "My son is a good man, but you make sure he earns your affection, Love. Keep him on his toes." Keegan grinned and replied, "Always." Then Siobhán and Morgan set off to explore the ball, eventually joining hands as they went. Muireann and Calder shared a look and a small smile at the blossoming romance between their parents, then she began to float over toward Ula, content to watch the familiars' antics for a while.

Once they were alone again, Keegan sighed deeply and said, "Damn. I thought the Fae on the homeworld were extra, but I'm beginning to think we bring the extra with us." Calder laughed and said, "I think maybe it's a bit of both." They continued their stroll, planning to enjoy the rest of their time before midnight came, and Keegan's family was formally introduced to the other Fae.

Shay and Niamh had been wandering around the gardens, trying to enjoy themselves and ignore the elephant in the room—or rather, the stalker at the ball. Cass had managed to stay within sight of the couple at all times, but he never came close enough to be construed as threatening. His presence was a promise of violence deferred. And as much as they tried to carry on with their evening, it was impossible to ignore the situation indefinitely.

Luckily, it was almost midnight, so they headed toward the World Tree at the center of the gardens. With any luck, the crowds of Fae gathering in that area for the costume change would at least discourage Cass from anything overt.

Things got increasingly crowded as they got closer to the

garden's center. Everyone wanted to be where the action was, and at midnight during the Samhain Ball, that meant the World Tree. Fae were nearly shoulder to shoulder as they waited for the big costume change, and excitement was at an all-time high.

Niamh spotted Áine off to their right, hovering over a floating tray of snacks, slurping down coffee at an alarming rate. She would occasionally stop to devour a donut, then it was back to pounding coffee. She heard her say, "Yum, hazelnut!" before she continued plowing through the food and drink. Lir was there, his Venom face pulled back, his little goat face enjoying his fair share of the donuts, and there was a raccoon holding a coffee cup and saucer, sipping the hot brew carefully, with Ariel the mermaid floating nearby on a wave of water.

Keegan and Calder were not far away, looking torn between exasperation and humor. Niamh raised a hand and waved, finally getting her daughter's attention and heading in their direction. Cara and Reilly were heading toward them from the opposite direction, and Niamh spotted Siobhán and Morgan sitting on a garden bench a fair distance away. Liam and Conor were a bit farther away, surrounded by a group of younger Fae, laughing and sharing a few pints.

Keegan returned her mom's wave but was soon distracted as someone wearing an incredible Buffy the Vampire Slayer costume walked up to the area directly in front of the World Tree. When she turned toward them, Keegan realized it was Deirdre! She couldn't help but exclaim, "Your costume rocks!" as she passed by. The High Druid turned toward her, gave her a smile and a wink, then continued to her spot in front of the tree. She turned to face the crowd, raised her hand, and, with a small flourish, released a chime that echoed throughout the gardens, signaling to the other Fae that midnight was almost upon them.

Everyone finished their conversations and turned their attention to the World Tree and Deirdre. The Druid waited a moment, then she said, "Fáilte and welcome to the Samhain Ball! I hope you've all been enjoying the festivities so far. All of the Earth costumes look magnificent, but it is almost time for the real party to begin. Our Fae costumes will be revealed as soon as midnight is upon us. As this is the first céilí of the new year, I hope all of you will participate in the opening dance. We want to see those costumes, after all! Those Fae who would like to return to Ireland for a night of mischief will be free to portal once the costume ceremony is complete. Remember, younglings, petty mischief only! Don't make me come over there!

"In addition to our traditional visits to Earth, this year, we have the reintroduction of a family into our Aos Sí society. Taoiseach Shay Ó Brien will formally welcome them home after the dance. Alright, Fae, prepare for the changeover!"

All at once, the little floating faery lights began congregating above each Fae's head, expanding in size until a golden glowing halo illuminated each of them. More and more lights kept gathering until everybody was positively beaming with the golden light. When it seemed like each halo was about to burst, Deirdre called out, "Oíche Shamhna Shona Daoibh!" A massive burst of fireworks exploded overhead, adding emphasis to her exclamation.

The crowd responded just as enthusiastically. "Oíche Shamhna Shona Daoibh!" The glowing lights above each Fae slowly descended around them, triggering the changeover to the Aos Sí costumes.

Keegan watched the transformations with more than a bit of awe. She'd known about magic her whole life, but growing up on Earth, it had to be hidden. Seeing a spectacle like this overwhelmed her with gratitude that she didn't have to hide who she was anymore.

She watched her mother and father turn into Cáer Ibormeith, a goddess of sleep and dreams, and Aengus Óg, a god of love and poetry. According to ancient history, Aengus had dreamed of his love, but when he found her, she was a captive, being held with other girls as swans. So, he turned into a swan, and they flew off together, singing a song so sweet that everyone who heard it fell asleep for three days.

Their costumes represented the couple's swan forms, with white iridescent feathers scattered throughout their hair, as well as covering their clothing, and the wings sprouting from their backs. Their eyes were outlined in glittery black to mimic the face of a swan, and their lips were colored a dark coral to represent a beak. The effect was breathtaking.

Cara was transformed into Clíodhna, a goddess of love and beauty. She wore a sparkling gown in shades of blue and green, and there were three brightly colored birds encircling her. Reilly became Ogma, a god of language and eloquence, wearing a bright red robe and a lion's pelt on his back. Whenever he opened his mouth to speak, ephemeral golden chains appeared to link his tongue to the listener's ears. His costume was completed with a large club.

Keegan then looked over at Lir and was utterly astounded. The familiar had transformed into the god Lugh, a massive warrior with curly blond hair, a green mantle, an intricately carved spear, and a large spectral dog with fur of every hue imaginable.

She turned to look at Calder standing beside her, only to find his costume had changed to that of Fionn mac Cumhaill, the ancient hero and leader of the Fianna. He wore a long forest green tunic and darker green hose, which Keegan was delighted to see left very little to the imagination. He also had a strange burn scar on his thumb and platinum blonde hair.

She giggled and said, "You are certainly working the blond vibe, aren't you?" Calder just stared back at her, mouth agape, rendered momentarily speechless by her costume.

She was dressed as Bríd, the goddess of fire, as well as spring, fertility, and life. Her dress was forest green, the same as his tunic, but with golden knotwork embroidered along the arms, hemline, and sides of the bodice. An elaborate tree of life, made of gold beads and tiny jewels, decorated the center of the bodice, with its roots woven around her waist and the branches intertwined up and around the deep V neckline. A wreath of spring flowers formed a crown atop her riotous red curls. But the real showstopper of this costume was the fire covering her from head to toe. In this case, the flames were just an illusion, but the effect was magnificent.

As she took in his expression, a sly grin spread across her face, and she put a hand on her hip, saying, "See something you like, Ó Faoláin?" He turned toward her with a look so intense she gasped. He looked ready to devour her, and the way that look heated her blood; she was ready to let him. He was reaching for her when they heard, "Ahem!" Keegan put her flaming hands on his chest and let out a sigh. Calder began steering her toward Áine and said, "Come on, Love. I think you're going to want to see this."

Over where Áine had been slamming coffee and devouring donuts just a few minutes ago, there now stood a female Fae with long, straight, bright-red hair, dressed in tight black leathers, with multiple weapons strapped to her body. In addition to all the weapons, the sheer amount of jewelry adorned with what appeared to be genuine rubies and diamonds was impressive. And topping everything off was an ornate tiara with more jewels than seemed possible.

"Holy shitturds, Batman! That is some serious freaking bling, girl!" Keegan exclaimed. Áine's smile could have lit up the entire garden. "I know, right? When we went over it at the salon, Dana said she could probably come up with some gold and a few gems, but this is over the top!"

Calder was very still. Too still. Keegan looked at him and said, "Hmm, I wonder where those gems could've come from." He tried to keep a straight face, but he couldn't help but grin at the look of surprise on Áine's face as she realized what he'd done. "Guilty," he said. "But it's a very small thing for an Earth Fae to bring forth gold and a few gems. Besides, I owed you back pay. Sorry, I'm still late on the crickets portion of your paycheck."

Áine looked at him sternly, then said, "Okay, Mud Boy, you're forgiven. But hurt my girl again, and I'll burn off more than just your nipples." Calder nodded and replied, "That's more than fair, a Bhanríon. But I have one more surprise. Try shifting to your phoenix form."

Áine looked confused but said, "Alright, why not?" She shifted to her phoenix form and was surprised to note that the tiara did not disappear with the rest of her costume but remained visible and shrank to fit the size of her current head. "Wait a minute, Keegan, did my tiara stay put? And shrink to fit my head?" she asked. "Yep, you've still got a little blingy crown." Then Keegan turned to Calder and said, "You realize she's never taking that off now, right? There will be no living with her after this."

"Nonsense," Áine disagreed. "I may wear the tiara for a little while, but I'll eventually put it away. Eventually." Calder shrugged and said, "Sorry, I felt I was in enough trouble to bring in the big guns." Keegan shook her head and said, "After this, I'll be amazed if she doesn't desert me and decide to go live with you and Lir."

Another chime rang out, and the Fae quieted as Deirdre, dressed as the goddess Badb, all in black with a multitude of raven's feathers and glittering obsidian decorating her long flowing gown, raised her voice and declared, "Let us all move to the meadow for the Damhsa na Tine Mhóir!"

Everyone began to wander toward the meadow, where

bonfires dotted the landscape, casting flickering shadows across the faces of the Fae. A group of musicians—primarily fiddlers, pipers, and drummers—began playing a reel, and everyone found a place around a bonfire. Keegan and Calder were soon skipping and spinning, laughing as they messed up the steps, but not caring. Keegan saw Cara and Reilly, her mom and dad, Áine and Lir, as well as several others in their group, including Muireann, who transformed from Ariel, the Earth mermaid, to Lí Ban, the ancient Irish mermaid. Ula was transformed into her companion, an otter, and they both lounged in her floating wave of water.

Her group even included Máire and Corley, who appeared to be dressed as The Morrígan and The Dagda, if her incomplete knowledge of Irish mythology wasn't mistaken. Although Máire's costume, which was skintight and full of black leather and crow feathers, did resemble Deirdre's Badb costume. Then again, that whole three-goddesses-in-one thing had always confused her a bit.

But Corley made an entertaining Dagda. He had a big, hooded cloak and a large staff, which was said to kill with one end and return life with the other. There was a bubbling cauldron that apparently was never empty on the ground behind him. He also had convinced Saoirse to play his pet pig. Keegan grinned and thought, *I bet he owes her one for that.*

As they were spinning around, a few fires over, she could pick out Siobhán, as the mother goddess Danú, dressed all in shades of blue and green with flowers and vines entwined in her hair and around her arms and waist. Morgan, who was never far from Siobhán this evening, wore the costume of Danú's beloved husband, Donn, god of the dead. He was clothed in white robes, covered with golden knotwork embroidered along the neckline, waist, sleeves, and hem. He also held the bridle of a spectral white steed, which pawed at the ground and snorted.

The dance ended with everyone applauding, out of breath but

happy and enjoying themselves. Keegan put her hands on her hips and took deep breaths, trying to slow her heart rate down. She finally saw the last few members of their group; they were a couple of fires down in the opposite direction. Liam was dressed as Goibniu, the metalsmith of the Tuatha Dé Danann, wearing a heavy smith's apron and carrying a large hammer. Conor had gone from Marilyn Monroe to Cú Chulainn, an ancient hero and demi-god with tri-color hair and multi-colored eyes. She also spied Croía, who was wearing the costume of Sadbh, a goddess of deer and transformation, and Colin, who was portraying Nuada, complete with a silver hand and the fiery Sword of Light.

Unfortunately, she also saw her aunt Étaín, dressed as Niamh Cinn-Óir, the beautiful, blonde Fae who long ago fell in love and spent three hundred years with the mortal Oisín, son of Fionn mac Cumhaill. Her asshat uncle Cass, playing the part of Oisín, of course, was also in that group, but neither of them was paying any attention to the other. Étaín seemed pretty drunk and rather pissed off. Cass just seemed obsessed with Niamh, as usual. *That whole thing is a problem for another day,* she thought. *I hope.*

As the music from the dance was dying down, Deirdre stepped up on a slight rise at the center of the meadow and sent out that chime one more time. She said, "That was fabulous! Alright, now that the obligatory first dance is done, younglings, you are free to head to Earth. There are four Druids at the World Tree who will open a portal for you. Remember, petty mischief only! Now off with you!" A large group of teenagers and a few young adults (at least they looked like young adults; they might be three hundred years old; it was hard to tell) took off for the World Tree, ready to have some fun and cause some havoc on Earth this Halloween night.

Once they had gone, Deirdre nodded to Shay, who joined her in the meadow's center. She whispered something to him, then took her leave. "Oíche Shamhna Shona Daoibh!" he greeted the assembled Fae. "And welcome to the Samhain Ball! We just have a little housekeeping to get through, and then we'll let you get on with your celebrations."

He motioned for Niamh, Keegan, and Áine to join him, so they made their way over to him and turned to face the assembled crowd. "This is the Doran family, Niamh and Keegan, and Keegan's familiar, Áine. Niamh left the homeworld for Earth before Keegan was born. They have recently returned. In addition, the Council seat recently held by Máire Daugherty will now revert to the eldest Doran sister, Niamh. Everybody give them a warm welcome!" This elicited polite applause and a few whistles and cheers.

As things were dying down and Fae began to disperse, a voice called out, "I'm sorry, but I have a question." Everyone turned toward the voice, which came from Máire, who now stood across the centralmost bonfire from Keegan and the others.

"You see, I've done the math. From the time Niamh left the homeworld to the time Keegan was born was a little over six and a half months. And we're supposed to believe her father was some anonymous human, and she was born two and a half months early?" she said, raising her voice to be heard clearly by all those gathered. "I think it is far more likely that Keegan's father was a Fae. And if he were a Fire Fae, there would have been no reason for them to leave." She paused a moment for dramatic effect. "So, it stands to reason that Keegan Doran is Dúbailte."

Gasps rang out across the meadow, followed quickly by muttering. Shay tried to dismiss the accusation as nothing more than rivalry among family members. "Now look, you have no proof of any of that. This is nothing but pure conjecture, brought forth by a young Fae who has plenty of reason to be jealous of a returning aunt who has just taken away her seat on the Council."

Máire opened her mouth to say something, but instead, she doubled over in pain, her hands pressed against her temples. *Destroy her!* screamed the tritone voice inside her head. *Kill her now!* Máire shook her head and replied within her mind, *No! I only wanted them both to lose face publicly so I could get my Council seat back. I'm not killing her!* Corley moved closer to her, ready to help however he could. Laoise and Saoirse drew near to the couple as many of the other familiars spread themselves throughout the crowd, ready to help as needed.

The crowd was growing more uneasy by the minute, Máire's accusation causing serious suspicion to fall on Keegan. Seeing Máire in such serious pain without an apparent cause just ratcheted the anxiety up even higher.

Then, Cass stepped forward and said, "What my daughter said may well be conjecture. She has no way of knowing who Keegan's father might be." He paused momentarily and walked around the bonfire toward Niamh and the others. "But I do. I was there."

More gasps and muttering, but this time, actual questions were being thrown out. "What do you mean?" said a Water Fae. Another Fae further back yelled out, "How do you know?" And still another shouted the real question everyone wanted the answer to, "Who is it?"

Meanwhile, Máire was struggling with the pain in her head, the voice inside urging her to take action, but still, she fought against the enemy's order to destroy her cousin. As Corley stood by her, helpless but determined to be there for her, he noticed that Laoise and Saoirse had joined them, and many other familiars were popping up among the Fae.

Cass practically strutted around the bonfire, relishing the attention. For all his faults and arrogance, Cass was a master storyteller. He played to his audience, heightening their desire for drama.

"I had started dating my lovely wife, Étaín, a few months before her sister disappeared. We were already very much in love, but unfortunately, Niamh had developed a bit of an obsession with me. Perhaps it was a misguided reaction to the grief from their parents' deaths, which had happened less than a year before, I don't know, but whatever the reason, she seemed to be following me everywhere."

Niamh was almost vibrating with her anger as she said, "You are a fucking liar! You were the obsessed one!"

Cass held up a finger, moving it back and forth, and said, "Now, now, Niamh, wait your turn. This is my story." Niamh just rolled her eyes, which normally would've made Keegan giggle, but unfortunately, what they were dealing with was no laughing matter.

Máire was still struggling with the pain in her head to the point that she fell to her knees as she tried to resist the voice. Laoise shifted to her white wolverine form and positioned herself directly before her girl. Máire's father didn't seem to notice.

"As I was saying, Niamh had developed an unrequited attraction to me, and no matter how gently I tried to let her down, she just kept coming. One day, I was on my way to meet Étaín when Niamh ambushed me, catching me by surprise, severely burning my hand, and causing me to fall against the side of a building. She quickly put up a wall of flame, blocking my retreat. I called forth my own fire, hoping to create a small window through which I could escape. Just as I was about to break through, a certain Air Fae joined Niamh, reinforcing her flames with his air power. I dug deep and almost broke free when suddenly the flames disappeared with a whoosh, causing me to fall forward. Then I felt a sharp pain in the back of my skull as he used a branch or something to club me over the head."

Someone in the back called out, "Oh, for fuck's sake, who was it?" There were a few nervous titters at that, although the crowd seemed to be growing increasingly concerned with the state of Máire, who looked very close to passing out.

"Easy, friend, we're almost there. I woke up with a hell of a headache, but I didn't want to make waves by accusing my girlfriend's sister of assault, so I just tried to ignore it and go on about my business. But Niamh wouldn't leave it alone and continued to follow me around for weeks like a lovesick pup. One day, she confronted me again, this time right outside the house of her Air Fae accomplice. I sternly rebuffed her. She said I didn't know what I was missing, but she would show me. She ran up to her accomplice's front door and pounded on it. He opened it quickly, obviously having watched what was happening in his front yard. She made sure the door was open wide, then threw herself into his arms and passionately kissed him. He enthusiastically returned the affection, and I left, disgusted but relieved that maybe she had finally moved on from her obsession with me. It was only a week or two later that she disappeared. And, as my daughter pointed out, Keegan was born less than seven months later."

Another Fae yelled, "I'm about to club you over the head if you don't bloody well tell us who this Air Fae was."

Cass gave a Cheshire cat smile and said, "Can't you tell? Maybe it's a coincidence, but Keegan and Shay have the exact same silver eyes, don't you think?"

More gasps and murmuring spread throughout the gathering, but before anyone could form coherent speech, Máire let out a primal scream and shot a blast of fire in Keegan's general direction. Laoise screamed, "No!" A shield of earth formed a few feet in front of Keegan, stopping the sloppy projectile of flame from getting anywhere near her. Máire collapsed into Corley's arms, who quickly picked her up and disappeared into the crowd, weaving his way quickly to the woods, where he could use both the darkness and the foliage as cover to get them out of there.

Laoise had a quick whispered conversation with Saoirse, who replied, "Go; I'll stay here and try to keep a lid on this!" The dog quickly took off after the retreating couple.

Pandemonium broke out as powers were called all over the meadow. Many Fae, who were already well on their way to drunkenness, began shooting at each other, taking the opportunity to settle old grudges or just cause general mayhem. The gathered familiars mitigated much of the damage, diverting or nullifying attacks whenever possible. Even so, staying unharmed required keeping your head on a swivel.

Keegan and Calder moved the short distance to Niamh and Shay and took a defensive stance, attempting to block any stray powers that came their way, and several ricochets came close. Cara and Reilly were heading toward them, but progress through that warzone was slowed to a crawl.

A piercing whistle that was very familiar to the Ó Faoláin brothers echoed over the meadow, followed by, "Liam! Conor! To me!" The two oldest brothers began making their way through the chaos to their mam. Calder looked at Lir and said, "Go help clear the way for them, Lad!" The púca, currently disguised as an ancient god, gave him a nod, then the familiar shifted to his nightmare horse form and took off toward the older brothers.

Áine, who had already switched back to her phoenix form, straightened her tiara, then swooped toward Lir and shouted, "Wait for me, Goat Boy!" The two began making swift progress through the rowdy, volatile crowd.

Shay, trying to use his air power to enhance his voice, kept saying, "Everyone needs to calm down! Please! There's no need for this violence!" Cass took advantage of the chaos he had created and moved around behind where Niamh and Shay were standing. As everything erupted and became more and more chaotic, he sent a fireball hurtling toward the Air Fae.

Luckily, Étaín, who had made her way over near her sister, had been expecting something like that, and she deflected the fireball with one of her own, sending it harmlessly into the bonfire. "You're not just a fucking liar, you're a fucking coward as well!" she yelled, finally completely over asshat Cass and his bullshit.

Étaín looked at her sister and said, "I've been an eejit, Niamh, and I wouldn't blame you if you never spoke to me again. I've been blind for so many years, caught up in my obsession with someone who did not deserve my love. I've hurt you terribly, and I've hurt my own daughter, so much so that our relationship may not recover. I will do my best to try and repair that relationship, and I'd like to try and be your sister again if you'll have me." Tears streamed down her cheeks as she finally admitted her failings to herself and everyone else. Niamh just reached out and took her hand, giving it a squeeze. She wasn't ready to forgive her sister, but she was prepared to begin the process. After all, as she'd recently been reminded, family is life, and her sister, however screwed up she might be, was still family. They would take it one step at a time.

Suddenly, a compact tornado dropped out of the sky and landed close to Keegan and Calder, so self-contained it barely stirred their hair. As the winds died down, Deirdre mumbled to herself, "Time to begin navigating the pain and chaos." She stepped forward then and, amplifying her voice, said, "Enough!" This caught the crowd's attention enough that active volleys stopped, but everyone's powers were still called and ready to launch while they waited to hear what the High Druid had to say.

"Cass Daugherty, I call you to come forth and be judged," she said. Cass, who had been trying to blend in with the crowd, suddenly found himself alone as those around him backed away. "What?" he exclaimed. "I've done nothing to warrant your judgment."

"Oh, but you have," she hissed at him. "Even if I hadn't seen the cowardly attack you just attempted on Taoiseach Ó Brien, even if I didn't believe that you were, in fact, the obsessed aggressor against Niamh, there is still an excellent reason you deserve to be judged."

"And what might that be?" he asked, with more than a touch of attitude. Deirdre took a couple of steps closer to him, leaned in, and smiled. "You deserve to be judged, Lad, not because you are part-Fomorian; if that were a crime, I would also be guilty, as would many of the Fae here tonight. But you have been communicating with and actively furthering a Fomorian plan to invade and subjugate the Aos Sí."

An older Fae nearby clutched his chest and said, "Oh, for feck's sake with the surprises! Me poor, old heart can't take it."

Deirdre did an admirable job of keeping the humor off her face, but her lips did give a bit of a twitch. Cass attempted to appear outraged and tried to refute her claims, but she was having none of that and cut him off immediately.

"Don't even bother denying it. I have friends among the Fomorians, the faction that opposes the invasion plan. They have supplied me with incontrovertible proof. Your fate is sealed, I'm afraid." Then she looked at him and said, "You don't deserve to dress as an Irish hero. Here, let me help you with your costume." She lifted a hand and, with a flourish, cast a glamour over Cass. A golden, sparkling mist surrounded him, then slowly dissipated, leaving behind a likeness of Balor of the Evil Eye, an ancient Fomorian enemy who looked like a hideous, one-eyed monster.

Cass growled as he released a burst of flame all over his body, instantly dissolving Deirdre's glamour. Then he poured a massive amount of power into his hands, quickly forming an immense fireball and throwing it directly at Deirdre.

Keegan and Calder were standing a few feet behind Deirdre, holding hands. As Cass released the enormous ball of flame, they both screamed, "No!" and each of them flung their powers, all of their powers, into a protective wall in front of the High Druid.

Their wall successfully blocked the fireball, but a bright, silvery light also erupted between their hands. Startled, they took a step apart just as the force from Cass's fireball hit Deirdre, making her stumble back into the couple, causing the three of them to fall into the circle of light and disappear.

In a field outside of Kansas City, Missouri, a bright, silvery light suddenly erupted in the middle of the trunk of a hawthorn tree. Three people tumbled out of the light, each landing painfully on various body parts.

Keegan, rubbing her elbow from the rough landing, looked around, then over at Calder, and said, "Well, fuck. We have got to stop doing that!"

***The End***

# AFTERWORD

I hope you enjoyed reading this book as much as I enjoyed writing it! If you'd like to help me out, please take a moment and review my book.

Thank you!

*M.A. Kilpatrick*

Also by M.A. Kilpatrick:

*Hunted Elements*, The Dúbailte Chronicles Book Two
*Hallowed Elements*, The Dúbailte Chronicles Book Three
*The Dúbailte Chronicles*, Omnibus Edition